THE HIGHLANDER'S CAPTIVE

Highland Rogues, Book 3

Mary Wine

ARE YOU SIGNED UP FOR DRAGONBLADE'S BLOG?

You'll get the latest news and information on exclusive giveaways, exclusive excerpts, coming releases, sales, free books, cover reveals and more.

Check out our complete list of authors, too!

No spam, no junk. That's a promise!

Sign Up Here

www.dragonbladepublishing.com

〉〉〉〉〈〈〈〈

Dearest Reader;

Thank you for your support of a small press. At Dragonblade Publishing, we strive to bring you the highest quality Historical Romance from the some of the best authors in the business. Without your support, there is no 'us', so we sincerely hope you adore these stories and find some new favorite authors along the way.

Happy Reading!

CEO, Dragonblade Publishing

Additional Dragonblade books by Author Mary Wine

Highland Rogues Series

The Highlander's Demand
The Highlander's Destiny
The Highlander's Captive

CHAPTER ONE

McKay land…

ROLFE MUNRO WAS up at first light. His horse wasn't quite as keen about being on the way home as Rolfe was, though. Rolfe clicked his tongue to coax the animal out of the stable.

"The horse is smarter than ye," Cora Mackenzie informed Rolfe.

"Only because he has yet to understand that we are going south," Rolfe responded as he rubbed a sure hand along the animal's back. "Where the weather is much finer than here."

Cora grinned. "I find it suits me."

Rolfe took a moment to lock gazes with Cora. His lips twitched. "There ye go again, lass, cutting me with yer lack of affection toward me."

"As if ye feel any different," Cora replied. She drew in a deep breath and grinned. "Ye should thank me for not wedding ye."

Rolfe chuckled. "Ye're happy."

"It's a fine feeling," Cora informed him. She grew serious. "And I need to thank ye for no' pressing the matter of a union between us."

Rolfe made sure the saddle strap which went beneath his horse's belly was snug but not too tight. "I do nae doubt ye'd have been a good wife, Cora."

His tone was edged with something Rolfe decided he didn't want to think too deeply about. Marriage was a matter for contemplation and solid judgment. He'd been afforded a good position in life. One which came with ample food and a warm bed, when many lacked those essentials.

But nothing was without a price.

As the next laird of the Munro, his marriage was one that would affect the entire clan. Their prosperity would rest solely on his ability to choose a partner who brought something of value to the union.

Rolfe looked again at Cora Mackenzie. With her red hair and fair face, she'd have been pleasing as a bride. The fact that she was Buchanan's only sister would have ensured she brought an alliance worthy of the Munro clan's approval.

But she was in love now.

Rolfe felt something shift inside him. It was a fact that whatever it was, he was left slightly uneasy after feeling it.

The reason was simple; he didn't need to get distracted by emotions.

Especially when it came to ones associated with marriage.

He'd wed for the logical reasons, and that was simply that. Such was his duty to his clan and his father. Detaching himself from personal opinions on the matter was simply the path of least resistance.

"Ye've used up yer share of luck, Cora Mackenzie," Rolfe said as he led his horse from the stable. "Best mend yer wild ways now."

"I'll help her settle into a mundane life," Faolan McKay spoke from where he was just emerging from the tower of the McKay stronghold.

Faolan wasn't too concerned about the weather. He'd put his kilt on over his shirt, leaving the wide bandage that was around his middle in sight.

"Faolan McKay," Cora scolded under her breath. "Ye'll be heading straight back to bed."

Rolfe watched the way Faolan grinned in response to his new wife's tone. "Can I no' even bid me friend farewell before ye take me back to bed woman? It's no' that I do nae enjoy yer passion for me..."

Cora pulled her skirts up and flew up the steps to flatten her hand against her husband's lips. Faolan's eyes sparkled with enjoyment before he clasped her wrist and tugged her hand away from his mouth. A twist and a turn, and Cora ended up next to her new spouse.

For a moment, Cora frowned. She had a wild spirit, one Faolan seemed more than able to combat. And there was something in her face that made it plain she enjoyed the way her new husband handled her.

That sensation moved through Rolfe's gut again.

It was envy, sure enough.

And he still couldn't indulge it.

Not now or ever. So, he mounted his horse and enjoyed the surge of anticipation filling him. Ice crystals sparkled along the ground, promising winter soon. His men took their cue from him, climbing into their saddles. The horses shifted but caught the spark of excitement running through all the Munro Retainers. The animals began to paw at the ground, eager to depart.

Rolfe turned and reached up to tug on the corner of his bonnet in respect. Buchanan was the new laird of the McKay, and every window and archer slot had members of his clan watching to see how Rolfe treated him.

Rolfe knew what it was like to carve out his place one cut at a time.

Just being born of the right bloodline didn't ensure anything. Not in the Highlands. Here, strength was a factor, as was the ability to do business. Rolfe cleared the gate and rode down past the church where Faolan's half-brother was resting with his wife. Malcolm hadn't been the eldest, and yet, he'd wrestled the lairdship away from Faolan.

Rolfe grinned, though. Faolan had prevailed in the end. Cora was part of that success.

Her nature would also ensure Faolan didn't grow too bored with his position.

Rolfe grinned and leaned down low over the neck of his horse. It had been too long since he'd had a reason to ride out of his father's stronghold.

Far too long.

He bared his teeth and indulged his need to ride as though he had naught on his mind save his purpose. Nothing was further from the truth, of course, but life had a nasty way of being that way.

Still, it was only a fool who didn't manage to grasp the moments of pleasure he might, when they were in reach.

Even if the reason he was riding south wasn't the best. Rolfe didn't dwell on the fact that his father had wanted to send his sister a letter. One delivered from Rolfe's hand. His father was dying. He'd been lingering in the grip of an illness for the past two years but had always maintained the image of strength. To have it drained away a little at a time was worse than death.

Now, Rolfe had his sire's last words tucked into the front of his doublet. It was more than a farewell to a sibling, though. As his sire weakened, Rolfe had stepped up to shoulder the weight of the lairdship. Rolfe understood his father was making sure the Leslie were ready for the possible shift in power. An alliance had been struck when his Aunt Euna wed into the Leslie clan. An agreement to back one another up.

Rolfe was already confident in his claim on the Munro lairdship. It wasn't an over-inflated ego supporting that belief either.

No, he'd been earning his place while keeping his private feelings hidden.

The letter was a gift. The last one his father might be able to grant Rolfe in this lifetime. It was an opportunity to ride free one last time. A chance to escape the burden of leadership and expectation.

Rolfe had no intention of wasting it.

>>>><<<<

Leslie land...

EUNA RECEIVED HIM in her private chambers.

As her nephew, it wasn't precisely improper. Rolfe still felt a tingle on his nape as he climbed the stairs up to the tower top room where his aunt was. Double doors awaited him at the top of the stairs. As befitting the lady of the keep, Euna had the entire floor. When the doors were opened, a middle-aged woman stood there. She lowered herself before sidestepping neatly out of the way.

"Rolfe." Euna held her hands out to him.

There was an archway in the middle of the room which would lead to his aunt's bedchamber. Heavy curtains were closed over it to provide respectability to the moment of having Rolfe come behind the doors of what was normally the domain of the females only.

The look on Euna's face sent another tingle down his back. Her eyes were overly bright and her teeth set into her lower lip as she tried to maintain a hold on her emotions.

"Ye...Ye are a man fully grown!" his aunt proclaimed with joy.

Her personal attendants had joined her, four middle-aged women. All of the matrons were women of the Leslie clan. Euna's marriage contract had been sealed before she was delivered to her groom and into the keeping of the Leslie at the tender age of seventeen.

Cora had balked at such a fate.

Aye, well, ye had the chance to keep her and didnae.

Rolfe focused on his aunt. Through the years, he'd meet her. The need to maintain a strong alliance meant Rolfe's father had ensured there were opportunities for them to interact.

"Just look at ye!" Euna exclaimed with a bright smile. She'd clasped her hands together as if in prayer.

"It is good to see ye as well, Aunt." Rolfe reached into his doublet and pulled out the letter. "Me father has sent ye his greeting."

He handed the letter over. Euna had no real privacy. To have gifted the letter in secret would have been to place his aunt in danger of being accused of plotting against her husband. On the surface, it appeared that Laird Leslie and Euna were amicable with one another. But only the pair of them truly knew what went on behind closed doors. More than one noble couple put on a united front when the truth was they loathed each other.

It was a harsh fact of many unions made for the benefit of the clan.

Ye are looking at yer future, laddie.

Rolfe tightened his grip on his belt. The edge of the stiff leather bit into his palms just enough to cut through his inner thoughts. Dwelling on things that could not be changed was of no use.

Euna handed the letter to one of her attendants without opening it. Her eyes were serious as she contemplated him.

Rolfe might have tried to excuse himself, but he saw the need in his aunt's eyes. She was struggling to maintain decorum. But her hands trembled, betraying her.

"Aunt?" he questioned softly. "What is troubling ye?"

"Seath," she uttered the name of her youngest son. Euna shook her head. "Me husband said I spoilt him, and it seems…there is truth to the matter, for he's gone riding off to do…who knows what in the name of making a name for himself."

Rolfe drew in a deep breath. Seath was nineteen years old. Just about the perfect age for doing something foolish. The question to be asked was whether or not the lad was in serious trouble or just in need of being scolded by his mother when he returned. Boys became men through stupid stunts, and mothers didn't always understand the need to allow them to run into walls. Even if part of the lesson was standing in place while their female relative railed at them.

There had been a time… Rolfe forced himself to focus as he heard his aunt sniffle.

"Gone riding where?" Rolfe asked in an attempt to console her.

"The lowlands," Euna declared in a rush. "He heard one of the Duncan brothers has managed to break his fool neck and widow his

English bride. Seath thinks to bring the girl back here for her widow's thirds."

Rolfe had to tuck his chin to keep his aunt from seeing the way his lips twitched.

Euna narrowed her eyes. "Why is it ye men think such an idea is amusing?"

Rolfe offered his aunt a shrug.

"It is nae something to make light over," Euna declared firmly. "If the girl has something of value, many will think to have it. By the time the news made it here, half the Highlands will have men on their way to steal the girl before she can be reclaimed by her family."

Well, that much was true. Rolfe couldn't deny his aunt's thinking. A widow was ensured a third of her husband's estate upon his death. If the girl had been wed into the Duncan clan, it was for sure they wouldn't be allowing her out of their stronghold, for she'd take their money with her. At the least, she'd take part of her dowry.

His aunt might be due her concern over the matter. When it came to money, blood often flowed. The Duncan were close to the lowland border. For news to have made it to Leslie land, it was a sure thing that Seath wasn't the only one who knew about the new widow.

"Seath only rode out a few hours ago." Euna came closer, her voice pleading. "Ye could catch him."

He could.

But it would be an indulgence.

A personal one.

"Fetch him back for me, Rolfe," she implored. "Before we are forced to pay a ransom for him."

Rolfe drew in a deep breath. "It might do him a bit of good to end up ransomed."

Ransom was a game in the Highlands. So long as Seath didn't make the mistake of crossing any land with a clan that was feuding with the Leslie, the youth only risked having his pride injured when he was captured.

"I know it," Euna said. "I just can nae shake the feeling that something terrible is going to happen to him."

Tears shimmered in his aunt's eyes. It had been a long time since Rolfe's mother had died. On Munro land, there was only him and his father. Rolfe realized his skin was remarkably thin when it came to female tears.

Even the threat of them.

He shook his head and retreated a step.

Retreated?

Christ!

"Aunt Euna…" Rolfe tried to find gentle words to refuse her request. "When ye read the letter, ye will see that me father is no well. I am needed back on Munro land."

Euna tore the wax seal, which was on top of the letter. She scanned the contents before returning her attention to him. Rolfe felt like the collar of his shirt had suddenly shrunk. There was a glow of impending victory in his aunt's gaze.

"Me brother tells me not to worry about him."

Of course his father had written such…bloody Highlander pride.

"Mary, get down to the kitchen and have provisions packed for Rolfe and his men. They are to have cheese and bread and mead."

Ye've lost, laddie.

Mary inclined her head to acknowledge her mistress before she turned in a whirl of wool skirts and disappeared.

His collar was biting into his neck.

"I am truly grateful, Rolfe." Euna's eyelashes were wet, but at least she appeared to have blinked her tears away.

Still, he felt the need to clear his throat.

Why hadn't his father wed again? Rolfe suddenly realized he had very limited skills for dealing with women, and while the lack of such accomplishments had never even entered his thoughts as being something he needed to address, now, well, it appeared he needed to get as far away from women as possible.

"I'll be on me way, Aunt."

Rolfe reached up and tugged on the corner of his cap in respect. He caught just a moment of his aunt's joy before he spun around and headed for the door. He might just be riding into a mess, but at least it would be one with men to face off against.

That was something he knew well how to deal with.

Ye'll have to wed at some point.

Alone in the stairwell, Rolfe didn't push the thought aside. Cora had been a much better candidate for a wife than he'd first realized. Headstrong and unbridled, she'd never have resorted to using tears on him.

Rolfe stopped at the bottom of the steps. Guilt nipped at him, and he acknowledged it as his due. His aunt's tears had been sincere enough. For a moment, Rolfe indulged his longing for his mother. His father was ill and had been for years. Rolfe didn't allow himself many moments of weakness, not with the eyes of the Munro on him.

But he did miss his mother.

And just as soon as he found his lackwit cousin, Rolfe was going to drag him home and watch Euna take the lad to task!

And then are ye going to find a bride?

As to that question, Rolfe got moving again without really thinking too long upon the matter. Since his father seemed to be seeing to writing letters to tie up his dealings in the world, it was just possible Rolfe would return home to a bride waiting for him. So there was no reason to waste any time on contemplating the matter.

Which left Rolfe grinning because it had been a very long time since he'd been afforded the opportunity to chase someone down. He grinned as he joined his Retainers. Their mood was jovial as they clustered around the table in the kitchen where the maids normally took their meals. The Leslie staff was scurrying around, making sure they had ample fare to fill their bellies before they embarked on their task.

The Head-of-House came back in, her ring of keys in her hand because she'd been to one of the storerooms. A maid held the corners of her apron to make a sack for several blocks of cheese. Her cheeks were flushed with excitement. For the rich fare was locked away now that winter was near. The Head-of-House replaced her keys on the front of her belt. Somewhere there would be a burly butler, charged with ensuring there was no flitching from the storerooms.

Food was life.

But for the moment, there was plenty as the cook sliced off wedges of the cheese and placed it on the table. Rolfe reached for a chunk. He enjoyed the waxy feeling of it as he lifted it to his mouth and bit into it. The dense, flavor-packed food made him grin. It wasn't gluttony that motivated them. No, as much as his men might be entertained by the idea of riding headlong across the moors, there was not one of them who didn't understand there was also risk involved.

The moors were often unforgiving.

And life was rarely ever fair.

So, they grinned and jested as they feasted. Enjoying the moment to its fullest before they faced the wrath of reality.

Rolfe admitted to their being an enjoyment in riding out of the gates of the Leslie stronghold. It was a different sort of feeling, though.

A harder one.

Sharper.

It was born deep in his gut and came hand in hand with other, darker feelings. Perhaps it had been the lack of a mother after he'd turned ten, but Rolfe recognized how much he indulged his ruthless tendencies. He enjoyed being hard. Ahead of him was a fight or at least the promise of one, and it was the truth that he leaned forward in the saddle, eager to get to it.

He really should have wed Cora when he'd had her under his roof. She'd have weathered his darker side well. Letting her go had been soft of him.

There ye are again lad…no stomach for hurting a lass.

Rolfe dug his heels into his horse and tightened his thighs around the beast. As the stallion increased its speed, he needed to focus.

Good.

It was his last opportunity to ride hard. Women and the matters concerning them would be there when he had to return to his place and take up his duties once more.

For now, he would ride.

⋙✳⋘

ANNIS WAS GOOD at going unnoticed.

Very good.

It was an exceedingly practical and useful skill, one she'd perfected in her uncle's home, but now it would seem it had its purpose under her husband's roof.

Late husband, you mean.

Annis found herself looking toward the body of her recently deceased husband. Lonn Duncan was lying in state now. She was on her knees next to his still form as she listened to the family discussing her. It wasn't any real devotion to her duty as his widow which made her ignore the ache in her knees and remain. No, she was there, so she might be overlooked as her fate was debated.

"The laundress says she's bleeding now, so there will be no issue," Benedicta Duncan spoke with no remorse for the indecency of the subject matter.

She watched the consummation of your marriage…she has no shame.

That was very true. Benedicta had been behind a tapestry at the time, but it didn't change how mortified Annis still was three months later.

"My seed or me brothers, what does it matter?" This time the voice belonged to Goron Duncan. He was the eldest of the Duncan brothers. "I will see to the matter."

There was a touch of lustful anticipation in Goran's voice that made Annis want to retch. There had been nothing even pleasant about her husband's nightly visits. Whatever could make men crave it so much? Awkward and messy. That was what it was. At least Annis understood why it was called her duty.

For it was indeed a chore.

"You cannot see to the issue when the laundresses have already spread the matter far and wide," Benedicta replied. "And there is the matter of yer wife. Ye'll need a divorce before ye can wed the girl. Christ! Yer fool brother has placed us in a mess! We needed a baby of her bloodline."

"I can breed her now and wait to legitimize it all later," Goron insisted.

"No." Benedicta's voice sliced through her son's argument. In the entire stronghold, only Benedicta dared to speak to Laird Goran Duncan in such a tone. She was the matriarch of the clan and no mistake. "Annis is already illegitimate. But born a granddaughter to Margret Clifford. If the English queen dies before Margret, Margret will inherit the throne of England."

"Aye, I know it," Goron replied to his mother. "Why do ye think I went to so much trouble to fetch the lass from England? Her dowry was nae so great either, not with her father being so young and his personal secretary doing his best to hide the young scamp's liaisons."

"She came with a signed and sealed acknowledgment of her birth from her father William Stanley and an archbishop. William Stanley is a lad now, but he will become the Earl of Derby, and if his mother outlives Elizabeth Tudor, he will be the crown prince of England."

"Well, Lonn is very dead and will no' be making ye a grandson with that blue blood mother," Goran said bluntly.

"It would seem ye have inconvenienced everyone quite a bit, Lonn," Annis whispered to her departed spouse. "How thoughtless of you."

Her humor was less than decent.

Still, Annis couldn't manage to scrape together much concern over it, much less shame. Not when Lonn had been every bit as despicable as his brother and mother. Her eyes narrowed as she recalled his temper when her mouthy courses had arrived.

"Ye are useless, Annis. Half me family saw me plow ye, and yet ye do nae have the good sense to conceive."

Annis could still feel the side of her face stinging from the vicious blow her husband had dispensed as her chastisement.

But the memory made her smile. It was a little expression of victory, for while Lonn might have had her at his mercy in bed, he hadn't been able to keep her from using her wits to deny him what he wanted.

There were concoctions to prevent pregnancy. Benedicta had evicted every soul who had arrived with Annis at the Duncan stronghold. Tears finally burned her eyes as Annis failed to stop herself from thinking of that moment when Aife had been torn from her side. But Aife had been more experienced in life. She'd known the Duncans might part them.

"Listen well, my sweet. Ye have always known yer blood is yer curse. I will teach ye how to keep yer waist slim until ye decide ye want a babe. It is the only thing I can do for ye now that this marriage has been agreed upon."

Annis felt her throat tightening up.

Aife had been…well, the maidservant had been her mother really. The woman who had borne Annis died in childbed. Every memory Annis had of love was at Aife's hand.

"I will never forget how ye parted us," Annis informed Lonn. She meant those words for the other members of his family as well, for they had all watched as she begged them to allow Aife to remain.

But no. The Duncans had wanted Annis entirely within their power.

"Ye will no be spying here, English bitch. The only attendants ye shall have will be Duncan."

That had been the last time Annis had cried.

So she blinked away the tears which had gathered in her eyes. Aife she'd loved. Annis would make the woman who had raised her proud.

"My wife is barren," Goron declared in a hushed tone. "A useless bit of baggage that can be dealt with."

Annis wasn't a stranger to such ruthlessness. That was sad, for she wanted to be shocked by Goran's veiled suggestion.

But she wasn't.

Well, at least ye are clear-headed instead of fighting off fear.

That was true. Annis needed a plan, and she needed it quickly, or all she would ever have of life was what someone else made of her.

Such is the lot of most women.

Annis tightened her resolve. Aife had taught her there was joy in life. But she'd have to muster her courage up and make a grab for it, or she didn't deserve it. What was the point of being created in the image of her Creator if she was naught more than a little mouse?

"We need yer wife," Benedicta informed Goron. "She is a Campbell. If she dies so young, her kin will ride down and raid us for certain."

"Simple enough to tell them she died in childbed," Goron countered arrogantly.

"We might be assured that yer brother's wife has no way of communicating with her kin, but a Campbell is another matter," Benedicta scoffed. "They are the most ruthless clan in the Highlands. They will have someone keeping a watchful eye upon their daughter."

"Then we'll deal with the laundresses," Goron decided. "I am Laird of the Duncan. Anyone who does nae want to meet an early end will shut their mouths and accept what we tell them about any babe Annis produces for me brother after his untimely death."

Benedicta was quiet for a moment. Annis felt an ache between her shoulders as tension drew her body tight.

Brood mare.

That was all she was to the Duncan.

It wasn't as if so many other women had much better lots, but Annis discovered herself chaffing.

Then you'd better think of a way to rescue yourself and find a better life.

For there was little point in escaping if she had nowhere to go.

"Are we agreed, Mother?" Goron proved how much power his mother had in the clan by asking.

"Aye," Benedicta said. "I will deal with the laundresses. Once they tell me the girl is finished with her courses, ye'll need to bed her."

Goron grunted.

"I mean often," Benedicta insisted. "Yer fool brother didn't take the matter to heart. Do ye think I do nae know who both of ye bed and when?" She made a scoffing sound. "We have one month to see the matter righted, so ye will make certain of it."

"Do nae worry, Mother, I'll be attentive."

Annis felt something inside her shift in response to the sound of Goron's voice.

Lust.

It was a word she'd only heard until coming to the Duncan stronghold. Now, it had meaning beyond the sermons she'd sat through. Now, she heard it in Goron's voice, and it stroked something inside her.

Awakening a need she'd been advised to quell, for women were expected to be obedient.

Annis stood up. Her knees stung, but her pride was growing.

You still need somewhere to go.

Yes. That was a fact. But there was no point in knowing where she was heading if she didn't have the things needed to make it there. Maybe she didn't have all the details of the plan worked out. But there was no way she was going to be sitting in her chamber like a little mouse when Goron came to use her.

Dead on the road with her courage beat a whimpering mouse in a castle.

And she didn't care who disagreed with her. She had one chance, and Annis was going to make the most of it.

Come what may.

⇥⇥⇤⇤

THE DOUGLAS CLAN turned out in good numbers to see their laird's brother laid to rest. Lonn was taken through the front gate of the stronghold as drummers and pipers played out a sorrowful tune. Annis took her place behind his coffin.

"I approve of the somber dress, Annis, for it sets the right example." Goron leaned down to keep his words between them. "But the circles beneath yer eyes?" He made a tsking sound. "We both know there was little warmth in yer marriage bed, so I can nae see why ye were weeping over Lonn's loss."

Annis quelled the urge to blister his ears with a very deserving retort.

He lacked decency.

Considering he has already discussed bedding ye before his brother was even in his grave, there is no surprise there.

Annis didn't look at Goron. The music was wailing around them. A breeze was gusting. The wool dress she'd put on was sturdy. An over partlet helped protect her chest and neck. It tied beneath her arms and had a hook in the front.

The weather was perfect.

It will numb your fingers and nose when you venture down the road.

It was still perfect for her purpose. The chill in the air afforded her the chance to wear her traveling dress to Lonn's service and interment. The chance to be outside the stronghold gates was too precious to waste. If the weather had been finer, she'd have had to wear a lighter weight dress and forgo a partlet or any over garment for that might have sparked suspicion.

As it was, there were several burly Duncan Retainers watching her. Clearly, Goron wasn't planning on allowing her any opportunity to slip away.

So, stop appearing so collected. A weakling doesn't need to be watched.

Wise words.

"How...*how*...how can you say such a callous thing?" Annis shook her head and allowed her words to carry to the Retainers watching. "He was your brother. Have you no shame?"

Goron's eyes narrowed in irritation. There was a flash of temper in them before he recalled how many of his clansmen were watching.

He reached out and captured her hand, giving it a squeeze to reprimand her.

"Terrible to be widowed so young, but do nae worry lass. The Duncan will take care of ye."

Annis didn't miss the promise in his tone.

"I do so...wish Aife was here."

Don't allow him to make you his mouse.

Annis looked straight at Goron and fluttered her eyelashes as though she was beginning to weep. "Why did you send my nurse away? I need her."

Disgust replaced the irritation on Goron's face. He released her hand with a snort. "Do nae wail at me, woman. Ye were here to wed. Time for yer nurse to be gone."

"But Aife was so old. She might have died on the road. Would compassion for one old woman have cost you so much?"

Two of the Retainers cast quick looks toward them. Both were mature men, and there was an unmistakable expression of disapproval on their faces. They found a reason to widen the distance between themselves and Annis.

Goron did the same.

Annis sniffed. Her pride didn't want to allow her any tears, but she ordered it to yield.

She was fighting for her life.

Fat tears trickled down her cheeks by the time the procession made it to the village church. There was a line of clergy waiting outside the stone structure. The bishop was framed by boys who held large incense burners. He lifted his hands and began the blessing.

Benedicta, for her part, was truly grieving. She stood next to the body of her son, honest tears in her eyes as she walked him to his grave.

Good, she will be distracted.

Annis felt a twinge of shame over the thought.

Well, that simply proves you are a decent soul.

Goron was closing the gap between them once more.

Annis hiccupped.

The Duncan laird went straight past her to stand on the other side of his sibling's coffin. The Duncan clan was ignoring her. With Benedicta being the matriarch, Annis had merely been a bride brought into the stronghold for a purpose. Her dowry was safely in the hands of the Duncan clan, her bloodline aside, keeping her tucked away and far from her family was the wisest course of action. Her widow's thirds wouldn't be demanded by her kin.

Goran's wife was at least a Scot.

While you are English.

And she was going back to England, where perhaps she'd find Aife.

That is not much of a plan.

It wasn't. Still, Annis slowly drifted away from the coffin. The Duncan clan members closed in front of her, seeking to be part of the ceremony.

Maybe she didn't know where she was going, but it was her only chance. If she went back into the stronghold, Goron would make sure she didn't have the opportunity to escape him.

So Annis stepped into the trees, forcing herself to move slowly. A sprint would have drawn attention to her. Instead, she clamped her control in place and moved at a steady pace. She wove between the trees, and they closed in behind her to form a barrier to shield her.

Her sturdy wool dress didn't draw attention to her. Once she was far enough into the forest, she quickened her pace. The daylight was both useful and incriminating. For it would help the Duncan find her. She headed deeper into the wilds, down an embankment. A stream gurgled at its bottom. Annis stopped and gathered up her skirts before she carefully made her way across it, one rock at a time.

She jumped the last foot, landing on a thick carpet of dead leaves and needles. It gave a little beneath her weight as she caught the musty scent of decay. There was a roar as the wind gusted through the forest. The dry leaves and bare branches beat against one another, producing an eerie sound that seemed to pick at her resolve to keep going.

Winter was near.

She wouldn't last long in a Scottish winter.

Then you had best get moving.

Annis nodded firmly, her mind set. She let her skirts down but kept a handful of the front of them so she could climb back out of the ravine. Her calves burned with the effort, and sweat popped out on her forehead before she reached the top.

A sense of accomplishment began to fill her as she released her skirts and looked ahead.

"Well, now, who do we have here?"

Chapter Two

Whoever was in front of her, he was overly large. Annis was startled but not ashamed to admit it.

At least to herself.

But as she took in the Scot standing only a foot from her, she stepped back, which was a grave miscalculation.

The slope she'd been climbing was steep enough that one little step backward meant she tittered off balance. The smirk on the man's face transformed into an expression of alarm as he realized she was about to go head over heels back down the way she'd come.

"Here now." He reached out, grabbing at her skirts.

The moment seemed to freeze, affording her the experience of watching it play out in slow motion. Annis felt herself pitching back, the sensation of falling gripping her.

And then she was jerked up by the waistband of her skirt. It bit into her middle as the man used considerable strength to haul her over the crest of the embankment.

She stumbled into him, hitting him with a whoosh.

He was hard.

Annis wanted to recoil, but he'd used too much strength to yank her toward him. She collided with him, and they both went tumbling to the ground. He clasped her to him as he fell. Her skirts went flying up to her back, baring her legs all the way to where her garters were tied around the top of her stockings just above her knees.

The arms around her were tight, binding her to the man.

And a moment later, laughter erupted around them.

"Now that is the proper way to steal a woman!"

"Can the pair of ye no' wait for a bit of privacy?"

"May day has long past, ye know."

Annis flattened her hands on the wide chest of the man and pushed herself up. He didn't unlock his arms, though, which mean she ended up sitting on him with her knees on either side of his lean hips.

He had fair hair and blue eyes, which were full of amusement at her expense. He loosened his hold on her, his arms opening, but he clasped both sides of her hips with his hands.

"Let me go this instant!" Annis demanded.

But she wasn't planning on waiting for compliance. She pushed hard, raising her lower body off his. The brute didn't release her hips, though, so she moved her leg over him. It all ended in a tangle of her legs and skirts.

But she managed to roll over to the side and across the ground, extracting herself from his grip. By the time she was facing up again, there was dirt stuck to her lips and twigs in her hair. She kicked to free her feet, likely appearing ridiculous if the increasing laughter around her was any indication.

But she got to her feet free and cursed.

"Seath…ye have the manners of a goat."

Someone spoke above her. Whoever had chastised the first man had amazing strength. He grasped her by her upper arms and pulled her off the ground with nothing more than a soft snort. This man didn't release her either, but she got the feeling he was making sure she was steady instead of enjoying her misfortune.

He had striking blue eyes.

Annis found herself fascinated by the deep color. Like looking over the rail of a ship. It was truly the first time she'd been so mesmerized by anyone's eyes. She stared into those eyes, her mind entirely blank as the moment seemed to encompass them, sealing out everything else.

"Cousin Rolfe? What are ye doing here?"

Rolfe blinked. The moment shattered. Reality rushed back, and Annis felt her cheeks catch fire.

Blushing?

She sucked in a breath as Rolfe moved her to the side.

"Aunt Euna heard ye've ridden down here," Rolfe responded to the younger man.

Getting a good look at both of them, Annis saw the difference between them. Rolfe was a fully grown man compared to the other. There was a hardness in him that the youth didn't have. She stepped further to the side, something rippling down her spine that she simply wasn't able to name. An awareness of some sort.

Whatever it was, she was very sure she didn't want to be too close to Rolfe. His attention appeared to be on his relative, but she caught his glance shifting to the side when she moved.

He was far too observant.

Hardened.

Annis took another step away from him. The younger man looked toward her. He frowned and reached for her.

"Well, me mother should no' have troubled ye," Seath declared.

Annis shot back a pace to avoid the younger man. Rolfe stepped in front of her.

"I wanted her first, cousin. So ye can just step aside."

"Catching is only one part, Seath." Rolfe braced his feet shoulder-width apart and faced off with his cousin. "If ye want to steal a prize, ye have to be able to keep her."

Prize?

Annis narrowed her eyes, for she knew that phrase well enough. Benedicta had used the word often to describe her to Lonn.

"Well, since neither of ye are going to be able to keep me sister-in-law, that makes ye both…losers."

Annis jerked around. Emerging from the gully, Goron was in the company of his Retainers. They climbed with ease, their swords drawn.

A solid grip closed around her upper arm and pulled her back. Annis went willingly enough as she caught a look at Goron's face.

He shot her a grimace that promised retribution.

"Ye're on me land," Goron growled as he faced off with Rolfe. "And the woman belongs to me."

"She seems to not like belonging to ye," Seath needled Goron. "As I can tell, the lass was intent on running away."

"Aye. Some women need to be reminded of their place. She was wed to me brother. Neither Leslie nor Munro should be getting involved with Duncan affairs. Especially on Duncan land. Get on yer horses and leave before I run ye through," Goron threatened. He sent Annis another hard look.

Annis refused to give up and looked behind her. Rolfe and Seath had also brought their men. Their Retainers wore different color plaids, but they appeared to be joining forces to challenge the Duncan Retainers.

The problem was, there were a great many Duncan. They were still emerging from the gully, their expressions grim. Rolfe had placed himself between her and the Duncan. Whether it was as a prize or in protection, she didn't know.

Protection? Are you taking leave of your senses? He wants to claim you as well.

Which meant it was up to her to take care of herself.

That's nothing new.

Annis tightened her resolve. She looked around, seeking out any way of escape.

The horses.

She blinked as she realized Rolfe had dismounted.

Horses were faster than men on foot.

That thought was barely through her head before she was grasping her skirts and hiking them high so she could run.

And she ran.

The horse wasn't any tame mare. It was a stallion. It eyed her as she came toward it. Annis tightened her grip on her skirts, refusing to be intimidated by the huge beast. The only plan she had was to get into the saddle before the creature tried to unseat her.

And then hold on for dear life.

Fate was suddenly of a mind to be helpful, for the stallion was near an outcropping of rocks. Annis stepped up onto it, making the distance to the back of the creature much less.

Still, it would be an effort to gain the saddle. She swung her leg up while yanking her skirts out of the way. In midair, it felt like she wouldn't make it. She cringed as she realized she would fall short and end up sprawled on the ground beneath the creature's hooves.

Perhaps it would stomp her to death.

Such would be a kinder fate than being left to the whims of Goron and his mother.

But at the last moment, she was pushed up, ending across the saddle in a heap of panting and sweat.

"Ye've got good instincts, lass," Rolfe said next to her ear as he joined her.

Annis gasped as she was suddenly surrounded by the man. He was a wall of muscle, and for some reason, she couldn't quite recall Lonn affecting her in the same way as having Rolfe against her did. She seemed to enjoy it.

You are a fool. Is this the time to notice such a thing?

It certainly wasn't. Annis tightened her thighs around the horse as Rolfe gathered the reins up. He leaned forward, pressing her down as he wheeled the stallion around and kicked it into motion. The animal knew its master well. The beast let out a snort before it was digging into the soil with its hooves, sending clods of dirt flying out behind it.

It wasn't precisely the way she'd planned, but Goron and the Duncan Retainers were falling behind them. She heard Goron shouting after them, but there was nothing more that he might do.

Rolfe chuckled behind her.

The sound was both pleasing and frightening. There was a hardness to Rolfe that wasn't fed with arrogance. No, it was just something she couldn't deny. It was in the way he carried himself.

Experience.

Aye, that sounded right.

While Seath was eager for adventure, he had yet to prove himself. The younger man had all the pride and exuberance, but he'd yet to earn Rolfe's effortless hardness.

Rolfe eased their pace as they climbed a hill. The stallion dropped into a walk. He gathered the reins into one hand and reached down to stroke the neck of the animal, which made him press against Annis even more. She shuddered. It was an involuntary response.

She heard him let out a sound of amusement.

"You needn't be so proud of yourself, sir." Her tone was tart at best, but the words were across her lips before her better judgment kicked in.

"Managing to no' get run through by yer kin is a fine matter to be pleased with," Rolfe spoke next to her ear. "I suppose ye are free to think differently, but ye were the one who ran toward me horse. Rethinking the matter now are ye?"

"Absolutely not."

"Glad to hear it." There was a sharp edge to his tone. It was clear he wasn't the sort of man she should trifle with.

Afraid of him? Weren't you determined not to be a mouse?

Annis started to wiggle. "Let me off this beast."

The arms around her tightened. Annis gasped at the sheer power in the man. But she also marveled at his ability to stop just shy of actually hurting her.

Lonn had never been so accomplished.

Or he never cared if he caused her pain.

It was sad to note that she wasn't too sure which way it really was.

Ha! Don't go thinking any man is different. Women are chattel.

Which was why she had to continue with her escape. But the steel cage formed by Rolfe's arms promised her it wouldn't be easy to argue her way loose.

Well, you will just have to plan for the right moment.

Frustration drew its claws across her patience, but there was little she might do except endure. At least Rolfe was riding away from Goron Duncan.

Far away.

That was one of her goals, so she'd take solace in achieving it.

And later on, she'd claim victory by slipping away from Rolfe Munro, too.

⇶✦⇷

"YE BASTARD."

Annis kept her expression bland as she watched Seath tear into Rolfe. There was an ache in her lower back from how many hours she'd been in the saddle, but she ignored it as Seath rubbed his horse down before coming after Rolfe.

Rolfe was still working on his horse and didn't turn to face the younger man.

"Look at me when I am talking to ye, cousin," Seath demanded.

Rolfe turned his head. "This horse just saved me life. And I will need him in top form if the Duncan decided to get their mounts and set out after us."

Rolfe returned his attention to the stallion. The horse seemed to nod its head in agreement. Annis discovered her gaze lingering on the way he moved his hands over the soft brown velvet of the animal's skin. The horse appeared to be enjoying it.

You might enjoy being stroked like that.

Where had such a thought come from?

Lonn's touch had never pleased her. The horse shifted to make sure Rolfe carried his stroking down to its haunches. A strange little tingle teased her belly. Annis looked at the ground as she tried to deduce just what it was. A flicker of heat, teasing her lower body and even making her cheeks feel slightly warm.

So very odd.

"The Duncan have lost her to the Leslie," Seath declared.

Rolfe stopped his labor and faced off with his cousin. Annis felt tension rippling through the air, and she wasn't the only one either. Many of the Retainers were watching from over the backs of the horses they were tending. The hushed conversations which had risen up after Rolfe had finally called a halt died instantly as everyone focused on the confrontation.

"As wet as the ground is, there will no' be too much difficulty tracking us," Rolfe informed his cousin softly. The control in his tone sent another shiver down her spine. "Unless the lass is no' worth very much, if so, there is no reason for ye to be so possessive of her, Seath."

The man was truly hardened, but unlike Goron and his heavy-handed authority, she discovered her gaze drawn to his face as he dealt with his younger cousin.

"I set out to steal her, so she is mine," Seath insisted. "Can I no' want her for me own?"

"Ye have lasses a plenty on yer own land and the neighboring land which border the Leslie. Why did ye suddenly take it into yer head to ride down to the Duncan and take one of theirs?"

"She's English," Seath said.

"Aye, I heard that much in her voice," Rolfe confirmed.

Rolfe might have realized she was English, but a great many of his men hadn't. They glanced her way, and their expressions were chilly, to say the least. Annis held onto her poise. It was hardly the first time she had been disliked simply for being who she was.

"Which makes me wonder even more just why ye rode down to Duncan land to take her. Do nae tell me again it was because ye craved her."

Seath didn't stand up to his cousin's advance. The younger man stepped back, earning a grunt from Rolfe.

"I want her widow's thirds."

"And do ye think ye will see them in yer lifetime?" Rolfe scoffed. "It will take a lawyer two decades to argue the case before the Duncan are ever brought to heel over the matter. Stealing her means they will fight until their last silver penny to deny ye anything of worth. Even if ye win in court, lad, they'll send ye diseased sheep as payment at best."

"Her worth is in her royal blood," Seath declared hotly. For a moment, there was a look of victory on the youth's face. But it faded as Rolfe's expression darkened dangerously.

Rolfe's gaze was suddenly on her. Annis felt it like a bolt of lightning. She didn't duck her chin, though. No, she knew how to stand up to those who wanted to make her lower her eyes in shame. She was who she was.

Rolfe's expression eased just a fraction. Or at least she thought it did.

Wishful thinking.

Possibly, still, she thought she caught a flicker of...well...admiration for her ability to look straight at him before he snapped his attention back to Seath.

"Elizabeth Tudor has very few royal relatives thanks to her father's affection for beheading those who might have threatened his claim on the throne."

"Margret Clifford is heir presumptive," Seath answered.

"Aye, and the woman has sons," Rolfe replied. "This appears to be a lass, Seath."

There was a round of chuckles from the Retainers watching. It was grudging, though, and died quickly, proving the men watching were undecided.

"The eldest son discovered how to use his cock early," Seath said without hesitation over the scarlet topic. "This is his bastard daughter."

Rolfe looked back toward her. His expression wasn't thunderous any longer. He seemed to be contemplating her with what appeared to be mild pity.

"That would explain why Goron Duncan was willing to spill blood over his brother's widow," Rolfe admitted.

"And she is my prize," Seath declared boldly. "Don't go forgetting it either."

"What I won't forget is how much trouble ye've taken on for yer men to deal with." Rolfe returned his attention to Seath. "Yer father should have taught ye to consider long and hard what price yer actions will have for the Retainers who ride with ye, Seath."

"The men riding with me know the prize is worth the risk."

"Then they are as foolish as ye are," Rolfe replied. "Royal blood is naught but trouble. Even a by blow is enough to bring the king's attention to ye. Do ye think James will sit quietly by as ye produce children who might have a claim on what he already considers his?"

"Margaret Clifford might yet inherit the throne of England."

"Aye, and then there will be an argument over which line to follow. Both James and Margaret Clifford are descendants of Henry VIII's sisters. Just because the one who wed into Scotland had it in her contracts that her descendants are written out of the line of succession of England does not mean those contracts cannot be broken now that it is so long after the fact. And do nae forget that James is the descendant of the older sister!"

"Better I have her than Goron Duncan," Seath said. "James and all the lowland clans think to wipe out us Highlanders. Well, I'll not stand by while they breed up a royal heir to help them bolster their case that they are superior to us."

There was a round of agreement from the Retainers watching. A deep sound that spoke of a long dispute.

"There is dissent between Scotsmen?" Perhaps Annis shouldn't have asked the question. There was more than one scathing glance sent her way for daring to interrupt. But Rolfe's lips twitched up into a grin.

Annis discovered herself mesmerized by the transformation that little curving of the mouth made in Rolfe Munro. His face became quite charming.

"Aye, lass." Rolfe moved closer to her. "The Duncan and lowlanders consider us in the Highlands to be savages."

"They only admit to liking us when they have an army invading!" Someone added to the delight of the Retainers clustered around them.

Savages.

Aye, she could see it.

Well, he was that, and yet, she decided the word seemed to be a compliment of sorts, for it carried with it a promise that he would rise to the challenges presented to him.

"I will change their minds." Seath came closer. Determination showed in his eyes.

Oh yes, you've seen that before.

Annis stiffened, detesting the way she was always viewed as an advantage for someone's ambition.

But Seath suddenly shifted to the side. Rolfe had sent his cousin skidding with a hard shove.

"Kindly do nae act like a savage," Rolfe admonished his cousin. "She's a lass. Not a mare."

Someone grunted.

It seemed Rolfe was alone in his sentiments.

You cannot be surprised.

And yet, she was, because Annis was looking at Rolfe, and there was a twinge of embarrassment in his eyes.

Annis didn't even blink. What was the point? Her earliest memories were of people standing over her as they discussed her bloodline merits.

Seath was less than contrite. He jutted out his chin and sent Rolfe a hard look. "She's me prize, and I intend to take her home."

He reached for her, and Annis jumped back. Seath's Retainers chuckled at his expense. Annis held her tongue, for she knew better than to trifle with a man's ego. Seath's expression darkened.

"Ye are coming with me," Seath said ominously. "If I have to bind ye."

Annis narrowed her eyes. Something flared inside her. A need so fierce, she curled her hands into fists, unable to maintain her poise.

"Ye're a goat, Seath," Rolfe muttered under his breath in disgust.

He stepped in between Seath and herself. His expression was unreadable, but he clasped his hands around his wide belt, making the storm inside her subside just a bit.

"Goron Duncan will have found his horses by now," Rolfe said softly.

Annis shifted back a step. She locked gazes with him.

"Yer choice is to ride with us off his land or stay here and wait for him to run ye down," Rolfe finished.

Seath began to voice his opinion, but Rolfe raised his hand, and his cousin instantly fell silent. In fact, all the men around them were eerily still. The wind rustled through the tree limbs sending a tingle down her back with just how intent everyone was on her response.

"You will take me off Duncan land?" she asked.

"I will," Rolfe replied.

She had no reason to trust him.

Well, you know for certain what Goron intends to do with you.

That was very true. So, she nodded. "I would appreciate your escort."

Rolfe stepped to the side. He extended his arm toward his horse. This time, there was no rock for her to use to mount the stallion. Annis ended up looking at the distance between the ground and the saddle as she tried to come up with a method of getting herself onto the back of the creature.

"Up with ye, lass," Rolfe muttered next to her ear as he clasped her around her waist. Annis gasped at the sheer amount of strength the man had, for he lifted her up and deposited her in the saddle.

Something rippled through her.

A sense of awareness that she'd never encountered before.

Some flicker of heat deep inside her belly that she couldn't quite grasp an understanding of.

Whatever it was, a second ripple shook her when Rolfe joined her. He swung up behind her, settling against her back.

You aren't a virgin.

She wasn't, and yet, Annis felt shocked to her core. For some reason, she was keenly aware of Rolfe.

How hard he was against her.

He reached around her, gathering up the reins in a grip that appeared far more confident than she could recall ever thinking any man's hands ever appeared.

You are being ridiculous.

Clearly, the stress of escaping the Duncan stronghold had been more intense than she'd realized. Her emotions were frayed, for that was the only explanation for the way she was reacting to her companion.

Rolfe Munro.

His name suited him. Rolfe…*Wolf.*

Emotional.

She truly was. Annis couldn't help but smile. Just a bit, and Rolfe couldn't see her face, so it didn't matter. She'd been taught to conceal her feelings from a young age. They were a weakness.

Annis stiffened her resolve.

The price of showing weakness would be exploitation. People wanted her blood for their ambitions. Seath Leslie was no exception. Neither was Rolfe Munro.

They were there to use her to further their means.

No noblewoman has it any different.

They didn't. Marriages were arranged for the advancement of the families. Even a peasant girl was contemplated by her in-laws as to her worth or at least how much work she might do.

It was merely the way life was.

Hard.

So it was best to make certain you gained as much as you might, for the winter would come with its cold and hunger. Allowing emotions to lead the way was a sure way to end in dire circumstances. Why suffer the harsher edges of life and emotional pain as well? Better to at least spare herself the heartache since she couldn't change how cruel fate often was.

So, whatever it was Rolfe Munro stirred in her, she'd simply have to resist the urge to ponder it further.

⟫⟩⟨⟪

THEY RODE HARD. The rain soaked them, and still, the horses carried them across the miles of muddy road. Rolfe felt his companion sag as her strength waned. She fought to remain straight and not lean back on him. But they couldn't stop. Not yet. A tavern would be the first place the Duncan would look. So he rode on until he spied a lonely house that he knew well. He should have seen her as a nuisance, but there was something about the way she had turned and run toward his horse that remained solidly in his thoughts.

She was strong.

And she didn't let overwhelming odds defeat her.

Careful, laddie.

Rolfe might have heeded his inner voice, except he suddenly asked himself just why he needed to be wary. She was strong. And everyone was prodding him to settle on a woman.

He could do worse.

But there was Seath to consider. The Leslie would support him in his claim on the girl.

Are ye thinking to claim her?

For some reason, he was thinking about it. She sagged against him finally, and there was a stirring of something inside him.

A very unexpected stirring.

And it was stirring his temper.

At last, they made it to a manor house that he knew. In the dim light of dusk with the rain still falling on them, it was as welcoming as a palace. Someone spied them and rang a small bell on the inside of the barn. Several half-grown boys answered the call, pushing open the barn doors so they might ride inside. The horses crowded in, happy to have shelter.

"Up the stairs with ye, lass," Rolfe encouraged Annis to head toward the stairs. "There will be a dry bed for ye and a warm supper."

Rolfe watched as she headed to the base of the stairs. He was trying to maintain his composure, but he turned to discover Seath glowering. The sight broke through Rolfe's attempts to master his temper. If his cousin wanted to fight, Rolfe wasn't going to back down.

"Ye'll not be taking me prize, Rolfe." Seath unleashed his temper.

Rolfe faced off with his cousin. The Leslie Retainers were all cluttered around, clearly wanting to hear what Rolfe intended to do. His captain, Sholto, stood off to one side, making sure the Munro Retainers held their tongues.

The Leslie were on the verge of fighting.

A prize was a prize. They'd ridden out to claim one and clearly weren't interested in being denied what they'd earned.

Poor lass.

Rolfe pushed his misgivings aside. Royal blood was more than just taking a bride to irritate a neighboring clan. This lass was something which might tip the balance of power, and he'd be a fool to overlook what men would be willing to do for such an advantage.

When it came to power struggles, there was no fairness. Only winners and losers. What separated the two was often spilled blood.

Ye want to protect her.

He did, and what Seath didn't yet know about life was that fighting hard was only half the battle. Fighting smart was more important, and Rolfe knew how to use his wits as well.

"Keep yer voice down," Rolfe ordered Seath. "To take a prize is one thing. To be cruel to the lass is nae necessary. So far, she thinks there is merit in riding with us. Keep shouting, and she'll know otherwise. Which means the lot of ye can divide up who is standing watch to ensure she does nae try to escape. Since ye keep reminding me that she is yers, my men will no' be helping ye with that task."

Seath bit back his next comment as he contemplated Rolfe's words.

There was a shuffling among the Leslie Retainers. They were tired. The day had been long, and the road wet. Every one of them wanted to sleep.

Understanding dawned on Seath. Rolfe watched the way his features softened. Behind him, his Leslie Retainers began to grin. Rolfe didn't care for the fact that those men were enjoying having duped the girl. But it was a small price to pay if Seath didn't realize Rolfe was playing him.

What was her name?

The Leslie Retainers viewed her as a prize. A name would make her more human. Their mothers and sisters had names. The lass was English. And that was the word they wanted to keep her labeled with.

He wanted to plant his fist into Seath's face for it.

Rolfe's men were watching him, waiting to take their cue from him. They were strong and knew it and weren't immune to the allure of taking home a good prize.

Yer men would win the day if it came to a fight.

Rolfe found the thought uncomfortable. He didn't need to sever the bond his aunt had made when she was wed into the Leslie clan. Highland clans liked to think they could rely only upon themselves, but the truth was the world was larger than just the land a man was born on. Rolfe had had that lesson impressed upon him early. To be next in line for the lairdship was to think of the repercussions first.

"Ye're right, cousin." Seath grinned. "I'm behaving like a goat. No point in making work for meself if there is another way of getting the same thing. Better to be a horse. Horses are smart."

The Leslie Retainers began to talk. They were pleased with themselves and their master.

"Bring some ale!" Seath called out.

The tavern was a small one. It boasted a decent common room and a loft room, which might be rented. The tavern owner's daughters answered the call for ale. They carried large pitchers into the room, sitting them on the long trestle tables. Seath's Retainers happily settled down to partake of the beverage. Bread and bowls of stew came next.

The Munro Retainers were slower to take their ease. They looked to Rolfe to see what he planned to do.

"Rest, lads," Rolfe said. "We've a hard day of riding to accomplish at daybreak."

The Munro Retainers nodded and sat down. They didn't laugh as hard as the Leslie, for they were further from home. A man who let his guard down was a foolish one when out on the road.

Rolfe took a seat. He reached for a bowl of stew and grabbed a chunk of bread. His hunger wasn't a priority. But making sure he had strength was. So he ate while he had the chance.

But he stayed away from the ale.

His men followed his actions, not drinking. Filling their tankards with water and wrapping up in their kilts to catch the rest they might. Rolfe watched one of the girls carry a tray up the stairs. The door opened when she knocked on it, and the tray was handed off.

Good. The only thing worse than a kicking captive was one weak from starvation.

Not that he had a great deal of experience with captives.

Ye seem to be thinking about acquiring one.

Rolfe frowned. This time when his misgivings stirred, they were too strong to push aside. He didn't like the situation.

Didn't like it a bit.

But Seath wouldn't let the lass be.

Better Seath than Goron Duncan.

Goron Duncan had a wife. If he got hold of the English lass, either the man would kill his wife, or his wife would murder the little English lass to keep her place. Goron's wife was a Campbell, after all. No English girl would do well against her.

Ye still do nae know her name.

Rolfe wanted to, and that made him grind his teeth in frustration. He couldn't care about her. Not beyond decency. Seath was a man now. A young one, but he'd dig in on this matter, and Rolfe couldn't very well argue when he had a mind to keep the lass as well. Interfering would be disastrous to their relationship.

So why did it still sound like a good idea?

>>>><<<<

THE MORNING WAS misty.

Annis woke early and made her way down to the common room, where there was a pot of porridge at the hearth. A stack of pottery bowls was there, and after she filled one, the ceramic heated and warmed her hands while she walked to a bench.

Breakfast was a quick affair even as she lingered over the last bites.

But she made herself put the bowl down and stop procrastinating. She had a plan. And most importantly, a purpose. The Highlanders were gone, granting her a measure of relief. It would seem Rolfe had taken Seath in hand, dissuading the younger man from his ideas of making Annis his prize.

Good.

It was for the best.

Still, Annis had always had it pressed into her how many people would fight over her blood. It seemed strange to have the common room so empty.

Too simple.

So she went outside, but she went through the kitchen. The mist distracted her, though. It hugged the rooftops of the buildings as the water tickled her nose. It was chilly and yet magical. For a moment, she lamented the need to go.

You don't want to leave Rolfe.

Annis quelled the thought.

At least she tried. The idea persisted like a need to sneak into the kitchens for sweet bread in the afternoon when she knew full well she'd get two strikes from the rod if she was caught.

You don't know the man.

He is a Highlander.

Even if she was wise enough to know most of the stories she'd heard about Highlanders had to be an exaggeration, that still left a solid bit of truth in the tales. Highlanders were hardened people, and Annis had to admit that Rolfe and his men truly embodied what she'd heard about their kind.

They didn't like the English at all. So it was best to be on her way.

"Good to see ye are an early riser."

Rolfe and his men were already up, saddling their mounts. In the early morning light, Annis might have expected to see a few blurry looks, but there wasn't a single one. And she was the last one to the yard.

Highlanders.

She was impressed and more determined than ever to part company with them.

Annis nodded to Rolfe. "I want to thank you for your escort yesterday."

Another man took the reins of the stallion Rolfe had been preparing. Rolfe turned his full attention to her.

"I will not trouble you further," Annis continued. She offered him a reverence. Touching one foot in front of her and then placing it behind her. She bent that knee, lowering herself in a curtsey. She'd been taught the respectful gesture and practiced it until it was polished. Rolfe, however, didn't return it as was customary.

Perhaps they didn't reverence in the Highlands. Annis forced herself to look past Rolfe to where the tavern keeper stood. For some reason, there were a few butterflies in her belly as she started toward him, making her final break with the Highlanders.

"Where is it ye plan to go, lass? Yer kin sent ye to the Duncan. If ye return to them, they will merely find another marriage for ye. Me cousin is a decent man."

Annis tightened her composure. A man such as Rolfe would only respect strength. So, she'd stand straight up to him.

"I have no dowry," Annis stated pointedly. "For the Duncan have it all. Furthermore, I am no longer a virgin and, as it would seem, barren. You wouldn't want your cousin to be saddled with a useless wife."

There. Those were the words no one would argue with. Barren was a curse, and yet for her, it was a shield to protect her from being a prize to be fought over. Strange how one thing might be both sides of a coin, depending on who held them.

"None of that answers me question, lass." Rolfe appeared to be intent on finding out the details of her plans.

"I'm English."

"Aye. I've noticed," he answered with a slight grin.

For a moment, she was distracted, for his face transformed with that tiny curving of lips. He wasn't handsome, for that was far too tame a word for him. No, rakish fit, and she discovered she liked it far too much.

You do not care for men.

That was very true. It had been a disappointment, for when she'd wed, she'd held onto a little bit of hope that she'd fall in love with her husband.

Such was the stuff of foolish fairy tales, though.

For there had not been anything in her dealing with Lonn which had been any better than bearable.

Duty.

Annis drew in a stiff breath. She focused on Rolfe, for she wasn't going to step back into the role of wife.

"Barren," she repeated.

"I heard ye the first time, lass."

"Good," Annis replied. "So it's best we part ways. You can explain to your cousin how he does not need to take on a woman who is useless to him."

Rolfe looked her up and down. It was a frank appraisal. She caught herself wondering if he liked what he saw.

Do not become distracted!

"It seems yer ruse is up, Rolfe." Seath suddenly appeared behind her.

Annis turned her head, but the younger man reached out and grabbed her wrist. She was sucking in a gasp as she felt a loop of rough rope go around her arm.

And something snapped inside her.

Annis turned on Seath in a spitting ball of rage. She lifted her knee and rammed it straight into his groin as she yanked her hand away from the rope. As far as thinking went, she wasn't doing it. Instinct was ruling her, making her shove away from her captor.

Seath's face had been bright with a smile of victory. It faded as her knee struck its target. Pain flashed through his eyes as she shoved him away from her. He stumbled back a few paces but recovered quickly. Perhaps she might have been wary of him if she were in her right mind, but at that moment, all Annis could think of was fighting for her life.

But she wasn't going to win. Seath's men crowded in on her.

Someone wrapped their arm around her waist to keep her in place as another grabbed her arms and pushed them out straight. Seath's eyes narrowed. Annis caught a glimpse of his wounded pride, but it wasn't enough to get him to tell his men to release her.

No, he wanted his victory more.

He smirked at her as he wound the rope around her wrists. He knotted it tightly as the pain went up her arms. Someone slipped a strip of cloth with a knot between her teeth and tied it on the back of her head with no regard for the amount of hair they pulled.

"Ye are my prize," Seath growled just inches from her face. "Me cousin might be more crafty with his words in getting ye to come along peacefully, but I do nae care if ye spit and snarl the entire way."

He didn't.

But that wasn't what Annis found herself suffering a blow from.

Crafty?

She turned her head to look at Rolfe. He stood off to one side, his large hands gripping his thick belt.

Watching.

He wouldn't help her.

You were a fool to even think he might.

Seath chuckled. Annis jerked her attention back to him.

"Did ye think me cousin would help ye?" Seath inquired sarcastically. "English, ye do nae ken how it works in the Highlands. His aunt is me mother. I could cut your tongue out, and he'd no' interfere."

There was a round of amusement from his men.

The low, cruel sort of chuckles that chilled her blood.

Well, at least you know how to deal with this.

Annis had perfected the art of detachment early in life. When the majority of conversations were about her uses, it had seemed the best way to console herself. Inside her mind, she might find a place where she was more than a mare. A place where there was hope.

Which wasn't in Scotland apparently.

She let her eyes focus on a point just beyond Seath's shoulder. The knot inside her mouth was drying out, but she resisted the urge to grind her teeth.

Let him think her beat.

There was a grunt from Seath before someone was pulling her toward a horse. She was tossed up without warning.

At least your hands are bound in front of you.

Small mercies.

Oh, she was very accustomed to making bouquets of them!

So she pulled at her skirts to get them settled as the rest of the men finished making ready. The misty morning turned into a rainy day as they set off.

Small mercies.

They thought her whipped.

She didn't give them a reason to look twice at her. They'd all be sleeping quite soundly when she retrieved the knife stuck through her garter.

The only mercy she'd grant Seath Leslie was to not drive it between his shoulder blades before she went on her way!

⋙⋘

Duncan land…

TERIN CAMPBELL WAS no fool.

Even if her husband believed she was.

The Duncan stronghold was full of dark corners, for it was built of stone. She pressed herself flat against a wall and listened to her husband Goron talking with his mother, Benedicta.

"We'll not be letting the Leslie have her," Benedicta insisted. "How could ye think to abandon the chase?"

"Rolfe Munro was riding with Seath," Goron argued. "Without horses, we had no hope of winning the fight."

"And now?" Benedicta demanded. "Now...ye have naught."

"Lower yer voice, woman."

Terin smiled. Her husband liked to refer to gender any time he was feeling pressed upon. He truly did think his cock made him something special.

Her husband was a special sort of ass.

"I will get Annis back," Goron said. "But what is more important is having the right to claim any issue from her. Ye did not have the king's approval for her marriage with Lonn."

"Of course, not," Benedicta replied. "James would never grant it, considering he is eyeing the English throne for himself. Ye will no' get it either."

There was a smug chuckle.

"Well now. I might have a better chance of recovering me dear brother's widow if James were to think the Leslie were out to breed her behind his back. Better a Duncan than a Highlander. And I am a married man, after all."

There was silence for a long moment.

"Ye have some fine wits inside that head," Benedicta said. "We could sue for the girl's return. James might agree if he thinks we are intent on keeping her widow's portion. How strange to think yer wife has a use after all."

"Aye," Goron remarked. "I will set out for Edinburgh at first light to present the petition to the king."

"Aye," Benedicta remarked. "Once we have Annis back, we'll deal with yer wife. Divorce is messy. Far better to lose Terin to something tragic...a miscarriage perhaps. That way, we will maintain our allegiance with the Campbell."

"Terin is barren," Goron said. "I've spilled enough seed in her to know at this point. Bedding her now will nae result in a pregnancy."

"I do nae need her to be breeding to make it appear that she died having a miscarriage," Benedicta said. "Leave that matter to me.

Simply share her chamber tonight so it cannot be questioned."

Terin pushed back into the passageway, allowing the darkness to engulf her.

Barren?

She might argue against the charge, but in truth, she didn't know. The reason behind her ignorance was simple.

She was still a virgin.

Far enough away from the chamber where her husband and mother-in-law were talking, she turned and pulled her skirt up so she might climb the stairs. Her boots were soft-soled, so they didn't make any sound on the steps. Goron had stumbled into their wedding night so drunk, he'd fallen face-first into the bed beside her.

What she couldn't forget was the way his men had called through the open door.

"Do ye need any help?"

"Would ye like any help?"

"Come on now, at least share her mouth with us!"

Terin made it to a storage room. She was careful to walk across some pieces of firewood that were stacked next to the wall, for it wouldn't leave footprints in the dust. The door itself appeared to be chained shut, but it wasn't. Terin pushed it inward and locked it from the inside.

Her haven.

One of many throughout the stronghold. She'd identified many such places in case she needed to hide. Her husband might not even look for her.

Goron had no taste for her.

He'd awoken the day after their wedding, looked at the blood she'd smeared on the bedsheet, and grinned.

"Do nae worry me sweet wife. I will no' bother ye ever again." He'd raked her up and down and shook his head. "I like fire in me woman. Ye..." He'd pointed at her in the corner of their bed. "Are a mouse. If ye ever grow up, ye can suck me cock up to prove it. Until then, mind yer place, or I'll let me men break ye in."

She had been young.

And Goron's words had terrified her.

Now? Well, four years later, Terin realized she'd been correct to fear her husband, but shivering wouldn't do at all. Her father had wed her young. Just seventeen, and Terin knew why now. He'd wanted her compliant. Her sire had counted on her being too naïve to know just how terrible the world was or just how harsh a man Goron was.

She had her eyes open wide now. But back then, she'd not pondered just why the men escorting her to her wedding had looked anywhere but at her.

They'd wanted an alliance, no matter the cost for her.

Of course, now she'd run out of time. Benedicta would do precisely what she'd said she would, which left Terin with only one option.

She would have to act first.

CHAPTER THREE

ROLFE SENT SEATH into the dirt.

The hard connection of his fist against the younger man's jaw drew the attention of every man riding with them.

"What the hell?" Seath scrambled to his feet and faced off with Rolfe. "What cause do ye have to strike me down, cousin?"

"Cut her tongue out as I watch? Did ye learn that sort of thing from yer father, Seath?" Rolfe's voice was low. His men shifted as they recognized just how dangerously close their laird was to losing his temper. "To terrify a woman who is helpless with threats of being cut into pieces? Tell me—" he moved closer to Seath. "Did yer father ever do such a thing to me aunt?"

Seath's glowering ceased.

He stiffened, recognizing that he'd crossed a line.

Rolfe intended to make sure he realized he should have never gotten close to it.

The Munro Retainers wore dark expressions as they allowed their disapproval to show. The Leslie Retainers cast uncomfortable looks from side to side as they recognized how very dangerous the situation was.

Seath lifted his hands. "Ye said it already, Rolfe. I've the manners of a goat. I should no' have said such a thing, but the lass kneed me."

Rolfe sent another hard blow into his cousin's midsection.

"She is half yer size and English, as well!" Rolfe followed Seath and grabbed a handful of his clothing to keep him near. "If ye are man enough to have yer father's Retainers riding behind ye, then ye are too old to be making excuses for yer own words. Being in command means being aware of every word which crosses yer lips."

"Ye're right," Seath conceded. "I shouldn't have said it."

Rolfe made a low sound under his breath. He was fighting to control his temper.

But that was another trait a leader needed to have.

Self-control.

He released Seath. "I will be asking Euna."

"Me father treats me mother well, Rolfe," Seath defended his sire.

Rolfe drew in a deep breath and pointed at his cousin. "And yet ye learned it from somewhere. Cut her tongue out? Christ man! Ye should be grateful I waited until ye had her out of sight before I took the matter up with ye."

Seath snorted and opened his arms wide to indicate his men. "Yet ye lay me low in front of me men."

Rolfe's eyes narrowed. "Ye said it in front of yer men, so ye will be held accountable in front of them. Any man who rides with me would have a problem with what ye threatened that girl with, and if they don't, I want to know who they are, for I will not have savages at me back."

"I wouldn't have done it," Seath growled. "Ye are making too much of the matter. Taking it to heart. Ye've done yer share of prize stealing."

"The lass does nae know ye wouldn't do it. She's terrified, and ye should be ashamed for putting tears into a woman's eyes." Rolfe stepped up close to his cousin once more. "What do ye think this is Seath? Some moonlight raid where ye will only be thrashed for taking a few hens if ye are caught? That is a woman of royal blood. Not only was she wed to the Duncan, ye can be very sure the king will have an opinion about ye bringing her into the Leslie family line. What ye have done is not some simple prize snatching."

Rolfe was fighting back a wave of disgust. It was thick and hot, threatening to drown him.

Seath drew in a stiff breath. He straightened up and sent Rolfe a stern look. "I was not about to allow the Duncan to keep her."

There was a shifting among the men. They were all weighing the risk of taking the girl over allowing the Duncan to keep her. Rolfe would be a fool to overlook the need to utilize strategy when thinking about the matter. A royal blood heir would increase the power of the Duncan greatly.

It was not a matter to dismiss lightly.

"Threaten that lass in such a grievous fashion again, and I will take her from ye," Rolfe raised his voice so every man listening heard him clearly. "My word is me bond."

He turned and walked away before he gave into the urge to thrash Seath, as he so richly deserved.

"Ye're letting the lad off a bit easy," Sholto muttered when Rolfe stopped beside him.

His captain was someone Rolfe valued the counsel of. There was a touch of gray at the man's temples, attesting to the years of experience he had. Sholto appeared to be in complete control of his temper.

Unlike you.

Emotions were the devil's music.

"Mind ye," Sholto continued when Rolfe remained silent and started to rub his horse down. "It's a sad thing when ye have to step in. Seems the lad should have been brought up a bit better by his father or at least no' given authority over Leslie Retainers until he proved he was mature."

"Euna said she'd spoilt him," Rolfe grumbled. "It seems to have proven true."

Sholto nodded. "The little lass will be suffering his ill-temper."

Rolfe turned and locked gazes with Sholto. The older man simply sent him a look that made it plain his captain didn't see why Rolfe hadn't already thought the same thing.

Rolfe reached up and tugged on the corner of his knitted cap. It was a respectful gesture he received from every man riding with him, but offered it to Sholto in gratitude. His captain grinned before returning his attention to his horse. The man was whistling a moment later.

Aye, it's up to you now, laddie.

And he really shouldn't interfere any more than he already had.

But the look in her eyes haunted him.

What was her name?

Rolfe still didn't know, and it was bothering him more than it had before.

Ye're treading on thin ice.

Caring about the girl was going to bring about a whole load of trouble.

That is nae stopping ye.

It wasn't.

Sholto was still whistling, but he turned and looked at Rolfe. There was a wealth of meaning in the man's eyes. Unlike Seath, Rolfe appreciated the nudge from someone wiser. He nodded and turned away from his horse. As Rolfe walked toward the tavern they'd stopped at, he heard Sholto call out to one of the two younger lads who were riding with them to come and take over caring for his horse. The younger boys would enjoy getting a chance to work with the stallion. They would earn their place as Retainers in another year.

Everyone earned their way.

Rolfe was the son of the laird. He had his duty, and with such came a need to make sure he was careful with his words and actions, for they'd be scrutinized.

Seath needed more lessons in such things.

They'd stopped at a public house. It was large, and likely the family had fallen on hard times, so they'd welcome in guests to bring in some silver. The main room had tables and benches. A doorway opened to the kitchen where he could see the mistress of the house working at a stillroom table along with several young girls. A small bell was hung over the door so that when he pushed it inward, the top of the door hit it. A soft tinkling sound rang out, and a thin boy came hurrying into the main room to welcome him.

The youth was tall and lanky and maybe fourteen winters. He had an apron on and reached up to tug on his cap.

"Where is the lass?" Rolfe inquired.

The boy's eyes filled with uncertainty.

"I see me cousin warned ye to no' mention her." Rolfe withdrew a few silver pennies and one gold piece from his doublet. He held up the gold piece. "This is for me men. Is yer father here?"

The youth shook his head.

"Me husband was killed three years ago." A woman emerged from the kitchens. She was wiping her hands on her apron. "So, I offer hospitality to travelers in order to keep this house and feed me family."

"I am Rolfe Munro." He placed the gold in her hands. "I pay for me men."

The woman took the coin and weighed it in her hand. "Normally, I am not one to meddle in the personal affairs of me guests. However, I keep a Christian home, and I do nae need any trouble from the Church."

Rolfe dumped the silver into her hand. "Send some hot water and soap up to the girl. No one will behave dishonorably under yer roof."

The woman nodded, accepting his word on the matter. She turned around, intent on going back into the kitchen. "Take him abovestairs," she instructed her son.

The lad was quick to turn and start up the stairs. Rolfe followed him. The door he stopped in front of wasn't locked, and none of the Leslie Retainers were keeping watch.

Damn, Seath. He'd left the lass bound.

The youth was gone a moment later, the sound of the door bell summoning him back to the main floor.

Rolfe stood still for a moment.

It wasn't quite respectable to be alone with the lass.

Well, it is no' right that Seath left her tied up and tossed like a sack on a bed either.

He was guessing about just where she was, but it was likely a good guess. Rolfe hesitated a moment longer, feeling a strange stirring inside himself. Something he hadn't felt in years. A tingle of uncertainty surprised him because he was long past the awkwardness of youth when it came to the opposite gender.

Christ. Ye are acting like a virgin.

Rolfe rapped on the door before he pushed it in. The room was small. Just a loft space that had been built up so it might be lent for a few bits of silver. The bed was built into the back wall. There was barely room for the door to open. There wasn't a window because it would have let the heat out. The girl was sitting on the bed. She was a tussled mess. Her hair rising up in a cloud around her face. The gag was still between her teeth, and now her ankles were bound.

But she sent him a glare, which made it plain she wasn't anywhere near broken.

Whatever Rolfe had intended when he'd pushed the door in, he discovered himself lost in the way she looked at him.

Damned if he didn't like her spirit.

⫸⫸⫷⫷

ROLFE MUNRO GRINNED at her.

Annis wanted to growl in response.

Damn the man and his cousin for enjoying her plight.

Her fingernails dug into her palms because she was clenching her hands so tightly. It was a poor choice on her part because it made her wrists push against the rope binding her. The skin was already broken and bleeding. A new shaft of pain went down her arms, making her draw in a soft gasp.

Rolfe didn't miss it either.

Annis looked away, unwilling to allow him to see the pain glittering in her eyes.

"Here, lass," he muttered softly. "I'll free ye."

Whatever she'd thought he was there for, it wasn't to release her.

Annis returned her gaze to his.

Such amazing blue eyes. Almost like sapphires.

He froze when their gazes met. As if he felt the same shifting between them.

Don't be a fool. He sees you only as a prize.

Well, there was no point in quibbling over what had always been a part of her life.

Better to take the comfort you can.

There was a solid truth. Annis pushed her frustration aside and lifted her bound wrists. She refused to allow her pride to interfere. The night would be long and miserable if she remained the way she was.

Rolfe broke off the connection between their eyes to look at the rope knotted around her wrists. His expression hardened.

You are only seeing what you want to.

Maybe, but at least it was better than the chill of detachment. She knew how to take solace in being a person only to herself, but it was a lonely place. Solitary. In truth, Annis had no love for it. Hope flickered inside her, trying to ignite as she had looked into those blue eyes.

He tugged at the knots, finally pulling the scratchy binding away from her skin. The rope around her ankles didn't last long either. When he finished, he looked back at her, his gaze on the gag still around her head. Annis reached up, but it was knotted in her hair.

"Best allow me to do it."

Her pride was trying to rear its head, but all refusing his offer would do was gain her a bald spot. So she turned her head and felt him gingerly working to free the knot.

The sides of her cheeks were painful.

Annis worked her jaw open and closed a few times before she turned and looked at him. She quelled the urge to smooth her hair back.

There would be no primping for his benefit.

He seemed at a loss as to what to do next. It surprised her, touching off a ripple of sensation that she struggled to understand.

Was she touched to see he had compassion for her plight?

She shouldn't be. He'd watched her be bound and never raised a word of protest. Setting the example for his men.

"I suppose it's only fair that ye would no thank me," he said.

A dry little sound of amusement escaped her lips. His lips curved up into that grin once more.

He was a handsome brute.

Stop noticing.

There was a soft knock on the open door. Rolfe stepped away from the bed. There was a girl standing there. She was maybe sixteen, and her eyes widened as she took in Annis. Rolfe held the rope behind his back as she looked at him.

"Put it on the stool," Rolfe directed her.

Next to the door was a battered stool. It had several chunks missing from its edges, but it appeared servable enough. The girl sat a wooden bowl down. She had a handful of her skirt gathered up to protect her fingers where they grasped the handle of an earthenware pitcher. A little wisp of steam was rising from its top.

Oh my.

Annis couldn't help but be touched. Warm water? Her gaze flew back to Rolfe despite her determination to not look his way again.

He was watching her.

Their gazes fused, and something rippled across her skin.

She looked away quickly.

But not fast enough, for the feeling lingered. A flicker of heat teased the surface of her cheeks as the girl placed a small bundle on the bed beside her.

"No one will disturb ye." Rolfe started to follow the girl out of the tiny room, but he stopped and looked back at Annis.

"What is yer name?"

He seemed to be fighting the urge to ask her. There was a hint of frustration in his expression as he realized he'd lost the battle against his curiosity.

Good. At least she wasn't the only one failing to fend off urges.

Her lack of response made his eyes narrow.

"Ye prefer to remain naught more than a prize, lass?"

"It is what you and your countrymen make me," Annis replied before she thought to bite her lip.

"And yer kin?" Rolfe turned to face her completely. "Did they not negotiate yer marriage with the Duncan?"

Annis lifted her hand and looked at the bloody mess her wrist was after being bound all day. "There is a simple truth to my circumstances. Marriage is a ruse that hides so very much. Disguising abuse with positive words such as duty."

"Lonn Duncan did not treat ye well?"

Annis looked back at Rolfe. His tone had tightened, surprising her. But it irritated her as well, for he was only trying to lull her into compliance by seeming sympathetic.

He'd watched and said nothing.

"He never took a knife to me," Annis stated firmly.

Rolfe's expression hardened. Annis felt a shaft of apprehension go through her. Rolfe was quite clearly a dangerous man. It wasn't something that might be conveyed in words. It was simply there, in the way he held himself. This was not a man who would prove himself in any way except his actions, and he was hardened by those actions. And yet, she wasn't sorry she'd spoken. Let him disapprove of her. She'd not cower.

"Me cousin will not cut ye, lass." Rolfe's eyes sparkled with something that looked very much like a promise.

Hope flickered inside her.

Don't be foolish. You will only be disappointed when he leaves you to his cousin.

Annis averted her gaze, needing to stop herself from forming an attachment to him. Hope was a very dangerous thing for someone like her, for it would lead to trust.

He'd stood there and done nothing as his cousin threatened her...she mustn't forget that. Seath was his family, after all. She looked at the bloody, torn skin of her wrists. That was reality. Blood, pain, and being bent.

Be prudent.

Rolfe cupped her chin and raised her face so their gazes met once more.

Annis jumped. The contact between them was jarring. Her eyes widened, and his did, too. For a moment, her breath caught. He pulled his hand back, seemingly just as startled as she was.

It didn't make sense.

Annis blinked, trying to understand why she'd responded in such a huge way.

Rolfe let out a grunt. "Forgive me. I should no' have put me hands on ye."

His apology stunned her. His lips twitched again as he noted her surprise.

"I do have some manners, lass," Rolfe offered with a grin. "I asked for yer name because it seems callous of me to call ye English."

"Annis."

She'd spoken before she contemplated the wisdom of the impulse.

You want to be more than a thing.

She did. Oh, she knew better than to court friendship with anyone.

They'd only use her for their own gains. Yet, there was something about the way he looked at her that just made all of her logical arguments irrelevant.

"Annis," he repeated. There was a gleam of satisfaction in his eyes as he spoke her name. "Annis."

He reached up and tugged on the corner of his bonnet as though they were meeting at some harvest market fair. His grin became a wide smile that flashed her a glimpse of his teeth, and she felt utterly breathless. He was tall and handsome and paying her court. It was only a moment before he turned and left, leaving her with his image lingering in her mind.

Annis sat still, a silly little smile lifting the corners of her lips.

Foolish.

Yes. She didn't deny it.

But her heart was thumping in a way she had never experienced. She would have sworn she could still feel his fingers on her chin. Whatever words her logic used to scold her with, she just couldn't stop herself from admitting she'd enjoyed the encounter with Rolfe Munro.

After all, reality would resume long before she wanted to welcome her circumstances back.

So, she didn't bother to fight against the strange emotional response to Rolfe.

No, there would be time enough for that later.

>>>>><<<<<

ANNIS.

Rolfe paused outside the door.

A fine name for the lass. Annis.

"Ye look proud of yerself."

Sholto was halfway up the stairs, leaning against the wall. Rolfe stiffened, and his captain grinned.

"I followed ye on in because I suspected ye'd let yer guard down."

It was a fair enough charge. Rolfe tightened his expression as he descended a few steps.

"Not that the little lass is no' something I'd like to have me full attention on, mind ye," Sholto continued. "She is no great beauty, but there is a sparkle in her eyes that intrigues me."

"Well, ye can just forget her," Rolfe advised his man.

Sholto chuckled and fell into step behind Rolfe as they went back into the common room. The scent of supper was thick in the air now. Rolfe felt his belly rumble, but he went toward the open doorway, which connected with the kitchen.

"I already saw to the lassie's supper," Sholto called after him.

The same girl who had brought the hot water was busy loading up a tray. Rolfe looked at it before turning around. His captain was watching him, but Sholto's teasing demeanor had faded. His captain was seeing too much for Rolfe's comfort.

What do ye mean by that, laddie?

Rolfe honestly didn't know. That feeling was stirring again inside him. A sense of interest he hadn't felt before. It defied logic and left him struggling to nail it down so he could understand it completely.

Indecision was something he didn't need. His men couldn't see him wavering.

Ye are wavering.

He was. And it was a fact that Rolfe didn't quite have the resolve to chastise himself for it either.

Ye mean ye can nae find the detachment to ignore the little lassie's plight.

Rolfe drew in a deep breath. That was it, really. He wasn't detached. He was involved, and it was growing stronger. What stunned him the most was how little he wanted to stop the growing feeling.

Does that mean ye plan to leave Annis with him?

He didn't want to. Rolfe acknowledged that fact as he sat down to eat with his men. The conversation was hushed among the Munro Retainers as they sensed his indecision.

He didn't need a rift between Leslie and Munro.

His father was dying. There were matters he needed to attend to, and taking a prize from Seath wasn't going to help at all.

The supper tasted like dust in his mouth while Rolfe wrestled with the facts of his position. It was hardly the first time he'd not cared for the sharp edges of a situation. Yet, he couldn't recall being so uncomfortable when facing harsh circumstances before.

Ye shouldn't have learned her name.

Rolfe grunted at himself. Better to be uncomfortable than enough of a bastard to think of a woman as naught more than a prize.

The serving girl came back down the steps. A moment later, Seath settled down on the bench beside Rolfe. His cousin was chewing on his pride, his chin jutted out. Rolfe continued eating.

"I suppose I owe ye a word of thanks for helping me get my prize away from the Duncan. Together, our men made a formidable force," Seath managed at last.

Rolfe turned his head and sent the youth a stern look. "What is it ye plan to do with her?"

"Well, I'll see what me father has to say on the matter," Seath replied. "She'll wed one of me brothers at the least."

"Do ye think any of yer brothers care to have a captive bride?" Rolfe asked bluntly. "One who has been offered less than the same care ye give to yer horse? Ye've given her ample reason to run the first chance she gets. In case ye missed it, that lass is not afraid of striking out on her own. Ye left her bound. Do ye think she'll be happy to settle down and be yer wife, when ye have left her without even the opportunity to relieve herself?"

Seath shrugged. "I wasn't intending to forget about her. It's just the first time I've had to think about taking care of a woman." Seath sent Rolfe a grin. "We'll be home soon, and me mother will know how to handle her. And me father will be pleased to hear ye helped me out. As for the lass, she'll get over it in time."

Aye. That would be so. But only because she'd have little choice but to make the best of her circumstances.

The tension in the room dissipated, though. Even Rolfe's men accepted the apology. They nodded with agreement before relaxing.

Rolfe couldn't find peace with it.

He maintained his composure. Drinking and eating with a mild expression on his face. Only Sholto guessed there were deeper thoughts going on inside his head.

Good. For it would be much easier to dupe Seath when the moment came if the lad wasn't smart enough to see that Rolfe wasn't at ease at all.

Annis would settle down.

But she'd be doing it as his captive.

⫸⫷

Duncan land…

BENEDICTA WAS UP at first light to see her son off.

Goron took only a few moments to eat a large breakfast before he stood up and headed for the stables. His men had been following his example, shoveling porridge into their mouths. When their laird stood up, they grabbed every scrap of bread and cheese on the table, stuffing it into their doublets to eat while they rode.

Those with women were lucky enough to receive bundles as they hurried through the doorway. But the Head-of-House was quick to keep the unmarried members of her staff in the kitchens where there would be no impulsive kisses to fuel gossip and ruin reputations. Retainers didn't always return sitting up in the saddle.

Benedicta handed her son some letters.

"There is one for Lady Cameron," Benedicta said. "She is me sister and serves the queen—another for my uncle William. Do nae give it into any hand except his, or he will never see it. His secretary detests the Duncan."

Goron nodded. He tucked the letters into his doublet. He didn't care very much for the games of power played at court, but he understood their importance. His mother was very good at dealing with the shadow games. He pulled her close in a hug and used the embrace to whisper in her ear.

"Terin hid from me last night."

Benedicta gave him a confident smile. "Do nae worry a bit about it. I have everything well in hand."

Goron mounted his horse and raised his hand to order his Retainers to follow him. He rode out of the stronghold with thirty men behind. It was a force that would draw attention when he reached court.

He didn't spare a thought for what he'd left behind him. No, his wife was useless, or perhaps he should say she'd provided all the benefits she might. Her dowry was well and truly in the Duncan coffers, and enough time had passed since the wedding for there to be few if any questions about her death.

Evil?

No, he wasn't evil. Just ambitious. Any of his men who saw too much would keep their mouths shut because they'd realize his success was Duncan success.

⟫⟫⟩⟨⟨⟨

Leslie land...

THE MEN MANNING the Leslie stronghold walls saw them as soon as they rode through the village. There was a ringing along the top of the walls that grew as each tower began to alert the inhabitants of the castle of the return of the laird's son.

It was always a time when everyone rushed out, hopeful there was good news but always mindful of the fact that some of the men might well be returning slung over their saddles.

Euna stood on the steps which led up into the main tower. She was wringing her hands until she spied her son. Seath, for his part, wore a bright expression of victory. Even his older brother's dark frown didn't manage to make him stop preening.

But Torian Leslie had spied Annis.

And there was no missing the rope around her wrists.

"I've brought home a fine prize," Seath declared. Now that all the horses were through the gate and every man standing on his feet in good health, the Leslie were in the mood to celebrate.

Several Leslie Retainers made sure to surround the mare Annis sat on and lift her out of the saddle. Rolfe held up his hand, cautioning his men to let them have their prize. Rolfe dismounted as Seath bounded up the steps to greet his mother.

"Ye worried me half to death," Euna informed him.

"I'm not a lad anymore, Mother," Seath declared, still beaming. "I might tell ye there was no reason to trouble Cousin Rolfe, but I believe he had a bit of fun."

There was a round of amusement. Euna shared a look with Rolfe as Annis was pushed by her, into the stronghold.

"Do I want to know what me brother has brought home?" Torian asked Rolfe when he made it to the top of the steps.

Rolfe stared at the Leslie heir. Torian shouldered a great deal of the duties of running the clan, and it showed in the stern expression he wore while so many of his clansmen were busy celebrating a victory they didn't know the details of.

"The Duncan would have sent yer brother's head back to ye if I had no' gone after him," Rolfe informed Torian.

Torian drew in a stiff breath. He extended his hand. "Ye have me gratitude, Rolfe."

Rolfe clasped the other man's wrist and felt Torian close his fingers around his own. They locked gazes just as firmly before Torian was pulling away to follow Seath.

"Now, this promises to be right amusing."

Sholto made the observation as he flashed Rolfe a smile before he followed Torian into the keep to enjoy the show.

Rolfe slowly shook his head. Sholto's age had many advantages, one of which was getting away with enjoying scenes like the one about to unfold without anyone taking him to task over it.

Lucky bastard.

Rolfe took a moment to tighten his composure before he climbed the steps and entered the keep. Dread was filling him. Something else was building up inside him as well.

Something he feared was stronger than his discipline.

⇒⇒⇒⇐⇐⇐

SEATH WAS PROUD of himself. He gripped her by the upper arm and guided her into his father's study. It was a large room with stone walls. Inside, his father had a huge chair with armrests on it and the Leslie clan's crest carved into the back, which rose high enough above his head for it to be seen when he was sitting in it.

A throne.

Even if the man wasn't a king, Annis understood very well that when it came to Scotland, a laird was the authority as far as the clan went. Not that things were so very different in England. Her grandfather was the Earl of Derby, and his word was law on his land.

She'd seen the same on Duncan land. Benedicta had wielded her power like a queen. Lonn had been a prince in every way. As for herself? She'd been the well-blooded mare brought in for improving the family line, and her worth had always been measured by what she produced.

It would seem Seath Leslie was no better than Lonn Duncan. She might even tell him so.

You are courting disaster.

For some reason, Annis simply didn't care. For the first time, she realized that Aife had taught her how to make poison, so that she might save herself.

Rolfe came through the doorway. Annis found herself looking at him and regretting her thoughts about poison.

Why? He will not save you.

No. But he had at least made certain she was comfortable. It wasn't much, but it was all she had.

Seath shut the door firmly and turned to face his father.

"I've brought home a fine prize, Father."

Annis narrowed her eyes as he pointed at her.

"I could nae tell ye before I went, but she is a descendant of William Stanley, son of Margaret Clifford. Who is heir presumptive of England."

Laird Leslie had a head and beard full of gray hair. The way he sat contemplating his youngest son made it plain that a great deal of that gray had come from Seath's antics.

"Royal blood is not something to trifle with, son," Laird Leslie remarked as he looked Annis up and down.

"It is also not something to leave in the hands of a clan such as the Duncan," Seath argued. "Benedicta secured a Campbell bride for her firstborn and a royal-blooded one for her second born. Fate offered us a chance to keep her from keeping this one."

"Benedicta is scheming," Euna raised her voice. "I agree it would be unwise to leave a royal-blooded heir in her hands."

"A bastard, though," Laird Leslie remarked.

"With the English queen still a virgin so late in life, a bastard has value," Seath continued. "For there are very few English nobles anymore. Elizabeth Tudor is the last of Henry VIII's children, which leaves only his sister's line to inherit."

Annis struggled to maintain her composure.

You've been discussed like an object many times.

She had, so there was no reason for her mouth to be dry or her belly to be rolling. She'd not give the Leslie the satisfaction of seeing her heave.

"Goron Duncan will go straight to the king over her," Rolfe interrupted.

"Which will only lend more validity to her bloodline," Seath said.

Laird Leslie slowly smiled. It sent a chill down Annis's spine.

"I will happily wed her," Torian remarked.

Seath turned on his brother. "I stole her. She belongs to me."

"Her blood would be of most use combined with mine since I am the heir," Torian directed his argument toward his father.

Laird Leslie began to stroke his beard. He pegged Annis with a hard look. "Ye can be certain Benedicta impressed upon her son Lonn just how important it was for his bride to conceive. Ye are no' maiden."

"I am barren," Annis didn't hesitate to say. It was a lie or, at best, something she didn't know for sure. Still, she refused to worry about her soul. God would understand her need to protect herself.

"Three months isn't long enough to know for certain," Euna informed her family.

"And ye were running away when I caught ye." Seath pointed at Annis. "Did ye make sure ye did nae conceive? Me mother sends a concoction to both me and my brothers' mistresses daily to protect the laird's line."

"Seath," his mother admonished him.

Seath sent a look toward his mother. "Ye take care of me well, Mother. Torian wouldn't want that little laundress he fancies to give him a son any more than ye do. And I would not speak of such a thing normally, but this is royal blood."

"Seath is correct," Laird Leslie decided firmly. "No one in this chamber will repeat what is said. Better to be direct, so there is no misunderstanding."

Annis believed him because any concoction that prevented conception would be cause for charges to be brought against Seath's mother by the Church. Sentences were harsh, and even being the lady of Clan Leslie would not save Euna.

"Look at the way she is dressed." Seath proved he was more experienced than Annis had guessed. "Wool dress, partlet, two pairs of stocking, and boots." He stepped close to her. "Ye planned yer escape well. Slipping away when the Duncan were busy burying Lonn. Ye are smart." Annis remained quiet. "Ye made sure ye didnae conceive…didn't ye? I will make a better husband than Lonn."

"I will try to remember that when you are cutting my tongue out," Annis told him sweetly.

Euna gasped. Seath's expression darkened. But his brother Torian cupped her shoulder and pulled her away.

Torian had dark hair. He was a fine enough looking man if she were of a mind to notice his attributes.

"Seath says stupid things," Torian told her softly. "Do nae be fearful."

Annis sent him a steady gaze. She would not falter. Torian's eyes filled with the glitter of appreciation.

Oh yes, men liked spirit in women.

They liked to break it before casting aside their broken plaything and moving on to the next amusement.

Annis wouldn't make the mistake of thinking it was any form of affection.

"Cousin Rolfe already laid me low for saying that," Seath complained. "In front of me men no less."

"The more ye whine, the more convinced I am of how much ye deserved it, pup," Rolfe answered his cousin.

Laid him low?

Annis looked at Rolfe. She really didn't mean to. But it was impulse, her body moving before she thought the action through. She knew better, and yet, she was staring at him before she'd drawn a single breath.

He stared straight back at her. His expression wasn't stony. Not for a split second. No. For just a moment, there was a look of assurance there. And it warmed her.

Stop looking!

Annis shuttered and looked away. Her breath was no longer controlled. Inside her chest, her heart was thumping away too quickly for cool detachment. She couldn't have feelings for him. She simply could not.

For she'd suffer.

"Another reason she should be wed to me," Torian pressed his case.

"She is my prize!" Seath was incensed.

"Aye." Torian turned to face off with his sibling. "Ye took her and never thought beyond what ye could do, Seath. What ye should have been focused on was what ye should do to endear her to making her home here. If ye wed her, she will always recall how ye have treated her, and she'll poison yer children against ye."

Annis felt her detachment return in a rush. Torian's words were like the tide coming back in. No matter how many seashells you found on the beach, the water always came back to cover them up.

His kindness had a purpose. That was all. He'd kept silent just long enough to allow his younger brother to give him enough evidence to support his claim.

"There is no need for a wedding," Laird Leslie spoke up firmly.

Everyone turned their attention to him, proving what Annis had first thought.

He ruled supreme in the stronghold. Her fate was entirely in his hands.

He looked at his wife.

"Torian will take the girl as his mistress. They will be handfasted. If there is issue, a wedding can follow the birth of a healthy son. Beyond that, I agree that the girl has no purpose."

Seath started to argue. His father held up his finger.

"Ye have done a fine service for the Leslie, Seath. Ye will be given authority over Stags Tower for the winter. Ye shall leave tonight."

Seath shut his mouth. He was the youngest child. A position of his own was not to be shunned. Annis watched the way his mother slowly smiled until Euna was beaming. She clasped her hands together and inclined her head toward her husband.

Torian offered his hand to his brother. Seath didn't hesitate but reached out to clasp his brother's wrist and seal the deal.

"I will go and see that supper is laid out for us all," Euna said, voice full of excitement. "We've much to celebrate."

Seath followed his mother out of the study. Laird Leslie settled his attention on Rolfe.

"I'm grateful for yer assistance, Laird Munro."

"Me father is Laird Munro," Rolfe corrected him respectfully.

Laird Leslie nodded. "Aye…aye. Ye are a good son, Rolfe. And a fine nephew. I will nae forget the help ye have given me family. With winter so close, I know ye will want to be on yer way at dawn."

It was a dismissal as well as a warning to leave the matter alone.

No one in the room missed it. Torian had settled himself in front of Annis, making it plain who she belonged to.

Rolfe didn't look at her.

Do you want him to?

She did, and admitting it to herself sent a shaft of pain through her heart, for Rolfe reached up and tugged on his cap without ever glancing her way.

He'd laid Seath low for her, though.

It was just a scrap of compassion, and yet, Annis discovered it warming her heart, even as Rolfe turned and left the solar.

Gone.

Annis struggled to draw breath. Tears prickled her eyes.

Fool! This is what happens when you care about someone…they abandon you.

Laird Leslie nodded and made a low sound of approval in the back of his throat. He looked away from the door to where Torian stood.

"Best for ye to deal with the lass," he instructed his son. "We'll have the handfasting tomorrow."

"Aye." Torian inclined his head in deference to his father's will.

Laird Leslie made a motion for Torian to take her away before he moved over to his desk. Annis heard him rustling parchment as Torian took her by the upper arm and steered her toward the doorway.

His grip wasn't biting.

She should have taken solace in the fact that Torian seemed to know how to control his strength.

But Annis was too busy blinking back tears.

He is not unkind.

Actually, she didn't know that. Not one way or the other. Torian was a stranger and one with a mistress.

His father's word was law.

Torian took her up three flights of steps. He guided her down a passageway and into a chamber. It was located near one of the curtain walls which ran between the towers of the stronghold.

"This room gets fine light in the mornings," Torian remarked as he attempted to break the awkward silence between them.

The window shutters were closed tight, but there were two sets of them on each side of the chamber.

Airing it out would be simple.

Even in winter, the space wouldn't smell dank or musty.

Torian turned to consider her. He got as far as her bound hands before his forehead furrowed, and he was moving toward her.

"I begin to understand why Rolfe took issue with me brother." Torian pulled at the knots before freeing her.

The hours of being bound had left her wrists bloodied. Annis bit her lip as she held back a little cry of pain when the rope ripped away a few scabs.

"Aye, well, me father is likely right to settle ye with me," Torian remarked as his gaze returned to hers. "Ye'll no' be feeling very warm toward Seath."

Annis looked straight at him. His eyes were a gray color. Just a bit of blue but nothing like Rolfe's eyes.

Don't think about him.

Annis drew in a breath. It was time to put her best foot forward and try to forge a relationship that was at least congenial.

"Thank you."

The pair of words tried to stick to the roof of her mouth. They ended up crossing her tongue in a jumbled mess that lacked any sort of composure. Instead, she sounded exactly how she felt...dejected and forlorn.

Torian didn't miss it either.

The thing was, Annis caught a look of agreement in his eyes. He didn't have any more liking for their arrangement than she did.

"I'll send someone up with a meal." Torian sounded relieved to have thought of a way to escape the chamber.

And you...

Annis didn't plan on quibbling over the matter, considering she was just as happy to see his back as he left. She drew in a deep breath and let it out as the chamber door closed firmly behind him. Her shoulders were tense, and at last, she was able to roll them to ease the discomfort.

Alone.

Solitude had always been her dearest friend, for no one might judge her or discover some personal detail to exploit later. Annis sat down but wrinkled her nose when she got a whiff of herself.

Rolfe had sent her hot water and soap.

Stop thinking about him...were you not almost crying over his loss?

She really needed to heed her own advice. Rolfe Munro had been dismissed by Laird Leslie. If he was still inside the stronghold at first light, Annis would be surprised.

No, he'd be gone, and she would have to face her fate. So there was no point in thinking about him even if she admitted she would have liked to.

Admitting it, are you?

Annis smiled. A true, broad smile that made her feel good. She was admitting it. Rolfe Munro was a fine-looking man. Oh, he was vastly different than any man she'd ever met, with his knees peeking out from beneath the edge of his kilt, and the way he kept his hair longer than was fashionable in England. It just brushed his shoulders in the back.

He was rakish.

Perhaps there was something to be said for girls being attracted to the devil's tune. She could certainly see Rolfe enjoying the night breeze and wrapping himself in the cloak of midnight darkness. Every warning she'd heard coming from the mouth of the clergy suddenly transformed into a fascinating enchantment when she applied them to Rolfe Munro. All of those words had been crafted to make her avoid the night and darkness, but when she thought about them in relation to Rolfe, Annis realized they could be enhancements as well.

She drew in a breath and let out a little sound of laughter.

God! It had been so long since she laughed.

She let out another giggle and then more until the chamber was full of her mirth.

She could keep him in her thoughts.

Don't you mean heart?

Did she? Annis sat for a long moment and contemplated the question. She honestly had no idea. But with no one around, she was able to indulge her curiosity. She looked at the window shutters. They were dark now. Which only encouraged her to remain with her fantasies.

Tomorrow would be soon enough to face the light of day.

>>><<<

"TELL THE MEN to eat and gather as much as they can without attracting attention." Rolfe kept an eye on the passageway as he gave his orders to Sholto. "They are to meet me at the stables in one hour. We are not staying."

Sholto knew his tone. His captain didn't question Rolfe but nodded before looking both ways and heading off toward the great hall, where the Munro Retainers were sitting at the supper table.

Rolfe flattened himself against the wall. The evening shadows lengthened and enveloped him. He had to clench his hands when Torian brought Annis by.

Fight hard but fight smart.

Something his father had taught him before he'd fallen ill. It was a lesson his father continued to reinforce as he was undermined by disease and still managed to succeed through strategy.

Tonight, Rolfe would need a solid plan to take home his prize.

He moved down the hall to the other end of the stronghold. The laundry was there. Now he just had to figure out which girl belonged to Torian.

It wasn't hard, though.

More of a process of elimination. Rolfe watched those working in the laundry. The women who were too old, the pair of girls too young, and then there were a few in just the right age category. He watched them, his eyes settling on the one who seemed more brazen than the others. It was just a small bit, for she still kept to her place, but the other girls gave her deference and took the harder jobs from her. A small smile of achievement curved her lips when those girls weren't watching.

Rolfe waited to catch her alone.

"Are ye Torian's woman?"

The girl gasped. Her eyes went to the two feathers on the side of his cap, which were pointed upward to tell everyone he was the eldest son of a laird.

"Torian wouldn't like to know ye have sought me out."

"I wouldn't touch what is his," Rolfe assured her.

The girl's expression changed, becoming calculated. "Then...what do ye want?"

Rolfe looked around, making sure they were not being watched. "Ye've heard there is an English woman here?"

The girl nodded.

"Yer laird is handfasting her to Torian, and if ye plan to stop it, make sure ye are here when she is brought down to be bathed. See that ye are alone. Set her free before the gates close."

"The mistress could turn me out if she suspects I did such a thing." There wasn't real fear in the girl's voice. Rolfe kept his expression blank. She was setting him up for gain.

"In which case, ye will be welcome on Munro land," Rolfe replied. "But I suppose ye can simply wait for yer place to be taken by the English girl. I suppose ye know it will happen sooner or later."

Rolfe offered the girl some coins. "In case ye need to travel to Munro land."

The girl looked both ways before she took the money and pushed it deep into her cleavage.

"How do ye know the girl will come here?" she remarked. "I can nae go abovestairs without permission."

"Any good mother will have their son's bride bathed before the bedding," Rolfe replied. He used the word bedding just to make sure the girl didn't have second thoughts. He wanted her to know her status was on the line.

Her expression darkened. Proving he'd hit her weak spot.

"She won't be able to get far in the time it takes for a bath."

"Send her out of the gates. Don't tell her about me," Rolfe instructed the girl. "I will get her off Leslie land."

The girl slowly smiled. "Fancy her for yerself?"

Rolfe understood the girl's tone well enough. Just because what he wanted would benefit her didn't mean she wasn't going to press him for as much profit as possible. He held up a gold coin. Her lips rounded in a little expression of delight.

"Send her out of the gates. Cover her in an arisaid. Do not tell her I have paid ye for this service." Rolfe stressed his instructions. "And put the coins in yer sock, where Torian won't find them."

The girl took the gold coin and nodded. She dug the money from her cleavage and hiked her skirt up so she might hide the money away as Rolfe had said.

Rolfe turned away from her. He checked the passageway before he walked down it and made his way through the inner yard of the stronghold. His men were in the stable. They were curious, but he'd commanded them well through the years, so none of them was slow in making ready to ride regardless of the hour.

Rolfe caught Laird Leslie watching them from his room as they led their horses out of the stable. He turned and tugged on his cap. His uncle nodded approvingly.

Ye'll be losing that approval.

He would. Rolfe didn't stop, though. He mounted, and his men followed suit. It would take some time, but his uncle would hear at some point that Rolfe had Annis.

He'd weather that storm when it came, because he was taking her.

CHAPTER FOUR

"THERE WILL BE a handfasting tomorrow," Euna spoke softly to the maid in front of her. "My son Torian will be taking the English girl as his. If she proves fertile, there will be a wedding."

Iona inclined her head. The gold in her sock would damn Rolfe Munro if she told the Mistress about it.

But the tone Lady Leslie was using made it clear she was delighted to be able to tell her son's mistress that she was being pushed aside.

Iona held her tongue. She'd always had to look out for herself, and she was good at it. Why have a lover when she might have the laird's eldest son? It was possible she might have preferred someone else, but no one could do as much for her as Torian.

Euna drew in a deep breath. "Good. Ye know there is little point in arguing. Since ye have behaved and not caused a scene, I will make certain ye have a decent dowry. Come spring, we shall see ye settled with a good man. For now, stay away from my son and keep yerself chaste so a decent man will have ye."

Euna was waiting for her to lower herself. Iona felt every fiber of her being rebelling against her circumstances, but the chill in the air promised her harsh consequences if she chose to be rebellious.

So, she performed a reverence, bending her knee and lowering herself. Euna was pleased, granting her a small smile before the lady left the side room of the laundry where Iona worked.

A dowry? That would be very nice. Of course, there was more to gain if Iona managed to get rid of the English girl and please Rolfe Munro. Still, it was a fine idea to keep in her heart for later. Torian would wed at some point. It was good to know his mother would make sure Iona was taken care of so long as she behaved.

She wasn't heartless. Just practical.

"Curse and rot her." Iona began to put on a little show.

"Iona! Mind yer tongue. Ye can nae speak so about the mistress."

Iona sent her friend a hard look. "Torian loves me. I know it."

Darra stepped closer so her words wouldn't carry. "Perhaps he does, but his marriage was never going to be arranged according to his likes."

"It's a handfasting," Iona was quick to correct her friend.

"If ye wanted to wed a man for affection, ye should never have taken up with the laird's son," Darra continued. "Now, the best ye can do is hope the mistress finds ye a man ye can charm."

There was a clearing of a throat. Both girls looked up to see Ursula standing in the doorway. "Ready a bath. The mistress has ordered ye tend to the English girl, Iona."

So she'd know her place. Iona narrowed her eyes to maintain her stance of being upset.

Ursula sent Iona a stern look. Darra sat her iron aside. There were stacks of linens waiting to be pressed flat, but the mistress's orders took precedence.

Iona heard the large hook squeak as Darra pushed it into the hearth so the pot hanging off it would begin to heat up.

"Bring the soap," Darra called to Iona, as there was a splashing sound from a bucket that Darra poured into the tub.

Iona let out a snort before she went through another doorway to where the storeroom was. Ursula was counting linen caps, which another woman had brought her after ironing them. The maid was smiling because her measure of work was finished for the day. As soon as Ursula nodded with approval, she performed a little courtesy and left with a quick step, on her way to get her supper.

Iona rolled her lower lip in to keep from smiling. The timing was perfect. The cook was setting out supper, and everyone who worked in the laundry was hurrying to go to the great hall to get the best of it while it was hot.

"Do not wallow in bitterness," Ursula said in an attempt to comfort her. "It will only sour yer view of the world."

Ursula used one of the keys hanging from a ring on her belt to open a small cabinet. Once the door was opened, the sweet smell of lavender and rosemary came out. Ursula pulled a small piece of soap from the upper shelf that was normally reserved for Euna alone.

She held it out to Iona. There was a frank look on her face.

Iona took the soap without a word.

Ursula's belly rumbled low and long.

"Darra and I will see to the English girl." Iona forced a smile. "Go on and enjoy supper. It will not take more than the two of us to see to a bath."

Ursula looked undecided for a moment. But there was another sound of water being poured into the tub to prove that Darra was wasting no time in performing her assigned task. Ursula's belly rumbled again.

"I'll see that there is a good tray set aside for ye both," Ursula promised.

Iona inclined her head and turned to go and help Darra.

The laundry emptied out quickly after Ursula left, the rest of the staff taking the opportunity to get off their feet while their supervisor wasn't there to notice.

Which meant Darra and she were very much alone. Iona took a moment to look at the other rooms to ensure the others were truly gone. Another bucket of water was emptied into the tub, and she heard Darra let out a soft groan. Her friend was stretching her lower back when Iona returned to the bathhouse.

"Ursula said for ye to get yer supper now," Iona spoke softly.

"She did?" Darra questioned. "What about the English girl?"

Iona shrugged. "I suppose Ursula doesn't want her getting too spoiled by having us tripping over each other to serve her. If she produces a son, that will happen soon enough. Or she wants me to know my place. I didn't ask for an explanation."

"Of course not," Darra said.

Iona walked into the room. "Anyway, ye've already filled the tub. It will not take too much to get her bathed. Go on before ye earn a scolding or miss yer supper because Ursula puts ye back to work as soon as she returns. With Torian handfasting tomorrow, who knows what the mistress has ordered to be readied."

Darra needed no further urging. She wiped her hands and sent Iona a smile before she hurried out of the door.

Iona smiled, too.

Very sincerely.

>>><<<

SOMEONE RAPPED ON her door.

It took a moment before Annis realized she might invite the person in or not.

Choice.

It had been a while since she'd held that power in her hands.

"Come in."

The door pushed open. A young boy stood there. He was thin and lanky but every bit as tall as herself. He reached up and tugged on the corner of his bonnet.

"The mistress has sent me to fetch ye down to the bathhouse, Miss."

"A bath?"

He nodded. "I will show ye the way."

Annis stepped toward him, but something moved beside him. A man was standing on the landing outside her door.

Annis froze. It didn't take very long for her to understand what the burly man was there for.

To ensure you are here for your...handfasting.

The Retainer tugged on the corner of his bonnet and looked at the boy. "The bathhouse, ye say?"

The youth nodded again. "Lady Euna came and told Mistress Ursula to make a bath ready. I was sent to fetch her straight away before the light fades."

Through the open set of window shutters, a crimson sky announced the last hour of daylight.

"The cook is setting out the supper now. Best hurry, or ye will have naught until first light."

The boy turned and started down the steps. He looked over his shoulder and motioned for her to follow him.

The Retainer appeared undecided.

Annis made the choice for him. She went right through the doorway and started down the steps.

She wasn't going to stink if there was an alternative.

If the man wanted to drag her back into the chamber, well, he could give it his best effort. But the Retainer fell into step behind her. Once she made it to the ground floor, the scent of food began to tickle her nose.

"Hurry, Miss." The boy encouraged her, clearly fearing he'd miss out on the best bits of supper. He was taking long strides and made his way to what was the laundry.

It was on a far end of the stronghold. The aroma of food was lighter as the scent of soap grew strong. It was warm, too. The area had several hearths that had clearly been in use throughout the day.

"Just here, Mistress." The boy stopped in front of an opening in the passageway.

"Mistress." A girl stood just inside the chamber. She looked at the lad. "Off to supper with ye now, Brody."

Brody needed no further encouragement. He tugged on the corner of his cap a final time before he was half running down the passageway, his steps echoing between the stone walls.

"I am Iona."

Iona looked past Annis to where the Retainer had stopped. Annis stepped through the opening in the wall. Inside the first chamber, there was a low oven and several longboards where linens were ironed. The fires had been allowed to burn down, but smoke lingered near the roof in spite of there being a large door open to what would be the side yard.

"I'll see to her." Iona was speaking to the Retainer. "How much trouble can an English girl be?"

Annis didn't stop to take offense. Not when a bath would be her reward for moving forward. Another doorway took her into a chamber with a hearth. A black kettle was suspended over the coals, steam rising from its spout. The tub was nothing special. It was made of wooden slats that rose two feet up. It looked like half a barrel, only larger. A small lump of soap was sitting on a stool near the tub. Annis picked it up, inhaling the lavender scent.

"Torian loves me."

Annis turned to see Iona coming toward her. The girl was glowering; she was pursing her lips with disapproval. She stopped and propped her hands on her hips, clearly trying to decide what to do with Annis.

"Ye should leave," Iona declared.

Annis choked on a half-laugh. "There is nothing I would like more."

Iona suddenly smiled. "Good. Come on then. I'll show ye how to get out before the gates are closed for the night."

Iona hurried across the bath chamber to another door. She cracked it open and stuck her head out.

"Everyone has gone into supper," Iona informed her. "Take that arisaid and wrap it over yer head."

The arisaid was a length of wool that women tended to wear draped down their backs. They would belt it against their waists with a few flat pleats, but it might be raised up to cover their heads when it rained or wrapped around the upper body to keep warmth in. Since the fabric had only rolled edges to keep it from fraying, it could even become bedding.

Iona had tossed the arisaid at her. Annis caught it as the girl went back to the door and looked out into the yard again.

"Get going. They will close the gate at dark."

Annis was struggling to believe in the moment.

What have you got to lose?

Her wrists were already bleeding. They could only tie her up again.

You aren't worth anything dead.

Annis shook out the arisaid and wrapped it around herself. She draped it over her head and headed for the door.

Iona moved aside as Annis stepped into the yard. The feeling of the dirt beneath her feet was surreal.

Get going...you can marvel at the change of events later.

Her heart began to hammer away, but she made sure to keep her steps even and not too hurried. There were a few other women making their way toward the gates. The sun was a crimson ball on the horizon. Up on top of the walls, Leslie Retainers stood watch. But with the arisaid, Annis blended in well enough. She hurried along with those going to the village for the night.

Every second felt too long. But she kept walking.

Her belly rumbled. But she kept walking.

The wind blew cold, and Annis smiled.

Free? Was fate turning kind at last? She didn't plan to ponder the question too long. Instead, she waited until no one was near, and then she went off the road, into the trees where she might increase her pace. Once the stars came out, she'd follow them so she wouldn't walk in circles and make easy prey of herself.

And just maybe, she'd succeed in finding herself a decent life, at long last.

Just maybe.

⟫⟫⟫⟪⟪⟪

IONA WATCHED ANNIS make her way across the yard. At least the English girl knew enough not to run. Iona stayed in the doorway, watching until Annis had made it through the gate.

Satisfaction filled her.

But when she closed the door and looked at the waiting bath, Iona had her first doubts.

The mistress might have her whipped for losing the girl.

Iona worried her lower lip as she tried to decide what to do. A log shifted in the hearth, making her aware of just how quiet it was.

No one was there except for her.

So, she'd just have to make it appear as if Annis had indeed gotten the jump on her.

Better injured pride than turned out.

Iona looked around the room. She settled on a length of wood sitting near the hearth. She backed up a few paces and gathered up her resolve.

Just one good hit.

But it would need to be a hard one, to give her a good lump because someone would surely check. She drew in a deep breath, determined to do it right the first time.

⟫⟫⟫⟪⟪⟪

ANNIS SAW THE lights of a village.

They twinkled and beckoned to her. Her belly grumbled as she continued on her way instead of going toward what would surely have ended in her being able to get a good meal.

Suddenly Seath's inattention to her was a blessing, for he'd never searched her and found the silver she had sewn between the layers of her underskirt. The little lumps were there and more. Come morning, she'd be able to book transportation for herself. The Leslie would never know she had the means to escape their land.

It was the balm she needed to soothe the chill of the night and her hunger. Fate really wasn't so terrible after all. Annis had certainly had her share of ill-fortune. But now, she felt the scale tipping in her favor.

Fate, it would seem, believed in balance.

And now, it was her turn to prosper.

She was truly grateful.

⇒⇒⇒✺⇐⇐⇐

"GO AFTER HER," Euna insisted.

His mother was furious. Torian held tight to his composure. One tiny grin would be Iona's undoing, for his mother was looking for someone to make an example of.

Iona let out a few little sniffles to complete her look of being the one wronged.

He didn't believe her.

But he was also grateful to her, too.

"Torian," Euna raised her voice. "Go after her now."

Torian slowly shook his head. "I think the English lass needs to feel the chill of the night. Perhaps she will nae think to leave the castle so easily once she's spent the night shivering and hungry. She will nae have gotten far by morning."

Euna was quiet for a moment. "I suppose there is merit in what ye propose."

Torian nodded. "Do nae worry, Mother. It's not cold enough to kill her, and she can nae walk off our land in one night, even if she runs every hour until daybreak. I do nae care to make her hate me by imprisoning her. Better she realizes on her own that she needs to make the best of our union."

Euna wasn't pleased. She had her hands clasped but was patting one with the other as she contemplated how to vent her temper.

"Ursula." Euna turned on her staff. "Ye shall give ten blows each to these maids for not seeing to the task I assigned them."

Darra's eyes widened as her pallor whitened.

"It was my fault she got away," Iona appealed to her mistress. "I told Darra I could manage the task."

"Well then, ye can have twenty blows from the rod," Euna said.

"There is no need for this." Torian attempted to calm his mother. "Iona has a large lump on her head to teach her the folly of her choice tonight. If ye are set on me handfasting with Annis, better to not turn the staff against her."

Euna cast a look toward her son. A moment later, she left the bathhouse. But she didn't go far. Torian was surprised to find her waiting for him inside his chamber when he made it back there an hour later.

"Mother," Torian remarked as he closed the door.

Euna was sitting in a chair, a single candle lit to illuminate her face. Torian had his doublet in his hands.

He cleared his throat as he put it down, and his mother made it plain she knew precisely who had disrobed him and why.

"Ye think I do nae know Iona hit herself?"

"What if she did?" Torian took advantage of the privacy to speak his mind. "I told ye, Mother. I have affection for Iona, and she loves me."

"Well, there is the truth at last." Euna flattened her hands on the top of her thighs. "Ye think me harsh."

Torian let out a long sound of irritation. "I do nae want to marry or even handfast with that English girl. And... Annis wants me attention even less. Is it wrong of me to not fancy forcing meself on a woman?"

Euna narrowed her eyes. "I never told ye to force yerself on her."

"What do ye call it then?" Torian demanded.

Euna drew in a deep breath. When she released it, she appeared far older than Torian could recall ever seeing her. The sight deflated his frustration, leaving him listening as his mother began to explain.

"Duty." Euna shuddered as some memory passed through her. "I remember when me father told me it was my duty to wed yer father. To arrive here and cultivate affection for a man I had never met, no matter how little effort he applied to the match. To do everything possible to ensure I conceived a son as soon as possible."

Euna looked at Torian. "Yer father's mistress was named Isla. He adored her and the girl that came after her and the next one as well. So many told me how lucky I was to have borne a son so very quickly and how fortunate it was yer father continued to visit my bed through the years, for he never adored me and made that point plain."

Euna was lost in thought for a long moment. Torian discovered his mouth had gone dry as he faced the look of loss on his mother's face.

"I suppose it's best for the English girl that she had made good her escape."

His mother stood up. She looked him straight in the eyes. "Yer father will arrange a match for ye in spite of this. For he will never see his firstborn wed for anything less than the most he can get for the Leslie."

Torian drew in a stiff breath.

"So, I will give ye something I never had. A choice." Euna patted a small bag that Torian hadn't realized was sitting on the table just at the edge of the candlelight. "There is all the coin I have skimmed over the years but was never willing to abandon my children to use. A few bits of jewelry as well. It is enough to buy yerself a modest home and business. Yer father will disown ye, but if Iona will have ye just for yerself, then I make a gift of this opportunity to follow yer heart."

"Mother—"

Euna held up a finger that trembled. "I loved once. It was long ago, and my parents told me it was a serious flaw in my character for, as the laird's daughter, I had a duty to perform. I promised myself I'd remember the pain if my children ever told me they were in love. Iona was determined enough to hit herself on the head. So, I offer ye me blessing because happiness is a truly wonderful feeling."

Torian felt as though the wind had been knocked out of him. His mother slipped out of the room while he was reeling over her words. The candle flame flickered with the closing of the chamber door.

He suddenly realized that he had never thought to gather up what he needed to take Iona away and make an honest woman of her.

And an honest man of himself.

No, he'd enjoyed having a mistress while remaining in his position.

And his position meant no one dared to point out to him that he was taking advantage of his circumstances.

He felt shame nipping at him.

Would Iona want him if he were not heir to the lairdship?

Torian suddenly needed to know. He shrugged into his doublet and grabbed the bag, sticking it inside his doublet before he left his chamber.

Iona had a chamber of her own. It was a tiny room that had once been used to store food at the end of the harvest when there was an abundance of root vegetables. Now, it had a fine bed and even room for a privacy screen to hide a piss pot. No maid had anything as fine.

He rapped on the door.

"Yes?" Iona sounded annoyed.

Torian pushed the door in and stepped through. Iona was rubbing her eyes. Her expression changed the moment she realized it was him.

"Torian?" She smiled. "I did not expect ye again...tonight."

"Because I have already had ye?"

Iona sat all the way up. "Ye know I will always welcome ye."

Torian withdrew the bag from his doublet. He reached out and placed it in Iona's hand.

"Ye hit yerself."

Iona's expression became guarded.

"Everyone knew it, Iona. They said nothing in order to maintain my dignity."

"Ye did nae want the English girl." Iona defended herself. She looked down at the bag to avoid the topic.

"That is enough silver for us to leave and live together."

Iona dropped the bag instantly. Her eyes went wide as she looked to the side and tried to gather her composure before he saw her true reaction.

. But he saw it.

And it ripped something inside him.

"Yer parents are dead, Iona." Another jolt of shame went through him as Torian realized he'd chosen her for his mistress because he knew there was no close kin to quibble with him over having her outside the bonds of wedlock. "Ye were correct. I did nae want the English girl. So...I'm here to ask ye if ye want to leave with me and become my wife."

"Yer parents would never accept me," Iona exclaimed.

"They would not," Torian confirmed. "And me sire would disown me." He extended his hand. "Come with me, but know without a doubt that ye will only be having me and whatever life we build together. The Leslie will shun us forever."

She shook her head. "No...no...ye are the laird's heir! He'd have to accept me after I have yer son."

Iona was scooting across the surface of the bed. She ended up with her back against the wall as she continued to shake her head.

Torian let his hand fall to his side. Bitterness burned through him, even as he acknowledged he had no right to be angry since he had never thought to offer his hand to Iona before.

They had both used one another.

Acceptance settled into him. It was harsh and full of self-loathing. But he picked up the bag and pushed it back into his doublet.

"It seems we had an arrangement, Iona, and that is all it was." Torian looked around the room. "Ye will not be put out of this room. When ye find a man ye want to wed, come to me, and I will see ye have a fair dowry. Our relationship ends here, though."

"Torian, ye can nae mean to abandon me."

"I accept that I took ye as my mistress for me own selfish reasons. Those are my sins. Tonight, I will reprimand myself and demand more from myself. I suggest ye think about doing the same, for I was not the first to have ye, Iona. Think upon the matter. Respect is earned, lass. It's time for both of us to remember it."

Torian left the chamber. He stood for a moment, but Iona didn't call out after him. That pain came again, and this time, he made sure he focused on it. He wanted to remember what happened when he chose to use his position for selfish desires. He felt cold and alone in the passageway, completely abandoned.

He had no right to expect anything else.

Torian nodded and drew in a deep breath. He started walking as he let it out. His pace increased as he left behind the indulgence he'd so blatantly flaunted before his clansmen.

He'd make more of himself than he had.

It was a solemn promise.

>>><<<

ANNIS SMILED WHEN the moon appeared.

It was only half full, but so very welcomed.

Suddenly the night was not so dark. The beating of the bare branches as the wind went through them became soothing instead of eerie. Somewhere an owl cried out.

Annis drew in a deep breath and pushed herself onward. The ground was uneven because she'd left the road. She took her time, choosing her steps with care. A turned ankle wouldn't help her cause.

Her belly rumbled, and she ignored it. She climbed up another embankment and looked up to get another glimpse of the moon to restore her confidence.

Instead, she saw a man.

She gasped, stepping backward.

Her luck simply couldn't be so bad.

Annis turned, intent on fleeing. The need to escape flashed through her like black powder being touched off. In an instant, she was devoid of every last bit of control. Running was the only thing she could think of.

Whoever the man was, he jerked her to a stop by a handful of her skirt.

She let out a cry, unable to submit.

"Easy lass."

Rolfe Munro.

Recognition flashed through her, but it didn't settle her. Instead, it intensified the need to escape. But Rolfe pulled her back, his arms clamping around her like steel bands. She'd never felt such strength in a man before. No matter how hard she strained, his arms didn't move even a tiny bit.

"Release—"

"Be still," Rolfe whispered against her ear. "Ye are caught."

Her temper flared. There was something about Rolfe Munro that shredded her composure. She bared her teeth and clamped down on his hand.

He let out a grunt, but his grip didn't slack. Instead, he took the ends of the arisaid and used them like rope, winding the cloth around her so that her arms were bound to her body by the fabric.

"Are ye sure about this?" Sholto asked from somewhere close. "The lass is a great deal of trouble."

"No trouble at all," Rolfe declared as he tugged the fabric even tighter. She ended up hugging herself with the cloth, making it impossible for her to lift her arms away from her body.

One of Rolfe's men offered him a length of rope. He took it and crisscrossed it over her chest on top of the arisaid.

It was much better than having the rough rope against her skin.

Don't you dare find something pleasant about this moment!

"It's good to see that Torian's mistress did no' simply pocket me coin but did what I paid her to do."

Annis gasped. Her eyes were wide as she looked at Rolfe. There was a look of satisfaction on his face that dumbfounded her.

"Aye, lass," he told her softly. "I made sure ye would be shown the way out."

"Why?"

His eyes narrowed. In the darkness, she saw something flash in those orbs, which made no sense at all.

"Because ye told me yer name."

TORIAN WAS UP at first light.

His men followed him without explanation, as he expected. But he felt their curious gazes on him when he didn't go toward the village but rode into the woods. So late in the fall, there were mounds of dead leaves covering the ground. He stopped and looked at an area that was disturbed.

Turning his head, he looked toward the Leslie stronghold. The side gate which opened off of the laundry was nearly a straight line.

His captain, Liel, dismounted with Torian and looked at the broken up sod.

"She is clever," Torian said at last. "And no stranger to being hunted. We'll ride a bit and see if we find any hints of a trail."

There was a trail—one marked by the hooves of several horses. At night, overhead, there would have been light provided by the stars. Routes changed with the season because of the location of the constellations above.

They came to a stream that was flowing with clear water. Several fresh piles of manure confirmed that a group of horses had been there recently.

There was something else, though. A small scrap of wool. It was tied around a rock and left near the manure.

Munro colors.

Torian picked it up and stripped the wool off the rock before he tossed it into the river.

Liel frowned. His man was wondering why Torian was so relaxed. Several of the Leslie Retainers looked between themselves as they questioned just why he wasn't more passionate about the chase.

"She is but a lass," Torian offered in explanation. "Is it possible some of ye have not heard that me brother was sent off to Stags Tower? Do ye truly believe it was only as a reward for bringing the English lass to Leslie land? She will bring questions from the crown to our land. Me father is making sure Seath learns to think his action through before setting out."

His men weighed his words.

"Let's find a tavern to enjoy the evening in, lads," Torian suggested. "No woman should come between brothers. Better she is gone with Rolfe Munro. My parents will find another bride for me in time. One which will bring the Leslie good gains and no trouble."

His men accepted his promise.

Torian mounted and rode toward a village. He'd set himself some goals. Ones that would challenge him to be better than he had, to become the sort of leader the Leslie deserved.

He intended to keep those promises.

⇒⇒⇒⟨⟨⟨

"BECAUSE YE TOLD me yer name."

What manner of logic was that?

Rolfe and his men rode hard. She'd suspected he was different than Seath, and the next two days proved it. He kept her bundled, sitting behind her on the journey. Even as frustrated as she was, she had to admit he was a better captor than Seath, for her wrists were not bleeding, and her mouth was not dry.

But he was also far more attentive, never letting her too far from his sight. Her cheeks reddened as he turned his back to afford her privacy.

The third day was dark, though. The sky was full of black clouds, and the horses resisted being ridden into the wind.

"Keep yer head down, lass," Rolfe urged her as he tugged part of the arisaid up and over her head.

Annis shifted. His fingers were warm against her temples, and it touched something off inside her. It made her shift again because she was so keenly aware of the man.

He tightened his arms around her.

"Are ye really so unhappy about being mine, Annis?" he asked.

It was a fair question.

There you go, trying to find positive things about your circumstances.

Annis let out a huff. But it was true that she honestly wasn't sure if she was more irritated with herself or Rolfe.

"Telling you my name does not give you the right to kidnap me." Annis wasn't precisely sure why she voiced her thoughts. Once again,

Rolfe seemed to shred all the barriers she normally kept between herself and the world.

"Does it grant me the right to no leave ye in a place where one of yer in-laws has threatened to cut yer tongue out?" Rolfe asked quietly.

The memory of Seath leaning over her surfaced. It sent a shiver down her spine.

"Easy lass." Rolfe was smoothing his hand along her shoulder. "I have taken ye away from that."

He had.

She liked it.

There was just no way to hide the fact from herself. His body seemed to complement hers, the pair of them fitting together in a way she had frankly never imagined two humans might.

You are overtired.

Clearly she was.

The horses were, as well. Rolfe steered them out of the wilds and toward a cluster of buildings. It was a tiny village of sorts. As they neared it, though, they saw the town square with its stocks set up on a rough stone platform.

As they arrived, the rain turned to sleet. The icy onslaught was driven by the wind, which began to howl. The horse they were on tossed its head, wanting to break free of the reins.

"Easy…" Rolfe cooed to the animal.

His captain was already ahead of them, negotiating with a man who had emerged from one of the larger buildings. He had his plaid pulled up onto his head as he and Sholto came to an agreement. The door to the building was open. Inside, a small child stood in the doorframe. The little boy blinked as he stared at the new arrivals. Behind him, there was activity as the rest of his family worked in the kitchen.

"These are simple people, Annis," Rolfe spoke next to her ear. "Do nae involve them."

There was a warning in his voice that even the howling wind couldn't carry away.

See? You are so set on seeing the positive that you have forgotten that Rolfe Munro is very dangerous.

He was. But for some reason, Annis was seeing that fact as an advantage.

Goron Duncan would think twice about crossing Rolfe Munro.

Rolfe stopped and handed her down to one of his Retainers. The man steadied her as her legs wobbled after being on the horse for so long. Her arms were still bound tightly against her body. She felt oddly off-balance as Rolfe joined her and turned her to face him.

"Annis? Do ye understand me?" There was a warning in his blue eyes.

Indeed, he was truly a dangerous man.

But it wasn't the warning in those blue eyes which made her set her teeth into her lower lip. It was the snorting of the horses. The animals were being led into a warm building, out of the onslaught of the storm.

The warning glittering in Rolfe's eyes made it clear he'd take them back out into the elements if she didn't heed him.

His gaze lowered to where her teeth were set into her lower lip. Relief flashed through his eyes before he took her through the doorway.

"Right up the stairs, laird," a woman called from where she was working at a table in the kitchen.

Rolfe reached up and tugged on the corner of his cap, knowing the woman had ignored the fact that Annis was partially tied up. The air inside the building was warm. It touched Annis's face, showing her how cold she had been.

She had to think of the horses.

You won't mind having a warm bed either.

Rolfe took her abovestairs. The room was small, but it was warm. Once inside, Rolfe began turning her around and around. The arisaid came loose, allowing her to straighten her arms at long last.

She let out a soft groan.

While the wool was definitely more comfortable than the rope had been around her wrists, her shoulders ached.

"Here now, lass." Rolfe muttered as he reached for her.

She recoiled from him. He jerked to a stop and sent her a hard look.

"Ye find me so repulsive?"

"We're alone, abovestairs," Annis blurted her feelings. Her face was hot, and she distinctly knew it wasn't from the temperature inside the room.

No, she was blushing.

Understanding dawned on Rolfe. His lips twitched, and his hard expression eased into that rakish look she seemed to find so very attractive.

He reached out again, capturing one of her arms. He began to work the stiffness from her muscles, sending relief through her.

A soft sound of delight escaped her lips.

"Careful, lass," he muttered as he moved behind her to knead her shoulders. "Someone might get the wrong idea about what it is we're about with sounds like that coming from ye."

"Hardly," she groused. "Only men enjoy bed sport."

Annis blinked. She gasped when she realized she'd actually spoken out loud.

It was a scarlet topic.

How could she have said such a thing?

She pulled away from him, her cheeks burning. Rolfe was watching her, but she simply didn't have the nerve to lock gazes with him.

He suddenly took a step toward her and then a second when she retreated. She bumped into the wall, and he flattened his hands on either side of her.

Caged.

Her eyes widened, and her breath froze in her chest. For a moment, she was caught in the grip of sensation so intense, she was half certain she might pass out. It was so extreme, she discovered herself marveling at the very fact that she was capable of feeling it.

"I think I would enjoy proving ye wrong, Annis."

He wasn't mocking her.

No, he appeared to be very confident in his position.

Could such a thing be possible?

She suddenly couldn't remain still any longer. Annis flattened her hands against his chest and shoved him back. He moved and chuckled. Proving she was completely at his mercy.

"You beast," she growled at him.

One of his dark eyebrows rose. "Beast? I've rescued ye, lass."

"Rescued?" she asked incredulously. "I believe I have been bound for every moment I have been in your company."

His eyes narrowed slightly, but he lifted a hand and pointed at her. "What pray tell was yer plan when I found ye fleeing from the Duncan?"

His question cut through the surge of emotions she was experiencing.

"I was going to book passage on a ship to England," she informed him firmly. "And join the court of Queen Elizabeth Tudor. The Virgin Queen is well known for liking heirs to be in service to her and never allowing them to marry."

There. It was a solid plan, after all.

"I see." Rolfe propped his hands onto his hips. He suddenly looked at her from the top of her head down to her toes. "Seath never searched ye."

Annis stepped back again. She stiffened as his eyes lit with confidence.

You just confessed, you fool!

Christ! The man undermined her composure so very completely. She'd babbled like a simpleton.

"It's a fine enough plan, lass," he began in a soft tone. "And if ye did nae sound so very English, it might have even worked with a wee bit of luck."

"I would have managed."

"What ye would have managed was to get yerself sold into service as a courtesan. To a high-class brothel skilled in making women submit by burning the soles of their feet until they obey. Customers don't look at the bottom of a girl's feet."

Her eyes widened in horror. She curled her toes back instinctively.

She shook her head to dispel the image his words had created. "Scots are not so terrible."

He flashed her a smile.

"That was not a personal compliment," Annis assured him.

"Yes, it was," he said before he closed the distance between them once again. But he only flattened one of his hands on the wall beside her head. The other captured her forearm, just above where her wrist was scabbed over. He raised her hand up.

"I took ye from the man who caused ye to bleed."

He had.

"And I kept Goron Duncan from taking ye back to a place where ye were clearly no'...*pleased.*"

Her mouth fell open. The topic was so completely scandalous.

And yet, her insides were suddenly heating up. Could he really do better in bed sport? She had heard a few rumors about women seeking out lovers. Was there more to liaisons than influence over a man?

"Thinking about it, are ye, no?" he asked.

Rolfe chuckled again. She jerked her arm away.

But she trembled because of the fact that he didn't hurt her with his grip. Instead, his eyes darkened as he looked at her, somehow seeing deeper into her soul than she had ever felt another human do.

He flattened his hand on the wall once more, caging her as she shuddered.

He smelled good.

It was the strangest thing to notice, for it was more than just a lack of stench. No, there was something about him that she enjoyed so much, she drew in another breath and shivered as she recognized his scent.

"Aye lass," he said as he leaned closer to her. He was a whole head taller than she was, so his face was nestled against her hair. She heard him inhale and let out a low sound of male enjoyment.

He liked her scent?

The question completely confounded her.

"I suppose ye shall just have to be my captive, then."

It was such a strange thing, the way his voice affected her. So close to her skin, she heard and felt his tone. Annis was positive she'd never been so utterly aware of another person in her life, never been so tempted to place her hands on him.

But he pushed back, his eyes glittering with purpose.

"And since ye are me captive, Annis, I'll be taking yer dress with me."

Annis ducked under his arm and made a break for the door. Rolfe caught her by wrapping his arms around her and kneeling down. She went with him, of course, and ended up struggling as he controlled her.

"If I were of the mind to fornicate with ye, lass," he said, "I wouldn't need ye to take yer dress off."

Annis growled at him. His words sunk in as her strength was spent. "Then why...why would you say such a thing?"

"Because I believe ye will be far less likely to attempt escape in yer smock and hose."

It made sense.

She was still blushing, but Annis had to admire the way he'd managed to find a way to contain her without binding her.

He was still a beast. Clever, but a beast nonetheless.

His hand landed on her upper thigh. She surged back into action, heaving and straining to dislodge his arms.

"Be still, Annis." His tone had turned to one of firm authority. "Ye need yer strength, and I will nae leave that knife on yer thigh."

She growled at him.

He stroked her upper arms in response.

"Why don't you slap me?" It wasn't exactly something she should have asked. Honestly, she should have been wise enough to realize that if he hadn't taken to hitting her, putting the idea into his head was very foolish of her.

"Because I do nae have the manners of a goat," he answered firm-ly.

Her memory offered up the times he'd accused Seath of that. It left her anger deflated. Which allowed her to notice that she could feel his heart beating against her back.

"If you have better manners than a goat, release me."

Annis wasn't precisely sure what to think when Rolfe complied. He made a soft sound under his breath, and then she was free. He stood up and reached back down to lift her off the floor.

But he leveled a hard look at her.

"Give me the knife, Annis, and yer dress. I do want to take them from ye, but me men need their rest, and the horses have earned a roof over their heads." He made sure she got a look at the unwavering determination in his eyes before he stepped toward the door and turned his back on her. He put his arm out for her to drape her clothing over.

Not the manners of a goat.

No, but still the actions of a captor.

Annis was frozen. Rolfe drew in a deep breath and turned to look at her. "There is a warm bed behind ye lass and supper to be had. Outside this room, there is only an uncertain future for ye and freezing rain. If ye do nae see the wisdom in staying, call yerself me captive. For ye are staying if I must strip ye down to yer skin and sleep on this floor to get ye to remain inside this room."

The choice was hers.

Rolfe turned his back once more. His ultimatum hung in the air between them. Her belly rumbled, long and low, confirming how much she would enjoy staying.

"Is it so much to ask ye to trust me, Annis?"

"I don't trust anyone." It was another of those things that she likely should have kept to herself.

Rolfe had a knack for loosening her lips, it seemed.

He looked over his shoulder at her. "I'll have to work on changing that."

"Why?" It was an honest question.

He turned all the way around and studied her for a moment. "Because ye tremble when I touch ye, Annis."

She did.

And she stepped back as she shook her head.

She watched the way he closed his fingers into fists and stayed where he was, when the look in his eyes told her he wanted to follow her.

And press her against the wall once more.

And...

And what?

Annis was breathless as she contemplated what his kiss might feel like.

"Wait on the other side of the door," she ordered him.

It was the wisest thing she'd said during the entire conversation. But he didn't like it. His lips pressed into a hard line.

You might like his kiss.

Annis felt like screaming with frustration, but that still wouldn't have stopped her internal voice. It seemed to refuse to wear the shackles she had forced on herself for so very long.

Rolfe Munro was a very bad influence on her.

He suddenly grinned at her. "I suppose ye are being more prudent than I." Something flickered in his eyes, which set off another wave of heat in her belly. It was a steady burning now, impossible to ignore.

But what did it mean?

The door closed behind Rolfe as Annis was lost in contemplation. The man irritated her more than any other. Yet, it was different. Alone in the chamber, she admitted she enjoyed pitting herself against him, which was ludicrous because he was far stronger than she was.

Ah, and you like the way it feels to have his arms wrapped around you...

Her cheeks stung as she worked the hooks on the front of her dress.

Curse and rot the man for confusing her so greatly. She had a plan for her life. One she truly believed would make her happy. The bodice slid down her arms, and she opened the waistband of her skirt. The small hip bolster she wore was only secured with a single lace. Once it was open, she felt instant relief. The dress was made of sturdy wool, and she'd chosen it for her travels, but it had weighted her down.

The bed would be a sheer joy to lay in.

That didn't mean she was going to agree to being his captive.

Ha! Well, you are stripping at his command.

Annis finished with her dress and looked at her knife for a long moment. Helplessness gripped her as she laid the weapon on top of her folded clothing and admitted she had no choice but to comply.

At least it was Rolfe.

Annis decided she really didn't need to ponder just why she thought that way.

Really, she did not.

CHAPTER FIVE

"THAT LITTLE LASS is going to carve out yer liver." Sholto grinned while he made the observation as Rolfe came down the stairs. A few of his men added their agreement.

But it sounded a little too much like they might just be looking forward to it.

"Mind ye, I'm right happy to see she has some warmth in her blood after all," Sholto continued as he offered Rolfe a mug of ale. "Seeing as how ye seem intent on taking her home. The winter is bitter enough without a cold woman in the keep!"

More of his men laughed.

Rolfe discovered he was battling the urge to plant his fist into Sholto's face.

Over a woman?

He raised the mug to his lips instead, hoping to find some measure of calm in the strong brew. His captain slowly grinned at him, seemly understanding precisely what Rolfe was thinking.

He couldn't.

Sholto's grin grew wider, even as Rolfe gave the man nothing but a stony expression. He fixed his attention on the pile of clothing Rolfe had dropped on the tabletop.

Rolfe held up his hand as his captain realized what the pile of fabric was. "Leave it be, Sholto."

"Laddie…" Sholto began. "A wee word of advice for ye."

The captain was drawing the moment out. Rolfe wanted to stop him, but, at the same time, there was part of him that couldn't resist letting the man have his say.

Sholto held the dagger up. "If the lass took off her dress and all, seems ye should let her have this back because ye just might enjoy her taking a stab at ye."

The room was silent for a moment, and then his men burst into laughter. Rolfe tried to remain unmoved.

He truly tried.

But his lips twitched, and he ended up choking on his amusement as a couple of his men had to wipe their eyes on their forearms because they'd laughed so hard.

Sholto enjoyed his moment, basking in the glow of his achievement. As the laughter died down, he took the dagger and handed it to the girl serving bowls of stew.

"Do this young fool a favor and sneak this back to the lassie abovestairs and tell her ye did it on yer own." Sholto winked at her and added a few silver pennies for her trouble. "He's never had a woman throw herself at him before! And if she gets the better of him, we'll know to leave him home in the future."

Rolfe shook his head, but the girl scooped up the silver and the knife and was turning away before she saw him.

Damn.

But his lips were twitching.

Rolfe wanted to chastise himself.

Except that ye're excited about the prospect.

He was, and it shamed him because he truly didn't want to be in the same category as Seath when it came to the way he treated Annis.

Ye aren't.

His confidence was secure, though. He'd never hurt the lass.

But ye want to put yer hands on her.

He did, but more importantly, he wanted her to want him to touch her.

Rolfe drew in a deep breath and released it.

The desire remained.

In fact, it was more deeply rooted now. He lifted his mug to his lips. Something felt like it was growing inside him. A need. A desire. He wasn't precisely sure what the word was. Only that he didn't even want to push it aside anymore.

No, he wasn't going to let Annis go.

Captive?

Part of him enjoyed knowing she was his. Not because he controlled her, but because while she was with him, no one else might touch her.

She wants naught to do with ye laddie.

That wasn't quite right. Annis didn't want anything to do with any man. He grinned once more. This time it was a wide smile that he enjoyed.

He was going to enjoy changing her mind.

⟫⟫⟩⟨⟨⟪

Duncan land…

"YER APPETITE IS not very good, Terin," Benedicta spoke a little louder than necessary.

She was making sure her words carried. Terin heard the way the conversation in the hall decreased as those sitting close enough to the head table overheard.

Terin smiled at her mother-in-law. "Perhaps my prayers have been answered at long last."

Benedicta's eyes lit as Terin brought up the topic she'd intended.

Oh, ye believe I am such a fool.

Perhaps she was, for playing along. It was a dangerous game, after all. But such was life. At least the one which Terin had been born into. Being the daughter of a laird was something so many little girls dreamed of.

They had no clue how terrifying the reality was.

A simple girl had troubles. Yes, Terin understood every girl had difficulties.

Still, they weren't worried about being poisoned.

"A child at long last would indeed be a blessing," Benedicta expounded. "Ye must begin taking care of yerself immediately. Since this news has been so very long in coming, we shall take no chances."

The staff was loyal to Benedicta. Not that Terin blamed them for such. No, she was the new bride and just one of two. After four years, her worth had dwindled away.

But she was a Campbell.

Terin knew how to fend for herself. She took two eggs from the yard and put them in the small kettle next to the hearth in her room. After they'd cooked, she peeled the shells away and ate them as she contemplated how to escape being the next member of the family interned in the graveyard.

She didn't dare trust the food for the Head-of-House was loyal to Benedicta.

As she finished the second egg, Terin knew what she had to do. Murder was wrong. However, escaping a plot against herself was fair enough. If Benedicta fell victim to her own plot, it really wasn't murder.

Terin refused to allow the prick of doubt to dissuade her. She had the right to defend herself.

She lifted her face and looked toward the heavens.

"I should pray that ye will deliver me from all evil, but ye have given me good wits, so I hope ye will not judge me too strictly for using them."

Her choice made, she crawled into bed and slept while she could.

≫≫✄≪≪

ANNIS LOOKED AT the dagger.

Concealed beneath a folded linen napkin, the weapon seemed to mock her.

Had the serving girl done it because she was another young woman who understood what it was like to be trapped in a world controlled by men?

Possibly.

Was Rolfe testing her?

That seemed far more probable.

Was he working on building trust between them?

Annis discovered herself smiling after that idea crossed her mind.

She'd enjoy trusting him.

Maybe you would enjoy his kiss.

Now, where had such an idea come from?

Annis lifted another spoon full of her supper to her mouth and chewed it as she tried to decide what her mind was doing.

Lonn's kiss had left her mouth bruised. Such a messy thing, kissing. Nuns really did have the right idea to take vows of chastity.

But the surface of her lips started to tingle. When she used the linen to clean her mouth, she discovered that her lips were more sensitive than she'd ever noticed.

It made no sense.

Very much like having the dagger returned to her.

No sense at all.

But her legs were cold without her skirts, so she crawled into bed. The girl had brought her another thick piece of wool. Annis arranged it on top of her, snuggling down into the bedding as she shivered. Outside, the sleet was still hitting the side of the house.

Perhaps beast was a strong word.

Still, she rather enjoyed the word when applied to Rolfe, for it seemed to fit him so very completely, but in a way she found rather attractive.

Her lips tingled again. Alone and in the dark, she reached up and gently pressed her fingers against her mouth.

It wasn't unpleasant.

Nothing at all like the way Lonn had left her feeling when he'd mashed his mouth against hers.

So…would a kiss be pleasant?

She yawned and closed her eyes as her body grew warm. As she drifted off to sleep, she discovered Rolfe was waiting in her dreams.

And the kiss he gave her pleased her very much.

At least in her dreams, that was.

⟩⟩⟩⟨⟨⟨

Duncan land…

TERIN WAS UP at first light.

Most of the castle was still sleeping. She hurried to dress, brushing her hair and braiding it simply. The muscles along her neck tightened as her maids failed to appear.

She made her way down to the kitchens to find only the Head-of-House and two older women at work.

"Mistress Terin," the Head-of-House exclaimed. "Ye should be resting as the mistress instructed."

Terin smiled sweetly. She kept her attention on the Head-of-House, but she heard the two women behind her muttering to one another.

"Yes," Terin said softly. "I am simply famished. And it is so early, I thought to come down and fetch me breakfast."

"Well then." The Head-of-House clicked her tongue. The woman turned around but not before Terin caught the way the woman's lips twisted in victory.

"Here ye are." The Head-of-House offered Terin a tray. "Ye have saved Innis a trip up the steps."

"Thank ye," Terin said as she took the tray.

She paused in the passageway.

"Innis, keep the maids away from Mistress Terin's room this morning," the Head-of-House instructed grimly.

She hadn't guessed wrong.

Terin felt her belly heave, but she swallowed and maintained her composure. She hadn't picked the fight with Benedicta, but she'd bloody well not become the woman's victim.

It was no sin to want to live.

Terin withdrew a linen cap from a pocket in the side of her skirt. The household maids all wore them. She tugged it on and grabbed an apron off a hook on the wall before she headed toward the third tower where Benedicta's chambers were. The two Retainers standing at the base of the stairs didn't stop her.

Terin started to climb the stairs with the tray. At the top, two more Retainers were on duty.

Terin simply offered the tray to one of them. She kept her face lowered as she handed it off, and they never even looked at her face.

Her mouth was dry, but she refused to have mercy for someone who wouldn't have any for her.

She'd done what she had to in order to survive.

And there was still one last thing to do.

But first, she'd wait and see what fate Benedicta had planned for her.

"I do hope ye enjoy it," Terin muttered without a shred of remorse.

⇛⇚

ANNIS MARVELED AT the sun the next day.

"Aye." Sholto stopped beside her and drew in a deep breath. "The Highlands have their own opinion about every single day!"

She smiled at his explanation. The morning was still breaking, but it promised to be a fine day. The hens were singing out as Rolfe and his men saddled the horses.

"Glad to see ye do nae spend too much time getting dressed, lass," Sholto added with a wink.

Many of the other Retainers turned their backs to hide their smirks, but their choking and coughing didn't disguise their laughter very well.

Annis felt her temper stir.

Well, you have your dagger back.

Annis looked toward Rolfe and felt sick.

What? You are giving in?

She looked away from him as she wrestled with her feelings. The thought of spilling his blood horrified her. And yet, she was equally upset over the idea of not being able to do what needed doing to escape.

"Contemplating yer plan?" he asked from behind her.

Rolfe had followed her away from his men. Annis turned to discover him looking at her with the arisaid in his hand. He had a guarded look in his eyes, though, and his gaze lowered to her thigh, just for a moment, but that was long enough.

"So, you know very well the girl gave the dagger back to me," Annis stated the obvious.

"Aye," he responded simply.

He stood so confidently. There was no way to miss the way he was completely in his element.

Of course, she was the outsider.

The stranger.

Annis looked around. Nothing was familiar. She felt lost and so very alone.

The last emotion chafed her pride, and considering it was the only thing she had left, her temper flared.

"I do not need your pity," Annis announced firmly.

"Ye need me, Annis. If ye do nae admit it, then I pity ye for being a fool."

"And what does that mean?"

Her question made him tilt his head to the side as he pondered it.

"No one does something for nothing," Annis continued.

"True enough," Rolfe agreed. "Could I not just be taking ye because I do nae agree with the way I see ye being treated?"

"Noble brides can expect no less."

He stepped closer. "That does nae make it right."

Annis shrugged. "I have little liking for it." She blinked and thought of something new. "I can pay you to escort me to a place where I can secure passage on a ship."

He was quiet for a long moment. He drew in a deep breath and let it out. "Aye, I could do that. Ye'll need to winter with us and in the spring…"

"Spring?" Annis muttered in frustration.

"Lass, look at the ground. It's already freezing at night. We'll be lucky to make it home before the snow flies. If I take ye to the coast, I'll not make it home until spring. Me men have families, and me father is very frail."

Annis made a little sound under her breath. It was a sigh of sorts because the rising sun was making everything sparkle as the light hit the ice crystals.

Rolfe grinned. He tossed the arisaid at her and turned around to return to saddling his horse.

You would have a much better chance of making it with Rolfe's escort.

She really would. Annis fingered the wool of the arisaid.

You will be much more comfortable, too.

But she would have to trust him. It was a great deal to ask of herself.

Why?

Because it hurt when trust was broken or torn away, as Aife had been.

She snuck a look toward the Highlander.

Well, he wasn't a friend.

And yet, she didn't see him as an enemy either.

Rolfe Munro was the strangest of all the people in her life. For he'd been someone she detested, and now, he offered her security.

Oh, now that is a very dangerous idea.

Security was something she didn't allow herself to think about. She had worth, and it meant people would fight over her without any consideration for what she might choose. Far better to find solace and fortitude inside herself while being prepared for uncertainty.

Those couldn't be snatched away from her or written into marriage contracts.

Rolfe would take her home. Winter was so often a bleak season, but Annis discovered herself looking at the next few months as the most secure ones she'd ever lived.

So, you're going?

Rolfe's men were hardened. They were also incredibly capable and loyal. Even if she didn't agree, Annis wasn't foolish enough to not see that Rolfe would have his way.

But he'd offered her the opportunity to agree.

Was that just a sham to make his life easier?

Does it matter?

It did. At least to her feelings. She wanted to believe in him. Wanted him to be noble not just because of blood but because of his own accountability.

She wanted him to be the man she'd never allowed herself to dream about meeting.

⟫⟪

"GOING TO ESCORT her to the coast, are ye?" Sholto came close to ask the question.

Rolfe slid his gaze to the side, but his captain didn't heed the warning.

"As long as I have known ye, Rolfe, ye have never liked lying." Sholto came to the point with a stern look in his eyes.

"I didn't lie to her," Rolfe stated firmly.

For a moment, there was only the sound of the horses.

"I told her I could take her to a ship," Rolfe clarified.

"Aye, ye did at that," Sholto muttered.

It's still deception, laddie.

And his captain wasn't any more at peace with it than Rolfe was. Sholto had always been an example for Rolfe to follow in matters of morality. Rolfe gripped the saddle he'd been securing around his horse.

"I do nae want to hurt her, Sholto." Rolfe looked at his captain. "In deed or word, and I can nae leave her to me cousins, or the Duncan, or on the road alone."

Sholto was serious. Rolfe stood still as the veteran sent him a hard look.

"Ye have feelings for the lass."

Rolfe looked away, but Sholto grunted at him.

"It's not a bad thing," his captain remarked. "It's time ye liked a lass enough to wed. English…well, she's no' so terrible, and she is not yer cousin."

"I did nae say I was of the mind to wed her."

Sholto raised an eyebrow. "Careful there, lad. Say that too loud, and there will likely be a few men who will happily try their hand at impressing the lass since ye have made it plain ye do nae consider her yers. Pride always has a price."

Rolfe started to do precisely that, but something tore through his gut, which made him clamp his jaw shut. Whatever the feeling was, it was strong. So powerful he just stood for a long moment as he experienced its intensity.

When was the last time he'd felt in such a way?

He never had.

Except for his mother.

Humph!

There is was again, that inability of his to deal with females. Aunt Euna had worked him over, and now it appeared that Annis was able to undermine his thinking as well.

Rolfe looked back to where Annis was standing. She'd gathered up the length of the arisaid and wrapped it around her body. She had a contented smile on her lips as she faced the rising sun.

She was a fine-looking lass.

Oh, it wasn't the sort of beauty Cora Mackenzie had. This was different. There was a solid strength in her that Rolfe just couldn't stop enjoying.

Honestly, he should have seen it as folly.

Instead, he wanted to see her succeed.

Something new went through him. A need so powerful, he felt like it was searing a path through his soul.

It was the need to protect her.

Not that he could blame her for wanting to see to her own needs. Such an attitude made her strong, but the world was harsh, and some men were black-hearted.

Rolfe returned his attention to saddling the mare Sholto had found for Annis. She would likely be angry with his use of words to gain her compliance.

But she was going to Munro land.

And that was his final thought on the matter.

⤛⤜

ROLFE AND HIS men knew their country.

Annis found herself struggling to understand where they were as the next two days passed. They took to the forest, traveling along paths that she honestly couldn't call roads. Yet the horses didn't protest. Her companions seemed at ease or at least accustomed to the terrain.

She lost her sense of direction several times, but they never did.

The next morning the ground was frozen, and it didn't thaw until nearly noon. Rolfe urged them faster, as Annis felt the tension in his men.

Winter was not something to disrespect.

They arrived on Munro land the third day. It took several more hours to make it to the stronghold. Three towers rose up into the air. One was taller by a story, and they made a nice triangle. The stronghold was perched on the high ground. Behind the fortification, the land fell away at a steep angle adding to its strength when it came to defense.

There was newer construction in fount of the castle. Two large buildings stood in front of the towers; one was still under construction. They were more modern with windows and even gardens.

"Me father used to worry the Munro would be considered uncouth." Rolfe rode up beside her as she took her first look at his home. "He brought a man up from England to design the newer buildings."

"Yes, it looks much like what I'd expect to see in York," Annis said in complete wonder.

It was unexpected. Annis marveled at the buildings as they rode through the village which surrounded it. The village was thriving. There were a large number of blacksmiths working on anvils, their hammers hitting and filling the air with pinging sounds.

As they rode on, she caught sight of several looms being worked. Huge bundles of fleece were stacked up, giving her a hint as to how the Munro made their money. Fleece fairs had crisscrossed England and Scotland since the Roman era. Wool was the fabric of choice and more commonly used to trade with than silver or gold. The Munro land clearly sat on a compass point where fleece came down from the north. The blacksmiths would be needed to shoe the horses to pull the wagons, as well as make all the metal pieces used in harnesses and such.

And then, there was stone.

Annis turned her head as they passed a large open yard where stone was being worked into blocks.

"You have a quarry," she said.

"Aye," Rolfe remarked.

"Do nae let him be too modest," Sholto called to her. "The lad took it into his head to bring in stone cutters. His father thought him daft, and I am no going to say I was all too keen on the idea of rocks being profitable but...they make a fine manor house."

They did. Henry VIII had built several newer palaces in the style. Eighty years after his death, they were still only seen in more civilized places.

You are judging the Munro.

She truly was, and her cheeks warmed.

Rolfe is the one who laid his cousin low for binding you.

Annis blinked and took the needling from her conscience. It was justly deserved. She'd allowed Rolfe's kilt and hardened body to make her think his mind was not modern.

She cast a look to the side and saw him in a completely new light. He really was a fine leader.

⟫⟫⟫⟪⟪⟪

ANNIS LIKED HIS home.

Rolfe enjoyed knowing it.

Ye more than like it, laddie.

He didn't argue with himself. There was a feeling sweeping through him as he caught the way she was looking at him.

He wanted her to like his home.

What that meant didn't matter. He'd explore his thinking later. For the moment, he was home. All the arguing he'd done to bring stone cutters up from England was suddenly worth it. The new house was fine and modern. The second house was ready for its roof and, by harvest next year, they'd be eating inside it. Even his father had moved into the new house.

If pride was a sin, fine, he was guilty. Annis was sneaking another glance at him, and he turned his head, so their gazes met.

⇶⇷

HE WAS PROUD of his home.

Annis couldn't hold back her smile as their gazes met.

"It is a fine home."

Rolfe's lips rose into a grin. He reached up and tugged on the corner of his bonnet. The horses knew they were home and picked up their pace. The mare she rode increased her speed, making it necessary for Annis to grip the reins and saddle. The courtyard in front of the manor house was wide. The second house was set so it would form a square if two more were added.

People had begun to emerge. The windows which ran along the three floors of the huge manor house were all open now with people leaning out of them. The Munro were loud as they welcomed their laird's son home.

Rolfe swung out of the saddle. His action afforded her a glimpse of his thighs as his kilt flared out. She kept smiling as heat teased her in more places than just her cheeks. He was a flirtatious man, and there was no way to deny that she found it captivating.

Her mare came to a stop, and Rolfe was there to help her down. He reached up for her, his eyes glittering with excitement over being home.

"Come along, lass." Rolfe interrupted her musings. "Me father will be waiting."

Inside the manor house was a hall. It was not as large as the Duncan one, but there was something about it that Annis felt drawn to. It was long and fitted with many windows, which allowed the afternoon light in. Long trestle tables filled it with plenty of sturdy benches. Wooden platers with cheese and bread were already sitting out in anticipation of the evening meal.

It seemed so warm and welcoming. For a moment, just a brief bit, Annis allowed herself to think about how it might feel to have arrived as Rolfe's bride.

You are not staying.

She wasn't, but just because she was going to be on her way in a few months didn't mean she couldn't indulge her fantasy. After all, her private thoughts had always been her refuge from reality.

So, she smiled and felt a contentment she hadn't experienced in a very long time.

It was very nice.

"Father."

Rolfe looked up at the raised platform at the far end of the hall. A man sat there. A huge chair with a sheepskin draped over it so that the fleece might serve as a cushion for him. His face was thin, and he sat hunched over, but his eyes were bright as he gestured for his son to come closer.

"My son," Laird Munro declared happily.

Rolfe stopped and tugged on the corner of his cap. The respectful gesture earned approving nods from the men standing behind Laird Munro.

"It's long past time ye made yer way back home," Laird Munro chastised Rolfe.

"Aunt Euna sent me on a wee little errand," Rolfe told his father with a grin.

"Did she now?" Laird Munro asked. He smiled at his son, his happiness obvious to everyone watching.

Rolfe was so fortunate to have such a loving parent.

Annis was jealous but not in a spiteful manner. Instead, she watched intently as Rolfe went to his father, and they clasped wrists.

How often had she dreamed of such a relationship?

You had such with Aife.

"Rolfe, my son." Laird Munro pointed to his right. "I have a fine gift for yer homecoming."

Annis looked in the direction the laird pointed. Her breath caught in her throat as she saw the girl standing there. Hands folded one over the other. Lips set in a careful smile. It wasn't overly bright. No, it was pleasant and pleasing. Her hair was honey blonde, and her dress was a cheerful shade of green to complement her coloring.

Annis was frozen as horror went through her.

You have no right to be upset.

She didn't, and it meant absolutely nothing to her emotions as they surged up.

"This is Kianna Chattan," Laird Munro introduced the girl. "Yer bride."

The hall was hushed. No one moved. In fact, it felt like no one even dared to draw breath. A woman standing beside Kianna made a soft sound in the back of her throat, and Kianna immediately sunk into a courtesy.

Laird Munro chuckled. "She's a fine lass. A bit shy, but that is a good trait in a wife."

She wasn't shy.

Annis knew too well what Kianna was feeling. Staring at a sea of strangers, she was holding tight to her composure as she looked at the man her family had sent her away to be at the mercy of.

Oh yes, Annis understood.

"Rolfe," Laird Munro's voice had hardened. "Who is that?"

Annis snapped her head back to the high ground to discover Laird Munro looking straight at her.

And the man wasn't smiling anymore.

Annis lowered herself. It earned her a grunt from Rolfe's father. The silence in the hall was broken as people whispered about her.

No, about Rolfe.

Annis suddenly realized her presence might tarnish Rolfe's reputation, if not downright shred it.

She was English, after all.

"I am Annis Stanley. Your son has been compassionate enough to escort me through Scotland."

There was a collective gasp as her English accent touched the ears of the clan members. Laird Munro leaned forward, his eyebrows lowering as he contemplated her.

"Step closer," he ordered her.

Annis complied, but she hadn't taken more than two steps before several burly Retainers moved into her path. Their expressions were hard, and the look in their eyes made it clear they felt she needed to be exterminated.

"Blast ye, both," Laird Munro exclaimed. "Get out of the way. Do ye think me so old I can nae withstand anything such a little lass might unleash upon me?"

He was old. Annis kept her expression smooth because the Munro Laird was worthy of respect. Age would do the same to everyone in time.

"Come here, girl," he beckoned to her once his men reluctantly cleared her path.

Annis was careful to only go to the bottom of the high ground. She stopped, feeling the glares of the Munro Retainers on her back.

They will delight in striking you down if you make even a tiny move not to their liking.

Laird Munro wasn't content, though. "Up here lass."

"As you wish."

Annis climbed the steps and kept her hands clasped firmly in front of her. Laird Munro studied her for a long moment.

"Stanley?" he asked her. "I've heard that name. The Earl of Derby is a Stanley. Are ye his line?"

Annis nodded.

"Aunt Euna sent me after her youngest, Seath, Father. He'd gone down to Duncan land to steal Annis."

"Your son has been most helpful," Annis stated softly. "He has escorted me away from those who were set to scheme."

Laird Munro grunted. "Scheme? Aye. I have no doubt of that!" He looked at his son. "And ye brought her here?"

"I thought it better than leaving her where Laird Leslie could make use of the blood flowing through her veins to strengthen the Leslie power."

Laird Munro toyed with the end of his beard for a long moment. "Ye have always had a head for strategy, Rolfe."

The hall filled with muttering. At least it sounded somewhat kind. She didn't dare risk a look over her shoulder to see the expressions of the Munro. No, Laird Munro was watching her. She stared back at him.

"Ye're no weakling," Laird Munro muttered. He suddenly nodded. "Well, we've rooms above stairs. Finnea?"

The wall of Munro Retainers parted as a woman came hurrying from the back of the hall. She was wiping her hands on her apron and reached up to give her hair a pat before she appeared before her laird.

"Finnea is me Head-of-House," Laird Munro introduced the woman. "She'll get ye settled."

Annis lowered herself in a courtesy. The Head-of-House turned and swept her from top to bottom before she used her head to indicate the direction to go.

Annis followed her as she felt the Munro watch her leave. The manor house was connected to the stronghold by a passageway. It was much more rustic but sturdy. The Head-of-House led her up to a second-floor room.

"It's a bit musty," Finnea said as she looked around the chamber. "Open up the shutters, and it will air out just fine. I was nae expecting guests."

"I shan't bother you," Annis promised as she went to open the shutters. When she finished and turned back to where the Head-of-House stood, she found the woman offering her a kinder expression.

"Good," Finnea remarked. "I'm glad to see ye are not one of those pampered English nobles who think maids will be standing behind ye throughout the day to tend to ye every second and wasting hour after hour of daylight because they do naught but wait upon yer whim. Here in the Highlands, we need to use our time for more important tasks, or we'll starve."

There was no missing the subtle warning in Finnea's voice. Annis nodded obediently.

"Well, then," Finnea said in a brighter tone. "Now that ye know where the room is, come down and fetch yer linens from the laundry…"

The Head-of-House was already turning and going back through the door. Annis had to jump to follow her.

She wasn't imprisoned in the chamber.

Annis felt a wide smile lift her lips as she hurried to catch up with Finnea.

She wasn't under guard!

Her feet barely touched the steps because she was so elated. At the bottom of the steps, Finnea began to point out the different directions to go for the things she might want.

"The bathhouse is there near the back… And if ye want a pitcher of water for yer room, there will be some fine pottery ones in the storerooms. Ye appear healthy enough, so bring yer sheets down to the laundry and fetch up fresh ones when ye want them. My girls are busy with the last of the harvest, and we all need to eat this winter, so best to have them in the kitchens."

"Thank you, Finnea."

The Head-of-House stopped and turned to look at Annis once more. "If ye want to be thanking me, ye can lend a hand once ye have yerself settled. That is, if ye know anything other than embroidery."

It was a challenge. But Annis didn't mind the way Finnea was tossing it at her. Something shifted inside her, a feeling Annis hadn't experienced in so very long.

Need.

She was needed, and the next morning when she woke up, there would be more than just an empty day of waiting for her fate ahead of her. Finnea had headed off toward the kitchens, proving she wasn't going to be too concerned with what Annis did with herself.

Freedom.

Annis drew in a deep breath and felt like her shoulders were lighter than they had been in years.

It was more than just freedom to come and go. It was trust, too, for no one cared that she might be a spy or intent on putting poison in someone's cup. It was something Annis would not take causally.

⟫⟫⟫⟪⟪⟪

Duncan land…

IT WAS A cold day when they laid Benedicta next to her son Lonn.

But Terin noticed that there was not as much mourning as there had been before. No, now, unless she missed her guess, there was a very clear sense of relief. Benedicta had ruled over the stronghold ruthlessly.

Terin stood close to the body of her mother-in-law as the priest spoke the final blessing over her. Benedicta's face was pale, her lips bloodless, and Terin looked straight at the corpse.

Benedicta had intended it to be her laying there.

So Terin wouldn't flinch or feel even a shred of remorse.

Even God wouldn't reproach her.

But as they returned to the stronghold, Terin felt the mood around her shift. The Duncan were restless. With Goran away and his mother's ruthlessness clearly felt by many, the situation was ripe for a rebellion. A clan wasn't always run by the bloodline of the last laird. If enough of the Retainers decided to put the matter to a vote, someone else who was deemed fit to lead might take the position.

The hall was full of mutterings as the Duncan Retainers saw their opportunity to be done with the harsh rule they'd been under. Terin tightened her resolve because she might so easily be struck down if there was rebellion.

So she walked straight up to Lucas Duncan. He was the son of Goron's uncle. The younger son of the last laird, and there were many, many Duncan Retainers looking at him at that moment.

"I am a virgin," Terin announced boldly.

Whatever Lucas had thought she might say, it wasn't the words that crossed her lips. Around him, Lucas supporters were stunned.

"My father knows my marriage was never consummated, and I will prove it in front of the midwives." Terin held tight to her resolve. A midwives' council wasn't pleasant to endure at all, but she was fighting for her life at the moment, so her modesty was less important.

"Do nae listen to that Campbell bitch!" The Head-of-House broke through the Duncan Retainers and pointed a finger at Terin. "She...she poisoned the mistress!"

There was a rumble of disapproval behind her.

"I took the tray ye were ordered to prepare for me and gave it to Benedicta," Terin stated clearly. "She died by her own scheme. I suspected it was so, but ye, ye prepared the poison and handed it to me, knowing what would happen to whoever ate that food."

Terin looked at Lucas. "She held the keys to the stillroom. I have never been allowed near it, and half of the men standing behind ye know that is the truth, for they were tasked with watching me every moment of the day and night."

"Yet ye made it to the kitchens to get that tray," Lucas spoke calmly.

"I did," Terin said. "And lingered in the hallway to hear her telling everyone to stay away from my rooms for the day so my screams would not be heard. Should I have compassion for those who had none for me? I was sent here by my father and laird, and have done my duty."

Lucas drew in a deep breath. "Bring the kitchen staff here now."

It didn't take long for the entire kitchen staff to appear. They lined up, the senior maids in front, as those with no authority lined up in back and looked at the floor. Lucas held his hand up for silence as he contemplated them. His gaze touched on one of the young boys who was an orphan and worked in the kitchens.

"Come here, Tomas."

The boy had a mop of unkempt hair, which poked out from beneath his worn cap. He blinked but moved forward with the ignorance of youth. The lad was too young to understand the tension surrounding him.

Lucas bent his knees so he was eye level with the lad. "What is yer first task of the day, lad?"

"I must lay the fire," Tomas replied quickly. "I bring in the wood."

Lucas nodded. "Do ye rise early?"

Tomas nodded quickly. "If I do nae have the water warm before first light, I get the rod and nothing to eat until supper."

Lucas nodded. He reached over and pushed the boy's torn shirt collar back. Dark bruises decorated his neck and shoulders.

"Ye are a good lad to tell the truth," Lucas spoke softly. "Do ye remember breakfast two days ago? Who was up early?"

Tomas nodded. "Mistress Terin came and said she was famished."

"He's just a boy," the Head-of-House interrupted. "Terin often gave him treats."

Lucas shot the Head-of-House a hard look to silence her. But Tomas was shaking his head. Lucas returned his attention to the boy.

"Why do ye shake yer head, lad?"

"No one gave me treats," he said with lament.

"Ah," Lucas remarked. "Never?"

"Me mother did. Before she died. But when I came to the kitchens, they say treats will make me lazy."

"Do ye know Mistress Terin?"

Tomas nodded. "I would take her tray up every day."

"Did ye take it up to her two days ago?" Lucas asked.

Tomas shook his head. "I already told ye, she come down to the kitchen."

"Ye did say that," Lucas remarked. "Ye have a good memory, lad."

There was a shuffling of the Duncan Retainers in response. Tomas nodded.

"Do ye remember what the Head-of-House said after Terin took her tray?"

"She told everyone to not go up to the south tower for the rest of the day."

The Head-of-House started to tremble. She looked around, seeking someone to come to her aid, but even her staff was shifting back and away from her.

"Tomas, ye are a good lad, and I promise ye may have treats without fear of turning lazy. Go on back to the kitchen now, lad." Lucas looked at the line of maids. He pointed at one of the youngest. "Take the boy. Feed him. Comb his hair and wash his face. He is a Duncan and born the son of a Retainer who lost his life serving the Duncan. We raise our own."

The girl was grateful to have a reason to leave the hall. She grasped Tomas by the hand and hurried away. The promise of food had the boy eager to accompany her, and they were gone quickly.

"Mercy," the Head-of-House begged. "The mistress ordered me to do it."

"I've no doubt about that," Lucas said as he rose back to his full height. "But ye lied to me now about it, so ye are not innocent. And ye have beaten that lad simply because ye could. So...ye are not worthy of mercy. Terin spoke true. Ye do nae deserve compassion."

"We need a new laird." An experienced Retainer stepped forward and stated his view boldly. "There has been too much scheming and leaving a union with the Campbell's unconsummated shows Goron has no sense of duty."

There was a round of agreement.

Lucas looked at her. Terin stared straight back at him.

"If I challenge Goron for the lairdship, I might not win. Are ye sure ye want to proceed with an inspection? Goron is not one to suffer a loss of face."

Terin lifted her chin. "I was sent here to unite the Campbell with the Duncan. Yet, I am still a maiden four years later. I might have left and returned to me family if I had no sense of duty. Select yer midwives."

Lucas turned and surveyed the women of the clan. He pointed at several of them randomly, never choosing those who stood together.

Terin nodded and turned to go to her chamber. Behind her, there was a murmur of approval. The first she'd earned from the Duncan.

It would not be the last.

⫸⫷

Munro land…

"YE THINK I do nae know ye are displeased with me?"

Rolfe looked at his father. Cian's eyes were open as he pointed at Rolfe.

"I'd be a poor laird if I failed to arrange a match for ye, Rolfe."

Rolfe bit back the words which wanted to cross his lips. There was sincerity in his father's eyes. Age had ravaged him, and he was struggling to have a purpose as he faced his death.

"She appears to be a fine lass," Rolfe muttered. He watched the way his father studied him.

"Ye have changed, Rolfe." His father pointed at him. "There is something different about ye."

"I have just been gone," Rolfe assured his father.

His father was silent a moment before he nodded. "I'm glad to have ye home."

Rolfe sat beside him for a bit. The fire was crackling, warming the room too much for his taste, but his father felt the cold easily now.

After his father fell asleep, Rolfe left the room.

In the hallway, he allowed his feelings to show on his face. A bride? He didn't need one.

Yes, ye do.

His temper was flaring. Rolfe knew it was irrational of him to be so upset about seeing a bride waiting for him, and yet, he couldn't deny the way he felt.

He should greet her.

But instead, Rolfe turned in the opposite direction. There was a woman on his mind, and even several hours sitting with his father hadn't diminished the need Rolfe had to seek her out.

Leave her be, laddie. Ye have a bride.

Sage advice.

He didn't give a rat's ass for heeding it, though. Sensation was burning in his gut, and now that he'd tended to his father, there was nothing that seemed more important than seeking out what he wanted.

But he didn't make it very far. Annis crossed his path, a pitcher in her hands. She froze when she saw him.

Something new went through his gut.

His captive.

And he was going to make her his.

⋙⋘

ROLFE EMERGED FROM the lengthening shadows in the passageway. He was a man who walked with purpose, and being home hadn't affected that fact, either. He stopped when he spotted her.

Annis felt something jump inside her.

There was something in his eyes. A promise, a need, she wasn't sure precisely what it was, only that it made her feel breathless.

She'd never actually believed a look might do that to a person.

To you.

No, she hadn't, and she stood still, caught in the grip of it without any desire to break the spell.

He closed the distance between them and looked at the pitcher. "We've maids aplenty in this stronghold, Annis."

"I do not need to be waited upon," she assured him.

He tilted his head to one side, contemplating her. But a maid was walking down the passageway. Rolfe plucked the pitcher from her hands and held it out to the maid.

"Take that to Mistress Annis's chamber."

The maid had her hands around the pitcher instantly. She nodded, but Rolfe had his attention on Annis.

"Come with me," he said to her gruffly.

Rolfe wasn't leaving it up to chance either. He clasped her wrist and pulled her behind him.

"What are you doing?" Annis demanded.

"Taking ye where I can be sure no one is listening."

He was just pulling her past another set of maids when he answered her. The two women cast wide-eyed looks at them before they grinned. The sort adults wore when there were no children around to see.

Annis felt her face catch fire. Rolfe pulled her to the bottom of a stairwell and started right up.

"I will not go abovestairs with you," Annis argued.

He turned and tossed her over his shoulder.

"Rolfe!"

She'd meant to admonish him, but the word came out in a rush as she settled on his hard shoulder. He turned without hesitation and mounted the stairs.

He spun her loose at the very top of the tower. Cool air brushed up her legs before her skirts settled. Annis backed away from him. However, that only took her further into the chamber he'd carried her up to.

"Have you taken leave of your senses, Rolfe Munro?"

He leveled a hard look at her. "Why did ye defend me in front of me father and clan?"

Her temper deserted her. Annis discovered herself feeling uncertain as she looked at the seriousness on Rolfe's face.

"Yer wrists are still covered in scabs. So why would ye say what ye did?"

Annis shifted. She seemed unable to remain in place. She discovered herself tugging on her sleeve to cover the marks on her wrists, and Rolfe was looking right at her fingertips.

"You have agreed to escort me to the coast in the spring, so naturally, I see no reason to cause difficulty in your home. We should go forward, not dwell on what has passed," she muttered.

Rolfe had his gaze fused with hers. He was contemplating something, and it made a tingle tease her nape.

"Agreed. We should be clear on what the situation is now," he informed her softly. "I have not agreed to escort ye to the coast, Annis."

Annis drew in a quick breath. "You most certainly did."

He shook his head. "Ye heard what ye wanted, and I did nae correct ye for I do nae care to restrain ye."

Annis thought for a moment, recalling their conversation.

"I can pay you to escort me to a place where I can secure passage on a ship."

He was quiet for a long moment. He drew in a deep breath and let it out. "Aye, I could do that. Ye'll need to winter with us and then in the spring…"

Rolfe hadn't agreed. He'd said he could, not that he would.

Her eyes widened as she realized he'd let her assume he was in agreement.

"Well, perhaps I am gullible, but your father has presented you with a bride now. So, of course, you will want me gone," Annis spoke firmly. There. Now she'd made her expectations clear. "You will have to do your duty and wed her."

Rolfe was taking a moment to consider her argument. He slowly shook his head.

"What do you mean, no?" Annis demanded. "I do not belong here."

His lips twitched up again. This time, his grin was careless, and there was a glimmer in his eyes that made her heartbeat accelerate.

"Who treats ye better than I do, Annis?"

His question caught her by surprise. Annis found herself thinking intently about it.

"Well...You have been decent when others were not."

He nodded and stepped toward her. For some reason, she was captivated by his approach, staring at him as he closed the distance until she had to lift her chin because he was taller than she was.

"Aye," he said as he looked down at her. "I've disagreed with me kin over ye, lass."

Blood was the tightest bond. She knew it only too well. And yet, Annis felt something tear inside herself, as she thought she heard lament in his tone.

"I do nae regret it, Annis."

She stiffened as he appeared to know her thoughts. Annis looked away, feeling like the world was spinning, and her grip on her composure was flying away from her.

Rolfe cupped her chin and brought her face back. "But what draws me to ye, lass, is that ye would place yerself in front of me. Everyone comes to me for protection. They all want me to shelter them. Everyone except for ye. You put yerself in front of me."

There was a flash of appreciation in his eyes. Annis stared at it, warmed by the fact that he valued her effort.

But his attention lowered to her mouth.

"What are you thinking to do?" She gasped in shock.

"I'm thinking I would like to kiss ye."

The hold he had on her chin wasn't biting, but it was firm. Suddenly she recalled the bruising force Lonn had used when touching her and her belly heaved.

"I told you—" Annis flattened her hand against his chest and straightened her arms with all the strength she had. "I do not care for the touch of men."

He'd begun lowering his head, intent on placing his mouth on hers, but he froze.

A moment later, he stepped back. Annis drew in a deep breath. Sweat was trickling down the sides of her face, and her heart was racing so fast, she feared she might just collapse onto the floor.

But he'd withdrawn. She was caught in a moment of bewilderment, for men did not give way to the opinions of women.

At least, Rolfe was the first man she'd met who did.

Rolfe scooped her off her feet.

She gasped as he cradled her against his chest and turned around. He walked across the chamber and lowered her down. She looked around and realized she was sitting on a bed.

His bed.

Panic gripped her, and she rolled over onto all fours, intent on crawling off the bed. She only made it a foot before she was yanked to a stop by her skirts. Rolfe had sat down on the lower portion of her dress. He sat all the way down, his legs folded as he watched her. She had space between them, and yet was tethered unless she wanted to open her waistband and leave her skirts behind.

"What are you trying to do?" she demanded. Well, she intended to demand. What came out was a husky tone, which betrayed how unbalanced she felt.

"I'm waiting for ye to relax, lass."

Relax? That was the sort of thing she recalled the matrons advising her to do when they'd stripped her down and put her into the bed where Lonn would be able to deflower her.

This was different, though. Rolfe wasn't moving toward her. He might have reached across the space between them and grabbed her by the upper arm to drag her closer.

No, he sat and watched her. Waiting for her.

There was understanding in his eyes. A steady, controlled patience that eased the panic gripping her.

"I will wait until ye are ready, Annis."

"I will never be ready," she said. "Why do you think I want to go to the English court? So I never have to wed again."

Rolfe's mouth rose into that confident grin once more. Annis discovered herself looking closer at his gaze, wondering if by chance there was any possibility that she might be wrong.

He'd been so still that it startled her when he extended his hand. He held it out between them, his palm up in invitation.

Temptation needled her.

In fact, it was building up inside her as she looked between his eyes and the hand he kept between them. The silence surrounded them, and there was something about his lack of verbal pressure that made her think about yielding even more.

He was so very sure of himself.

She truly wanted to know if it was arrogance or not.

Annis laid her hand into his. The connection made her gasp. Just a tiny sound, but she felt like it was drawn from the depths of her soul. Her skin had never been so sensitive. Now, she felt every one of his fingertips as he closed his hand around hers. He drew her hand toward him.

Slowly.

So slowly, she became fixated on the way he was carrying her hand to his lips.

"In your English court," he spoke softly, "I understand a man will kiss the back of a lady's hand like so." The compression of his lips against her hand was light.

Yet, she felt it ripple up her arm, raising gooseflesh along the way.

Rolfe lifted his face and made eye contact with her again.

"And then, when they are bolder, they will kiss the inside of her wrist."

Her belly did a little flip as he turned her hand and lowered his mouth to the delicate skin on the underside of her wrist. While she waited, it felt like time was moving slower. As though she was living inside the moment, enchanted by his words.

This kiss was a bit firmer. It drew another sound from her, one Annis wasn't aware she could make. It was full of the wonder she was experiencing. Inside her body, there was a flood of new impulses, and all of them revolved around moving closer to Rolfe.

Her body tingled with a mixture of alarm and anticipation.

"The next pulse point is the inner arm, I believe."

He closed his hand around hers and twisted their hands so that their forearms were together. His motion drew her closer to him. She was leaning toward him, their upper bodies only one pace apart now.

"How..." Her lips were so dry. "How do you know so much about...the English court?"

She'd looked at him as she asked the question. Their gazes fused, and it was her undoing. His eyes were so full of intent. It stole her breath, filling her with anticipation so acute, surrendering to it was the only thing she seemed able to do.

Rolfe met her halfway, tilting his head to one side, so their mouths fit together. It was a gentle merging of lips, stunning her with how pleasant it was.

He cupped the back of her head, holding her in place as he kissed her. Rolfe took command, leading her in a gentle motion, moving his mouth against hers as he coaxed her into mimicking his motions.

Her belly tightened.

It was an insane twisting sensation that sent pleasure racing through her body. Never once had she suspected she might enjoy something so very much. The sheer level of it was beyond her grasp to understand. But that was all right, because all she really wanted to do was immerse herself in the sensation.

He shifted, trailing kisses up her cheek. Rolfe held her close, the hand on the back of her head cradling her skull as he pressed his face into her hair and drew in a breath.

Something new ripped through her. An awareness of him that stunned her with how very carnal it was.

You like it.

She did, and it made no sense because she had never thought such levels of pleasure were possible.

And he likes doing it.

Rolfe made a low sound as he inhaled the scent of her hair. It touched something inside her. A sense of knowing she was attractive, which had nothing to do with carefully crafted words. It was in the way his chest vibrated and the fingers gripping the back of her head tightened just a tiny amount.

"I'm getting too old to climb so many stairs..."

Annis let out a startled cry as Sholto came through the door. She wanted to scramble off the bed, but Rolfe's grip remained despite the way she wiggled.

The Munro captain looked up and took in the sight they made on the bed. He blinked and coughed. "Well, I did no' think the pair of ye would have progressed this far already."

Annis felt her face catch fire.

Rolfe released her with a frustrated grunt. She fought against her skirts as she tried to get off the bed.

His bed.

Christ! She knew it was his bed! She landed on the floor, and one of her ankles bent because she was in such a panic. But she righted herself and went running for the door. Sholto stepped out of the way just in time.

She heard him chuckling as she raced down the steps.

※》》》≪≪≪

"YE SHOULD HAVE knocked," Rolfe growled.

His captain was still laughing. Sholto had leaned forward and braced his hands on his thighs as he let out huge sounds of amusement.

Rolfe mumbled a word of profanity beneath his breath as he got off the bed.

Sholto drew his forearm across his eyes before he straightened and sent a look toward Rolfe. "Ye know...I'm rather relieved to see ye interested in a lass. A few of the lads were beginning to wonder, what with the way ye let that Cora Mackenzie ride away."

His captain let out a low whistle. "Cora was a fine looking woman. This one...well, I suppose there is something to be said for having a woman who is nae going to have too many men trying their hand at luring her away."

"Annis is fair," Rolfe defended her.

Sholto made a little moue with his lips. "She's not ugly, lad, and I admit she does appear to have a fine, plump set of tits."

"Mind yer tongue," Rolfe warned.

Sholto had lifted his hands up, as though he was gauging the way Annis's breasts would fit into his grip. Rolfe glared at him.

Sholto opened his hands and lifted them in mock surrender. "Aye. Aye. Well, I see how it is."

"Good," Rolfe responded.

"But I am curious as to just what ye are planning to tell yer father about that little bride he has contracted for ye."

Sholto always did manage to get around to the more serious topics, and he was right. His father's choice for a bride from the Chattan clan had been a wise choice, for they were allies.

"I'll manage it," Rolfe told Sholto.

He wasn't sure just how, but Annis's taste clung to his lips. There was no way he would forget it, and what was more, he didn't want to. Need was raging in him. It was more than lust. He was experienced enough to know this was different. It touched something, the memory of the way Cora had looked when he'd bid her farewell. The way she had looked at her husband made it plain she loved him.

Are ye in love, laddie?

Rolfe scoffed at himself. Love was, well, it was something he doubted he'd ever feel for a woman. Yet he admitted he wouldn't mind seeing Annis look at him as Cora had gazed upon Faolan.

"Are ye certain Rolfe?" Sholto asked the question seriously. "An English lass will not bring ye what many feel yer marriage should."

"I will manage matters," Rolfe repeated. "Haven't I done so for many years?"

Sholto nodded. "Ye've earned the respect of the Munro sure enough. What I'm cautioning ye against is losing it through one choice. The girl is here. Ye simply keep her. Perhaps that is what ye are thinking?"

His captain was making a solid point. Sholto wasn't blind to the fact that Rolfe had failed to go and greet the bride his father had selected. Plenty of others in the stronghold would know by now what Rolfe had made his priority.

Sholto was no exception. His captain had likely heard the whispers and come up to caution him over the choice he was making.

Even after he left, Rolfe continued to feel he was being pulled in two different directions. Practicality had always won over his emotions. It was a well-worn path that should have come very naturally to him.

He needed to greet Kianna.

That path didn't lead to Annis. Rolfe didn't claim to understand just why he was so opposed to anything which would keep him away from her.

Yet he was.

All the way down to his bones.

Of course, the biggest problem was that his men would understand it even less.

CHAPTER SIX

I T WAS TIME to be useful.

Annis awoke the next morning, still tired.

Because you were dreaming of Rolfe's kiss.

It was true, which made her groan even more. The dark hours of the night seemed to intensify the memory of the way it had felt.

She'd never imagined she might like it. Her body had somehow turned traitor after just one kiss.

It had been more.

As she brushed out her hair, Annis admitted Rolfe had done more than kiss her. He'd waited for her. Touched her gently. Enticed her.

Was that seduction?

Stop thinking about it!

She needed to heed her own advice. Annis finished her hair and turned toward the door. There was a household below her, and, without a doubt, there had to be something she could do to keep herself busy enough to still her thoughts.

Finnea had an exciting house to run. There was the old stronghold and the new manor house. In her search for the Head-of-House, Annis discovered there were new kitchens built along the back of the great hall. They were simply a marvel.

High ceilings, which allowed the smoke to rise up and away from those working. Huge hearths, which were large enough for an entire side of meat to roast in. Great chimneys rose from these hearths to help further vent the kitchens. There was far more room for work tables and five coppers where water was kept heating at all times. The last thing was the sinks. They were overly large and set against the far wall. They drained right out the wall, and when Annis ducked into the courtyard to investigate, she discovered the water went down a stone gutter and over an embankment.

Truly a marvel.

The old kitchens were still in use as well. With the last of the harvest recently brought in, there was an abundance of food in need of processing and storing. Finnea was in the old kitchens, supervising the making of fruit jams. The scent of sweet apples was thick, making Annis smile.

"What do ye seek, Mistress?" Finnea asked pointedly.

Annis smiled and inclined her head in respect. "I have come to be of use."

The Head-of-House was surprised. Two scoffing sounds came from somewhere in the back of the kitchens. Finnea snapped her fingers, and whoever it was fell silent instantly.

"Let me see yer hands," Finnea ordered.

Annis stuck her hands out, turning them after a moment. Finnea studied Annis's hands before raising her attention to her face once more.

"Can ye make a shirt?" the Head-of-House asked.

Annis hesitated. A shirt was a private thing, for it would touch the skin. Finnea clicked her tongue at Annis.

"Ye are a blue blood, so it stands to reasoning that ye would have been taught how to handle a silver needle."

The work in the kitchen had slowed as the maids watched intently. Finnea wasn't having any of Annis's hedging.

"Come with me," The Head-of-House instructed firmly.

Finnea wiped her hands off and headed out of the kitchen. Annis was suddenly staring at the staff, who were all looking straight at her. She turned quickly and followed the Head-of-House. Finnea went down a passageway and up two sets of stairs.

"This was the ladies' solar," Finnea shared as she fumbled with the ring of keys on her belt. "Back when the laird's wife was alive."

She fit a key into a lock on a wardrobe and turned it. The lock was stubborn, resisting at first, but the Head-of-House didn't relent. There was a grinding sound as the lock moved and opened. Inside there was the scent of rosemary and lavender.

"If ye were raised properly, ye know what to do with fine linen such as this." Finnea looked over her shoulder at Annis.

On the shelves of the wardrobe were carefully folded lengths of fabric. They'd been stored with bog myrtle to ensure moths and other insects didn't feast on the precious cloth.

"I've women aplenty who know their way around a kitchen and root cellar. What we do nae have is a tailor. The Fraser lured ours away with a fat purse and a buxom blonde."

Finnea drew in a deep breath. "Mind ye, I would have found the man a companion if I had thought he was so lazy as to not want to do the chasing himself, like an English—" Finnea's voice trailed off as she realized she was being insulting, but a bubble of amusement escaped Annis's lips.

Annis pressed her hand against her mouth, but Finnea grinned at her.

"Some men are beyond understanding, eh?" Finnea asked good naturally. She sent Annis a questioning look.

Annis nodded. There was a hint of mischief in the Head-of-House's eyes, one Annis wanted to share.

It had been a very long time since Annis had had a friend.

"The laird has shirts, but it's young Rolfe who has worn his threadbare, and the ones he has are nae the best, for he would not answer when the last tailor was here and go for a fitting."

Finnea stopped and contemplated Annis for a moment. "I know it is no precisely the thing to ask a woman who is not related by blood or marriage, but ye are here, and that Chattan child is far too young for me to be trusting her with linen and silver needles."

As Head-of-House, Finnea had a dilemma. Annis didn't doubt that the woman was torn as to admit it to her or not. As an outsider, it was likely Finnea would rather have Annis believe everything was in good hands.

"I spent many hours perfecting my stiches," Annis said. "My nurse considered it an essential skill."

Finnea's eyes brightened. Annis smiled at her. "If this is the task ye set me, I shall not quibble. You are the Head-of-House. You are in charge of deciding where everyone is best placed."

"Aye, well, the one who will test yer sincerity is the laird's son." Finnea made a sound under her breath. "Ye'll need some measurements off the man, and he will not make it simple for ye."

Finnea stopped abruptly, and a new gleam entered her eyes as she looked at Annis. "Then again, if the rumors are true, Rolfe just might make himself available to ye."

Annis felt her cheeks burn with a blush.

The Head-of-House offered her a saucy grin. Surprise flashed through Annis, and Finnea chuckled at her.

"Ye're the right age to enjoy the way the young aird looks at ye," Finnea remarked. "As ye have already done yer duty to yer family and are widowed, well, it seems fate has decided to put ye here. No reason not to enjoy it, eh?"

Finnea pulled the key to the wardrobe and the solar off her belt, and offered them to Annis. The gesture stunned Annis.

"The young laird brought ye here," Finnea explained as Annis took the keys. "I have no reason to distrust ye, and the snow will keep ye right here if ye need to be found. I imagine ye will want a smock, as well, since ye came with naught. Ye may have the cloth for one. Keep the keys. I have two sets of kitchens to manage."

The Head-of-House left a moment later.

Trust.

Freedom.

Annis couldn't contain her smile. Happiness was bubbling up inside her.

"Ye're the right age to enjoy the way the young laird looks at ye."

Annis was back to thinking about how much she'd enjoyed Rolfe's kiss.

You crave more.

She did. Reaching out, she fingered one bundle of fabric. Opportunities should not be wasted. She knew it very well.

What are you thinking to do?

Annis honestly didn't know. But she was more alive than she had ever been, and she liked the feeling.

So she wouldn't be pushing it aside.

Even if it leads you astray?

Why was morality always so contrary to what she wanted?

Are you admitting you want Rolfe?

Perhaps it was time to face the matter head-on, instead of waiting on Rolfe to corner her. Annis pulled a measuring tape from a small box and felt her belly flutter. But she wouldn't give into the little nervous sensation. She looked through the wardrobe, finding a short stack of paper. She took one and carried it over to a writing desk. The ink was still wet. She unrolled a quill from a length of wool that had been wrapped around it to keep the tip from rusting. Dipping it into the ink, she wrote down the measurements she would need.

Something shifted inside her as she finished. Annis grinned when she realized what it was.

Anticipation.

And she wasn't going to run away from it.

≫≫≪≪

"I EXPECT YE to marry that Chattan girl!"

Rolfe stood still as his father pointed at him.

"And do nae be thinking I have not heard ye had that English strumpet in yer room," Laird Munro continued.

"She is not a strumpet, Father."

His father grunted at him. "Why do ye defend her? Why would ye argue with yer own father over an English woman?"

"I am not arguing, Father. Ye taught me to be truthful." Rolfe kept his tone even and respectful. "No matter if I like or dislike a situation, the truth should always be spoken. Annis is not my mistress."

His father shut his mouth, clearly wanting to rage at him but, at the same time, agreeing with him.

"She was in yer room." Laird Munro nodded. "I heard it plainly."

"She was in me room," Rolfe admitted. "I carried her there."

His father's eyes widened.

"And I will tell ye plainly, Father, I fancy her above all women I have ever met. But she is not my mistress, and she has told me she will not have me."

His father merely grunted and waved at him. "I'm too tired to fight with ye, Rolfe."

Rolfe tugged on the corner of his cap. "Rest easy, Father."

Laird Munro closed his eyes, but he opened them again when he heard the outer door to his chamber close behind his son.

"Daeg," he called to his personal man.

The Munro Retainer stepped forward. "My laird?"

"Take the English girl and make certain she is never found by me son."

Daeg lowered his eyebrows.

"Do ye think I would tell ye to do it if I were nae thinking of the Munro?" Laird Munro said to his man. "I am close to me day of judgment, man. Very close. But I have to choose, do I leave the clan I was entrusted to lead into chaos? Me son has shouldered the weight well. He's only rebelling because that lass is here, distracting him.

So…take her away. And keep the matter quiet. It will be better if it is done swiftly."

Laird Munro watched Daeg, and his second man, Matterson, nod and leave. They were good men whom he had burdened. Oh, it was for the best of reasons, yet he'd told them truthfully. His judgment day was coming soon.

Still, for now, he was Laird of the Munro.

And his son would mind him.

>>><<<

ANNIS MOVED THROUGH the passageways. A chill lingered in the stone. In the older towers, the walls were very thick. Now that winter was gripping the land, the passageways would be cold until well into spring.

As far as useful, the temperature would make for good food storage. She passed a few maids and younger boys who were carrying vegetables and fruit to an open door. They left what they carried and went back the way they came. The maids looked at her, their lips curving up as they recognized her.

It seemed her presence in Rolfe's chamber hadn't gone unnoticed by anyone.

Well, fine then.

Annis held tight to her resolve. Perhaps this was what it meant to be a wanton. She was going back up to Rolfe's chamber, and if they ended up in bed, so be it.

Wanton.

Perhaps.

What made her grab a handful of her skirts in order to climb up the steps, which would take her to the tower top chamber Rolfe slept in, was the fact that wantonness felt so very much better than the apprehension that had filled her whenever Lonn had summoned her. The world suddenly offered more than duty and cringing compliance.

It was as though she could see colors for the first time. The contrast was simply overwhelming. No lecture or pearl of wisdom delivered to her over the years was going to stand up to the onslaught of impulses, and the reason was she was happy to be carried away.

She lifted her foot, but suddenly a hand clamped down on her mouth. She was drug back against a solid body as she clawed at the arm connected to that hand. The need to fight flashed through her. Annis kicked and pulled on that arm, but a hard impact on the back of her head ended the battle.

>>>><<<<

MATTERSON HEFTED ANNIS up and tossed her over his shoulder. Daeg was watching the passageway. He whistled when it was clear.

Matterson didn't think.

He kept his attention on his task.

When the laird gave orders with the clan's best interests in mind, a man had to not take tasks to heart. Some things were difficult. It was best to get them accomplished without any unnecessary personal involvement.

In the stable, he laid his burden in a cart and tossed a leather cover over her. A horse was already hitched to it. Daeg climbed up into the driver's seat, and Matterson joined him. The horse began to pull them through the yard. Sleet was falling, so anyone around was in a hurry to get where they were going. Their horse picked up its hooves, eager to finish its task.

Matterson was eager, too.

Because the sooner he finished, the faster he might drink until he forgot what it was he had done.

>>>><<<<

BEING GONE SO long meant there were many things that needed his attention. Rolfe entered his study to find a line of men and some women waiting on him. The Retainers who helped keep order near his personal study were doing their best to keep the peace, but there was spit on the floor, showing that whatever disputes were waiting for resolution, they were heated ones.

"I will hear all of yer cases," Rolfe promised as he went into his study. Sholto rolled his eyes as he pushed the door closed.

"An unruly lot today," his captain stated the obvious.

Rolfe dug deep for patience. His father was still laird, and yet, he'd not managed the clan in a long time. Disputes had to be heard, or they might erupt into fighting. Friends would take sides, and a matter between two men might easily grow into a dispute involving whole families.

"Bring in the first complaint," Rolfe instructed Sholto.

His captain went to the doors and opened them. Outside, there were four Retainers tasked with keeping everyone on the other side of the door until it was their turn. The first pair of men entered, their expressions angry.

"Laird."

They greeted him tersely. Rolfe settled in to begin. Several hours later, he had only managed to clear half of the line. The arguments were heated, and each new one tested Rolfe's patience. The hours flew by, testing his limits because his emotions were threadbare. He picked up a mug and drank from it, but the water it contained wasn't what he craved.

Whiskey seemed far more appropriate.

"But I have waited a long time!"

Sholto had opened the doors to admit the next dispute. Rolfe looked up as his captain tried to block the way, but whoever it was ducked right under his captain's wide arms.

Rolfe caught a flash of Kianna Chattan's legs as she bundled her skirts up and entered his study like a fox being chased by hounds.

"I must see the laird now," she declared in a huff.

Sholto grunted, but the doors fell closed with a bang as Kianna let her skirts down and stood in the middle of the study, a flicker of pride in her eyes.

Rolfe blinked. He hadn't really looked at her, and now, he discovered himself shocked. "Ye are...young."

Sholto had turned and started toward the girl, but he stopped as he took her in. His expression turned to shock as he rocked back on his heels.

"Overly young," his captain exclaimed in growing horror.

Sholto's dismay was something Rolfe agreed with. He swept Kianna from head to toe again but felt no relief. Her body had matured, but her face still had the freshness of youth. Even now, she was bold enough to push past his Retainers because she hadn't grown old enough to be held accountable like a full adult. Laird Chattan was a bastard for sending her to wed.

"How old are ye, lass?" Rolfe asked.

Kianna blinked, clearly not expecting the question. "Sixteen," she muttered after a moment.

"How long have ye been sixteen?" Rolfe inquired suspiciously.

"Two weeks."

Bastard.

The Chattan had sent a fifteen-year-old bride to him.

Rolfe gripped the arms of his chair. She was far too tender. He was suddenly grateful they had a chaperone. He drew in a stiff breath, trying to swallow his distaste for her. Oh, it wasn't personal; she was just far too young.

"Lass, I realize I should have greeted ye, but I have important matters to attend to right now."

Kianna nodded. "Aye. Very important matters. I tried to tell yer Retainers how urgent it was for me to see ye, but they kept blocking me way."

Sholto rolled his eyes behind her. "Come away, lass. It is time for work, not pleasantries."

"There will be plenty of time for us to speak later," Rolfe informed her as Sholto gripped her arm. "Go on with ye."

"But yer father's men took yer mistress away, and if she is gone, ye will press me for a wedding."

Kianna finished in a rush, her expression filled with urgency. She gasped as she realized what all she had said, her hand flying up to cover her mouth.

"What I mean is…ye brought her home, so clearly ye like her, and yer father brought me here so suddenly…maybe we could wait to wed," she finished in a rush.

Rolfe was out of his chair. He'd closed the space between them, alarming Kianna. Rolfe controlled his temper. The girl's eyes were filling with unshed tears.

"I am not angry with ye, Kianna," he offered in way of soothing.

Kianna might have been young, but she wasn't timid. She cleared her throat and nodded. "Since she was in yer room just yesterday, ye must still want her. Yes?"

"I do," Rolfe confirmed firmly. "What did ye see?"

"Well, as I was left on me own, I thought to explore a bit and…" Her voice trailed off as she realized how intently Sholto and Rolfe were listening. But she drew in a breath and found her courage. "I saw yer mistress going back up to yer chamber. A man hit her on the head and carried her away over his shoulder. I tried to get in here for hours in order to tell ye to go after her. Yet the men outside yer door kept pushing me away."

"Ye have done well, lass," Rolfe told her.

"Will ye bring her back? At least for the winter? I know I must wed ye but not just yet." She pleaded with wide eyes.

"I could not agree with ye more," Rolfe said. He'd started for the door but turned and looked at Kianna. "There is naught wrong with ye, lass. I'll explain matters to ye later."

Outside his study, six of his Retainers stood watching him. Rolfe didn't hesitate to command them. "Someone has stolen me prize."

There was a collective growl.

"I'm riding out to reclaim her."

The staff of the Munro stronghold flattened themselves against the walls of the passageways while Rolfe and his Retainers hurried toward the stables. Younger Retainers were pulled out of the line by more experienced, harder men, proving his men supported him one hundred percent. By the time they had mounted, the force Rolfe rode out of the gate with was formidable.

He didn't temper his mood.

Someone had taken his woman, and by Christ, he was going to take her back.

No matter what.

»»»—«««

ANNIS CAME AWAKE too slowly.

There was something she needed to deal with, some matter which could not wait. She felt it pounding through her, urgency growing stronger with every second that she fought against the fog holding her down.

But she could not rest.

She fought the urge to sink back down into slumber. There was pain, but she surfaced through it, opening her eyes. Memory rushed in, intensifying the urgency filling her. Panic was nipping at her, but she held it back, grasping at her wits.

"Awake, are ye?"

Annis rolled her head to the side. A huge man sat with his back to her. His kilt was the same colors as Rolfe's, though.

"I did nae like hitting ye," her captor remarked. "I was just following me laird's orders."

Annis recalled the way Rolfe's father had looked at her before she'd assured him she was there only as a guest.

"The laird is nae a bad sort," the Munro Retainer continued. "But well, after it got out that it took only a day for ye to be found in young Rolfe's bed...well...the laird felt he needed to keep his son from making a mistake which would affect the entire clan."

The main refilled the small pottery cup he was drinking out of. Annis went to sit up and discovered her hands were bound tight.

The man let out a huff. "I've a daughter yer age."

He lifted the cup and drank deeply.

Fear nearly crippled her. The tone of his voice told her how torn he was. It also let her know he was devoted to his duty.

Pity didn't help the dead.

Annis sat up. Her ankles were secured with thick rope as well. Her heart was racing as she sat up and looked around, seeking any bit of information that might help her escape. The man had his back to her. Was it because he respected Rolfe's claim on her? If so, it might be the reason she'd woken up.

Hope flared inside her.

"I need to use the...necessary."

Her captor grunted. "As if I'd fall for that. Ye'll stay bound, lass, because I do nae care to put me hands on a woman me laird's son claims as his own."

"Yet you have abducted me," Annis argued.

The man looked over his shoulder at her. Only for a moment, though, before she was looking at his back once more.

"I have to follow me laird's orders."

"The laird told us to get rid of her," another man said as he came in the door the first man sat facing.

"We've taken her away," the first man insisted.

"And now we wait?"

The first man looked at the second. "Ye did what I told ye?"

"I did."

The first man placed another cup on the table and filled it. The second man considered his options. Drinking was better than bickering, it seemed, for he sat down next to his companion.

They haven't killed you.

Her head was throbbing from being hit, but that was far better than death. Annis tried her strength against the rope binding her wrists, but it held firm. The rope around her ankles was different. She reached down and began to pick at the first knot.

"Rest while ye can, Mistress." The first man was looking over his shoulder at her. "It would be right uncomfortable for ye if I had to bind yer arms behind ye."

Annis let the knot go. He turned his head away once more. She was lying on a bed. It was a nice one with ropes strung beneath it to support the pallet. There was a pillow, too. Frustration was nearly driving her insane, but she straightened back out on the surface of the bed and closed her eyes.

She'd need her strength later.

⋙⋘

GORON DUNCAN HATED court.

James VI of Scotland was more like his English cousin Elizabeth Tudor than Goron liked. He was waiting to see the king, and it didn't appear that he'd be granted that audience anytime soon, for the king was busy and didn't appear to place fellow Scotsmen above other pursuits.

So, he waited.

"My Laird."

Goron looked up as one of his mother's personal Retainers appeared. Goron instantly stood. Benedicta would not have sent the man if something was not very urgent.

"My Laird, yer mother has died."

"What?" Goron demanded.

The Retainer nodded. "She's dead. And worse, for it was discovered she intended to kill yer wife but died by her own murder device."

"My mother does nae make careless mistakes!"

The Retainer's eyes widened. Goron cursed as he realized he'd just admitted to knowledge of his mother's intentions to murder Terin.

The man was gone a moment later. Goron erupted in a rage, but his own men had been sitting about and were half drunk. No use when it came to riding down the Retainers who had come from the Duncan stronghold. His men ended up looking at him as they waited to see what he'd order.

"Ready the horses," Goron said through clenched teeth.

"We're no waiting on the king?"

"A parchment signed by the king will be bloody useless if my cousin Lucas gains the support of the clan."

His men were sobering up fast. They'd all be cast out with him if Goron lost the lairdship. They hustled to saddle the horses. They left behind anything that wasn't essential, riding light and hard for the Duncan stronghold.

Goron had never been one to rein in his temper. Today, he indulged in that trait, allowing his anger to turn into rage.

His mother was the only person he had ever loved.

What was Terin? A useless bit of baggage. He was going to make sure she suffered. When he got his hands on her, he'd ensure her death was long and painful. Campbell daughter be damned.

He was Laird of the Duncan. Anyone who tried to take his place would die.

SOMEHOW, ANNIS FELL asleep.

Someone pounded on the door, waking her.

"Who is it?" her captor asked.

"Jasper Chattan." The door pushed in. "Ye sent for me?"

Jasper Chattan had to duck beneath the doorway. He straightened up and flashed a cocky grin toward Annis. He had a head full of midnight black hair, and it was long, part of it tied back, so it didn't fall into his eyes. His shoulders were as wide as the doorway, and he propped his hands on his hips as he stared at her. Appearing as huge as Goliath.

But his gaze was on the rope binding her wrists.

"An interesting invitation, Matterson Munro," Jasper remarked. "It's the truth I'm contemplating smashing yer face in for treating a lass like ye are, for I can nae see a reason for it."

"I told ye it was a waste of time to send for him," the second man said to Matterson. "Now he knows we took her."

"Shut yer jaw," Matterson warned his companion.

Matterson looked back at Jasper. "Rolfe Munro brought her home with him."

Jasper's playful grin melted into a hard line.

"The laird ordered me to take her away, and I heard ye were still here after delivering yer sister," Matterson continued.

"Aye." Jasper answered with a shrug. "There is naught but winter and me mother's watchful eye waiting for me at home. I thought I'd enjoy a bit of yer local brew before departing. But, I'm a bit unclear as to why ye have invited me here where there is a bound captive?"

"I do nae kill women."

"Are ye thinking I do?" Jasper asked softly. There was a dangerous edge to his tone, which Annis found very reassuring.

"The young laird brought this woman home with him," Matterson began. "I'm thinking that since ye brought yer sister here for an alliance with the Munro, it makes sense for ye to take this lass back to

Chattan land. Rolfe is a devoted son, but I suspect he'll challenge his father over this lass. And it's the truth that Rolfe has been running the Munro for many years. This is the first time he's set his eye on a lass. Chattan land is the one place he can nae go without crossing a line since yer sister is waiting to wed him."

Annis felt her insides twist. Something tore, flooding her with a sense of desperation. It was the most perfect way to permanently separate her from Rolfe.

She needed to escape.

But her bonds held tight. Worse than the rope refusing to yield was the fact that Jasper was looking at her now in a very serious way. All playfulness had vanished, leaving her facing the man he was when life demanded it. He wasn't half grown like Seath.

No, he was very much like Rolfe.

Hardened.

"Rolfe will be yer laird soon," Jasper remarked. "Ye said it yerself, he's acted as laird for many years. Why are ye risking his ire over taking his woman away?"

Matterson stood. "Duty is nae to be shirked. Yer sister is here, but she was not when the young laird brought this one home. It was bad timing. The old laird ordered me to see this one taken away."

Jasper locked gazes with the Munro Retainer. "My sister wedding him was to forge an alliance. Taking his woman might destroy that, and he might take it out on me sister."

"The young laird is not a man who would hurt a young bride," Matterson said firmly. "Rolfe has always devoted himself to the Munro. No need for this lass here to be hurt. She just needs to be somewhere Rolfe can nae go to fetch her. I will bring yer sister back to ye meself if she is treated poorly."

Jasper thought for a moment before he extended his hand, and Matterson clasped his wrist, sealing the deal.

"Ye are a man of yer word. My thanks for sending for me. It would be a blight upon my sister's future to have innocent blood spilled in her name. Kianna is not that sort of girl."

Matterson grunted. "I suggest ye get on the way."

Jasper nodded. He passed Matterson, coming toward her. The muscles along her neck tightened as she tipped her head back because of how tall he was.

"Do nae be any trouble," Jasper warned her.

He pulled a knife from the top of his boot and sliced through the rope around her ankles. Annis gasped because the motion was so swift.

He knew how to use a blade.

Well, you are free from the bindings.

He gripped her hand as he hesitated before cutting the rope on her wrists. They locked gazes. He had topaz eyes. He sent her a stern warning before jerking the blade of the weapon up and through the rope coils.

Annis held her tongue. Oh, it wasn't because she was feeling beaten. No, it was because she was able to walk toward the door and go through it.

She'd find a way to escape.

And do what?

Now there was a question.

You had been on your way to see what would happen if you indulged in your liking for Rolfe's kiss…

That need to escape flickered back to life inside her. Only this time, she was very sure she wanted to run back to Rolfe.

He had a bride.

It was a sobering thought. She'd been an unwanted bride and knew the feeling Kianna must have experienced when she saw Annis returning with Rolfe.

So maybe she should go with Jasper Chattan and make the best of her new circumstances.

Something in her rebelled at the mere thought. Annis bit her tongue. Even if it wasn't what she wanted, she had to think of Rolfe.

MARY WINE

He had a position to be mindful of. Denial was spreading through her. Like blood through a piece of linen when she'd pricked herself with a needle. The pain was so small and yet excruciating.

You are being emotional.

She was. There seemed no way to control it either. But at last, she found solace in her circumstances.

Affection truly was insanity.

⇥⇤

HE NEEDED SNOW.

Rolfe glared at the sleet. A fresh blanket of snow would have given him a trail to follow. Instead, the sleet simply made a mess of the roads, leaving him struggling to gain hints as to the direction his father's men had taken Annis.

The horses didn't care for the chill either.

There were two main villages outside of the Munro stronghold. He ground his teeth with frustration as the wind picked up and the bare tree limbs made an eerie rustling sound.

Like death.

Or, in this case, the end of…

Of what, laddie?

He wasn't certain. Only that he would stand in the sleet for the rest of the week if it meant he'd be able to recover Annis.

"Perhaps it's for the best," Sholto voiced what the rest of Rolfe's men were likely thinking. "This is yer father's word on the matter."

"And my bride?" Rolfe turned and looked at his captain. "Me father was too old to see that the Chattan sent a child. Duty be damned. I will not be bedding her anytime in the next few years."

"Some men would."

Rolfe grunted. "Enough, Sholto. I know ye mean well. Yet do ye truly need to hear me confirm that I will not wed Kianna until she is a

154

woman fully grown? I agree that it is time for me to wed. Now. Not in three years when Kianna grows up."

His captain sent him a hard look. "Me words are not for ye, lad. But for yer men. Some of them have not thought the matter through, and the weather is making them think poorly of ye."

Rolfe cast a look toward the Retainers behind him. A few of them offered him a shrug, confirming that Sholto was correct.

"I've shouldered every expectation of me, Father," Rolfe addressed his men. "The Chattan girl is not fully grown."

"So ye seek an English woman?" one of his Retainers asked. The man didn't shirk away from the hard look Rolfe sent him. It was a question all his men wanted an answer to. They'd followed him without the answer, which only proved how much they deserved one from him.

"She is a royal-blooded bastard," Rolfe informed them. "The Duncan thought to improve their standing through a marriage with her, and me cousin Seath stole her for the same purpose."

Understanding lit his men's faces. Several of them grinned as they nodded.

"A fine prize, then."

"Better ours than in the hands of others."

"Worth bringing back."

Rolfe felt victory stirring inside him. He might have shouldered the weight of running the clan, but this was something he might very well have lost the battle over, for Kianna would mature in time.

The fight wasn't won, though. He wouldn't be so naive as to think a few words would be the end of any debate over his marriage.

But it would do for the moment.

"It looks like fate is feeling kindly toward ye, lad," Sholto remarked.

Rolfe nodded, but his captain pointed toward the road. Two Munro Retainers were making their way back toward the stronghold.

"Matterson is yer father's man." Sholto identified one of them.

Rolfe knew it well. He mounted and rode toward Matterson, but one look at the man's face, and Rolfe knew Matterson was set in his thinking. Rolfe edged his horse up besides Matterson's.

"I can nae disobey me laird," Matterson told him firmly. "When he is gone, I hope ye will remember loyalty should never be broken." Matterson remained steadfast, never flinching. "Ye have a bride to welcome."

"Go back and take a good look at Kianna Chattan," Rolfe instructed his father's man. "Ye will see welcoming her would require a lack of decency that I am very glad I do nae have. She is too young."

Matterson's brow furrowed.

Rolfe looked forward. He had a direction now. The village up ahead would have someone in it who would have seen Annis. If not her, then his father's Retainers. It was a place to head.

As he rode off, he took hope from the fact that Matterson didn't call after him. It didn't mean Annis was still alive, but at least his father's man hadn't confirmed there was no reason for Rolfe to keep searching.

CHAPTER SEVEN

"**I** COULD BE sitting in a tavern. By a warm fire. Drinking strong brew."

Jasper Chattan rode up beside her. He cast Annis a long look. She knew what he saw. Her head was drenched. Water trickling down the sides of her face. At least wool was warm even when it was wet, for she was soaked to the bone. Jasper, along with his men, had the back portion of their kilts raised up to shield their heads.

"Do ye not know what an arisaid is, woman?" Jasper inquired.

Annis looked at him with narrowed eyes. "I failed to dress for an abduction this morning."

"Well, lass, ye are in Scotland now."

Jasper still had a slight curve to his lips, but it was clear she'd shocked him with her English accent. He was contemplating her in a new way now, clearly attempting to decide what she was worth.

"What are ye to Rolfe Munro?"

Jasper reverted to his hardened core as he asked the question. She was facing the future laird in him. Something he'd been raised to embody. No matter what was said in England about Highlanders, Annis had learned that she shouldn't allow the bare knees peeking at her to allow her to doubt that Jasper had received an education every bit as detailed as one her own father had been subject to.

He was not a man to toy with.

Or, in her case, to trust.

"Rolfe stole me from his cousin Seath," she answered.

Jasper's horse didn't like walking so close to hers. It tried to pick up the pace. Jasper took a moment to rein the animal in.

"What were ye doing on Leslie land?"

"I was wed to Lonn Duncan," Annis answered.

"Was?"

"I am widowed." Annis decided to stop waiting for him to pick at her with his questions. "I would very much appreciate an escort to a port where I can arrange passage for myself back to England."

"Perhaps I'll just take ye back to Seath," Jasper responded. "The Leslie are good fighters, which makes them the sort a man should keep as friends."

"Seath was sent away in disgrace for bringing me home."

"I notice ye did no' say that Rolfe would thank me for bringing ye back," Jasper spoke again.

"I know what it is like to arrive as a contracted bride," Annis answered truthfully. "And I would not care to know I placed Rolfe in the position of earning his father's ire."

Her words were true and yet, so very difficult to push past her lips. Rolfe was worthy of her effort, though. So, she drew in a deep breath and kept her chin level as Jasper contemplated her.

Jasper made a low sound in his throat. He suddenly kneed his horse and moved to the front of the column of his men. The next few hours dragged on. Jasper kept their pace slow as the sleet continued to thrash them. It was drudgery, to say the least. Pure misery as Annis opened and closed her hands over and over to keep them from going numb. Restoring circulation to her fingertips, though, only made certain she felt the icy bite of the sleet.

Jasper finally stopped late in the afternoon. He found a spot protected from the wind-driven onslaught. The horses were pleased to shelter against the rocky outcropping.

But the Chattan appeared somewhat surprised to be stopping.

"Build up a few fires, lads," Jasper encouraged his men. He gave her a shove forward. "We need to dry out our little guest. She is nae so accustomed to our fine Highland weather."

There were chuckles in response. Annis suffered them with grace. She was cold and had no intentions of choosing her pride by denying it.

Jasper's men began to build two large fires. For how hardened they all appeared, the work progressed slowly. At last, there was a flash and crackle as orange flames began to lick at the wood they had pulled from the forest.

"Warm yerself, lass." Jasper came up behind her once more. "I do nae need ye catching a chill."

"I shall do my best not to," Annis replied as she stretched out her hands. The heat from the fire made her realize just how cold she was. Annis warmed her hands as she tucked her skirts back and squeezed her legs together to hold the fabric away from the fire.

She drew in a deep breath at last, feeling the chill dissipating from her flesh. Jasper's men had left one fire for her, while they clustered around the other one. They'd added more wood, so it was larger and hotter. Steam rose off their kilts as they spoke and laughed.

A tingle went down her back. Something was on the tip of her tongue, but she'd been so busy warming herself that she hadn't really thought about what it was. A whistle sounded from behind her, and the Retainers in front of her snapped to attention.

They'd been idle.

Waiting.

Annis whirled around. A hard arm suddenly clamped around her waist as Jasper appeared right next to her. He flashed her a grin as he pulled her a couple of feet from the fire. He winked at her before focusing on the road they'd come down.

Rolfe was riding straight for them.

Soaked to the skin, he was leaning low over the neck of his stallion as he bore down on them.

She gasped, recoiling, but Jasper held her firmly by his side. Rolfe swung out of the saddle.

"Rolfe Munro," Jasper called out to him. "Interesting to see ye out here…in this weather…while me sister is back at yer stronghold."

Rolfe came to a stop. Jasper still had her clamped against his side. Annis wiggled and then pushed at him when he didn't allow her to place distance between them.

"Release her, Jasper." Rolfe's tone was hard and dangerous.

It stunned Annis, stilling her as she tried to decide just why she enjoyed knowing he was angry.

"I do nae care to have a fight with ye, Jasper." Rolfe appeared to be battling his temper.

Jasper chuckled. "Do ye think I can nae see the value of this little lass?" He turned his head and looked at her. "She fits quite well against me."

"Get yer hands off my woman!" Rolfe ordered.

"Yers?" Jasper let her go.

Annis stumbled away from him. One of his men had to reach out and pull her back to prevent her from stepping right into the fire.

"Ye heard me, Jasper. Annis is mine, and I will have her back," Rolfe declared.

Another jolt of sensation went through her. It was rich with gratefulness and joy overhearing that he'd come for her.

But the next thing Annis felt was fear. Jasper propped his hands on his hips and faced off with Rolfe. Her eyes widened as she realized neither was lacking when compared to the other. They were like bears making ready to fight.

Over you…

She was sick unto death of the fighting over her.

But she was helpless to do anything but watch.

"Ye have a bride," Jasper informed Rolfe. "And it seems yer father does nae want ye to have this little English sweet. I will take good care of her." Jasper smacked his lips.

In the next moment, Rolfe knocked him to the ground. They collided with brutal force. Annis jumped at the grunts that came from them as they rolled and began to punch one another. One of the Chattan Retainers drug her away from the men.

She had to stop them.

Whoever was behind her twisted her arm behind her back to control her. Pain erupted in her arm and shoulder from the hold. The tiniest movement made it excruciating. She ended up gasping as tears burned her eyes. She shoved her hand over her mouth, determined not to distract Rolfe.

He was fighting for his life.

>>>><<<<

ROLFE WANTED BLOOD.

The intensity of his emotions was a new sensation, but he didn't stop to contemplate the wisdom of following those feelings.

No, he drove himself toward Jasper, the sight of his arm around Annis setting off a blaze of need to beat Jasper down.

And Rolfe gave it his all. None of their men interfered. But Jasper was enough to take on. The man was hard and experienced, and he didn't yield an inch. Rolfe took as many hits as he delivered, the pair of them heaving as blood seeped from their noses and lips.

Rolfe turned and hammered Jasper with a hard punch delivered to his underbelly. It knocked the wind out of him. Jasper lay on his back as he wheezed and tried to get breath into his lungs. The sight was enough to allow Rolfe's temper to subside. He was on his haunches, his fingers still closed tight into fists.

Mud stuck to his back, and Jasper was filthy, too.

"That was a good fight," Jasper said.

Jasper let out a half cough, half chuckle. He rolled over and got to his feet. When he grinned, there was blood in his teeth, but his eyes were alight with enjoyment. He stuck his hand out and waited for Rolfe to grasp it.

"Are ye mad?" Rolfe demanded honestly.

Jasper shook his head. "Yer mother died a long time ago. Rolfe Munro, I tell ye, I adore me mother, but ye have no idea how hard it is to enjoy a good fight with me mother in the stronghold!"

"If yer mother is so protective, how in the hell did she allow Kianna to be sent to me? Christ man, she's not fully grown," Rolfe voiced his complaint, still unwilling to dispense with hostility.

"Aye, well, as to that." Jasper sobered. "Me mother was away when yer father's proposal came. Very bad timing. Me father said he owed yer father a debt from years ago and, what with yer father being in his last days, me father felt he had to agree or never settle the debt. Why do ye think I was lingering in yer village? I hoped ye'd take a look at Kianna and release her."

A moment of silence stretched out between them.

"Kianna knew ye were waiting?" Rolfe asked.

"Aye," Jasper confirmed. "She is me little sister, man. I was ordered by me father to bring her here, but that doesn't mean I intended to leave her." He pointed at Rolfe. "I expected ye to do the right thing and send her back home."

"Ye might have told me ye were waiting," Rolfe groused. "I did nae take a good look at yer sister until she barged into me study today."

Jasper frowned. "So, me sister is not worth enough of yer time to greet when she's been sent to ye and separated from everyone she knows?"

Rolfe shifted. "I admit I was distracted."

Jasper growled softly but in a very appreciative manner. Rolfe narrowed his eyes at him in warning.

"So this fight…" Rolfe asked.

Jasper smirked, showing off the blood in his teeth again. His back was to Annis, and he wiggled his eyebrows. "Ye owe me, Rolfe Munro. The little English lass will think ye fought hard for her."

Rolfe had fought hard. His ribs ached, and one side of his jaw was going to swell, but it suddenly didn't matter at all. He looked past Jasper to see Annis watching him, her face twisted with concern.

For you, laddie.

Rolfe nodded. "I owe ye."

He realized he'd never meant something so much in his life. Did it make sense? No, and he wasn't going to contemplate it, either. Annis was his.

This time, he was going to make very sure she knew it.

"Christ," Jasper muttered beneath his breath. "How can any woman make a man look like ye do at the moment?"

Rolfe sent Jasper a firm look. "When ye see one looking at yer sister the same way, ye'll know he's the right man to leave her with."

Jasper's grin faded. In his eyes, Rolfe caught a flicker of curiosity. Well, he knew the feeling. It had plagued him while Cora Mackenzie was sitting in his hall, just placed there by her brother and his father in the hope there might be some reaction from him.

Cora had stirred nothing in him.

Unlike Annis.

"I'll bring yer sister down to ye in two days," Rolfe promised.

Jasper was all business now. "And yer father?"

Rolfe drew in a stiff breath. "We shall each have to handle our fathers. Unless ye want me to keep yer sister. I swear I will not lay a hand on her. Annis is a proper chaperone if ye worry yer father might arrange another match for Kianna."

"I will take Kianna home, for I dare not show me face to me mother if I do nae," Jasper said. "And me father will see the error of his way or me mother is likely to beat him nearly unto death."

Rolfe grunted. "But not all the way?"

Jasper's lips were twitching once more. "Ye might think that is a kindness. In fact, it's the very reason me father will be glad to see me returning with Kianna, for being locked in a stronghold all winter long with me mother intent on making him suffer is a fate he'd gladly die to avoid. Kianna is her only daughter, ye understand?".

His own father wouldn't be so easy to appease. Rolfe didn't care. He'd made his choice, and it was there, in front of him. He grasped Jasper's wrist for a moment before he moved past him toward his goal.

And it was time to claim her.

>>>><<<<

ROLFE DIDN'T WASTE any time.

He had her back in the saddle moments after he'd clasped Jasper's wrist. The Munro Retainers mounted and followed them as they turned back toward the Munro stronghold.

The pace was dramatically different, though.

Unlike the hours riding with Jasper, now Annis had to hold tight and move with the motion of the horse or suffer the bouncing around against the saddle. The weather was growing colder as the horses moved faster, sensing home.

The Munro stronghold was a beautiful sight. Even draped in shadow because of the half-moon. They rode up as the Munro scrambled to bring out candles to illuminate the yard.

Rolfe caught her as she slid down the side of her horse. He was warm and hard, making her gasp.

"How are you not chilled?" Annis asked in wonder.

She should have pushed away from him, but there was something about being in contact with him that warmed her from the inside out.

Something flickered inside her. A need she honestly didn't want to think about. No, she wanted to act upon it.

"I'll warm ye, lass," he muttered.

His tone was thick with promise, and it stroked the flames inside her. The darkness was suddenly a welcome companion, for it enveloped them as Rolfe turned and clasped her wrist. He tugged her along behind him as boys came out to take the horses into the stable, and men hurried to find shelter from the relentless sleet.

Inside the stronghold, noise came from the kitchens where Finnea was ordering the fires stoked up and stew warmed for the returning Retainers.

Rolfe pulled her straight into the passageway. He made good on his promise because her cheeks warmed as maids hurrying toward the kitchen saw them heading into the shadows.

"Rolfe, everyone will know," Annis protested.

"Good."

He tugged her the few remaining steps to the top of the stairs and right through the doors which led into her chamber. He gave her wrist a tug and sent her into the room.

"I want every last stable lad to know ye are mine, Annis."

He picked up a length of linen, which was folded next to the pitcher of water. He gave it a snap before closing the distance between them and beginning to rub her wet hair.

He was so close.

Her cheeks were hot, and her breath was quick. She could smell him, and the water on both of them just made her acutely aware of him.

"But your father—" Annis tried to voice an objection.

Rolfe's hands stilled. He held her head in place as he locked gazes with her. "I respect me father. Do nae worry, I will address this matter with him."

He drew in a deep breath. Annis caught the look of distaste in his eyes, but determination was burning brighter.

"Get out of yer wet clothing, lass."

Rolfe started to turn away. She reached out for him, unable to bear the separation.

"I would not be the cause of disagreement between you and your father."

One side of his mouth twitched up. "Because...ye want to protect me again, lass?"

Annis set her teeth into her lower lip. She suddenly felt poised on the edge of a cliff. The impulse to just let go was so strong.

"I can nae resist the way ye shield me, Annis. Everyone comes to me for what they want. Ye are nae content to be sheltered." Rolfe's expression became intense as he spoke.

Annis discovered herself speechless. She'd always been consumed with surviving. No one had ever noticed when she did things for them.

He seemed to sense her thoughts as though he shared them. He turned back to face her.

"I will nae let ye slip away, lass. At least not until I have done me best to tempt ye into staying."

Moving forward and lifting her off her feet, he pressed her against the wall, her thighs wrapping around his body as she looked down into his face.

Suddenly she just couldn't hold herself back any longer. She framed his face with her hands, trembling as the skin-to-skin contact awakened a need inside her which swept aside every other thought. In that moment, there was only him and the fact that she wanted to be even closer.

Leaning down, she pressed her mouth to his. Kissing him with a slow motion as she tried to mimic the way he'd kissed her. He let her take the lead. She felt the way he controlled the urge to take command.

It was only a moment, and yet, it felt like an eternity. They were sealed together inside the space between heartbeats while she marveled at the way it felt to press her mouth against his. Never once had she imagined there might be so much bliss in the entire world.

She shuddered, and he shifted. Slipping his hands from beneath her thighs to her bottom. She slipped lower, until her mons was against his groin. A soft sound escaped her, one so breathless and needy, she didn't recognize it.

He kissed her harder. Taking command of the moment as he held her against the wall. His mouth was firm, moving over hers as he pressed her lips against his, so his tongue might tease hers.

It was nothing short of jolting.

She'd never been so close to someone before, and yet, she wasn't close enough. Her passage felt empty, her core heating up so that her dress was suddenly too hot. She wanted to shed the layers of fabric and pull his clothing off as well. She slid her hands down his face to his neck, where she tugged on the buttons holding his shirt closed.

His chest rumbled with a growl.

He allowed her legs to slip down until she was standing. It frustrated her, making her pull at his clothing more. But a moment later, he was plunging his fingers into the valley between her breasts.

She gasped.

He lifted his mouth away from hers, locking gazes with her as he pulled the tie which held her bodice closed, and opened the knot. Once released, the weight of her breasts started to push the bodice open. He pulled loops of the lace free, all the while watching her reaction.

How did she feel?

Desperate.

They weren't progressing fast enough. Her need was growing with every breath.

He parted the sides of her bodice and slipped his hands inside. She gasped as he cupped her breasts with nothing but her chemise between them.

"I like hearing that sound from ye, Annis," he said. "For it tells me ye enjoy my touch."

She did.

And he knew it. She caught the flicker of awareness in his eyes before he lowered his head and placed a kiss against the top of one of her breasts.

"Oh….my…" She was leaning back, trying to arch and offer her breast to him, but the wall behind her made it difficult.

He lifted his head and pushed her open bodice over her shoulders. With the sleeves still attached, she was suddenly trapped by the garment, her arms held to her sides and slightly behind her.

Something shifted between them. Her belly twisted as she caught the glint in his eyes.

"I want to claim ye, lass," he said darkly. "But first, I am going to prove that yielding to me will be worth it."

He'd stroked his hands down her side and made short work of opening the waistband of her skirts. Once opened, the water-soaked wool headed for the floor and puddled around her ankles. Her underskirt and hip roll had all gone with them, too. But her bodice was still holding onto her.

"I want ye to crave being mine, Annis."

He caressed her face with one hand. The motion so slow and sweet. She lifted her chin, immersed in the sensation. He angled his head so he might press a kiss against her throat.

The connection shook her to the core.

She was still at his mercy, her arms held back by her bodice, and yet, that knowledge intensified the moment.

He might take his pleasure, yet he was focused on her enjoyment.

She had to be dreaming. Reality had never been so kind.

He placed his other hand on her hip and squeezed. Her eyes flew open at the bolt of awareness that went through her. Rolfe was waiting for her, his eyes looking into hers, watching for her response.

"My bed will be a place ye anticipate going, lass."

It was a hard promise and, deep inside her belly, a need to yield completely to his demand was smoldering. She didn't feel the chill any longer. Her skin was warm, and he was hot against her.

"Show me." Annis wasn't certain when she decided to voice her thoughts. It wasn't really a decision.

A reaction.

Aye, he drew impulses from her, one after the other. His lips pulled back from his teeth, but it wasn't a grin. No, he was baring his teeth at her; that beast inside him responding to her. He pressed his knee between her thighs. Grasping her nape as he pinned her to the wall.

"Yer husband was a bastard for not sharing the pleasure with ye, Annis." He tugged her chemise upward, the wet fabric sticking to her skin. "Even an arranged marriage can be better if a man is nae selfish."

There was a dark promise in his tone. Some whisper of forbidden fruit drew her toward it without a care if she was damned for tasting it.

He stroked her from her hip to her mons. Never hesitating about touching her in so private a place. His knee kept her thighs parted when she would have closed them out of reflex. His fingers delved between the folds of her sex, drawing a strangled cry from her.

"Ye are nay frigid, lass."

"I'm not?" She blinked because it was a question she'd pondered. Right then, though, she didn't seem to have the focus to think.

Not when his fingers were stroking her.

It was unheard of, and yet, she discovered herself breathless as he continued. Pleasure was radiating upward from each penetration.

In...

Out...

Need was building up inside her passage, making her ache. Between the folds of her sex, there was something new. A spot that throbbed. The pleasure seemed to be centered on it, and Rolfe appeared to know exactly how to coax it.

She opened her eyes. It was no longer enough to simply experience the moment. She wanted to participate.

His eyes were glittering with intent. It was hard and dark, but the sight made her bare her own teeth at him.

"I'm not afraid." For the first time, she wasn't. It was like the shell of her youth had finally cracked and fallen aside.

"Ye are my woman, now."

He sent his finger straight into her sex. The little pearl at the top of her sex was far more sensitive than she'd realized. Direct contact drove a cry from her.

And then another as he continued to rub it.

Remaining still was impossible. Yet he held her, his body hard and his grip binding. Both only enhanced the moment. Somehow adding to the attraction. It made no sense, but she was far beyond grasping anything.

Something was building beneath his fingers.

A rising tension that had her thrusting her hips toward him.

Whatever it was, it burst a moment later. Pleasure twisted through her and snapped in an explosion so bright, it burnt everything she thought away. She was left withering. Encapsulated in the moment. The intensity was so extreme, she'd have called whoever tried to tell her it was possible a liar.

But the experience was real.

It gripped her.

Wrung her.

And dropped her back into reality as a panting, shivering mass of spent flesh.

Rolfe held her steady. His head tucked against her head as he stroked her hip. It might have been forever before she noticed the cool air once more, and her breathing settled. Reality slammed into her as she realized he hadn't taken her.

"You didn't…"

She heard him inhale the scent of her hair. "No, I did nae."

He pushed away from her, pausing to place a kiss on her lips. There was arrogance in his eyes, but all she managed to feel upon seeing it was that he'd earned it.

"I've proved meself to ye, Annis."

He kissed her. This time it was hard and full of intent. His mouth was firm, schooling her on the motions.

Then he backed away, eyeing her from head to toe. Her eyes widened as she realized what she looked like. In naught but a smock, one breast completely in sight and the hem barely covering her mons.

⇶✦⇷

DISHEVELED.

She truly embodied the word.

Rolfe indulged in a long look at her.

His.

Her lips were swollen from his kiss and her features softened by her climax. He suddenly understood the difference between lust and affection, for she was the most beautiful creature he'd ever seen, and the throbbing in his cock only enhanced the moment because he'd held back in order to ensure she had a reason to join him in bed.

He reached up and tugged on the corner of his cap. "I look forward to courting ye further, Annis."

Her eyes widened, confusion appearing on her face.

"I'm going to enjoy helping ye lose yer innocence, lass."

⇶✦⇷

"YE BROUGHT THAT girl back."

Cian Munro wasn't happy. Rolfe faced his father, reaching up to tug on his cap.

"What is the meaning of that?" his father demanded. "When ye do

171

nae respect my decisions."

"I have someone to introduce ye to, Father."

Cian was momentarily distracted. Rolfe stepped to the side, allowing his father to see Kianna Chattan. She lowered herself.

"Closer, lass." Rolfe raised her up with a motion of his fingers. "I want me father to get a good look at ye."

"I have seen the girl."

"Have ye Father?" Rolfe asked softly. He reached out and clasped Kianna's arm to move her forward.

Once she was directly in front of his father, Rolfe moved to stand beside his sire. His father grumbled, looking at Rolfe instead of Kianna.

"Kianna has told me she turned sixteen two weeks ago," Rolfe informed his father softly.

"Two weeks ago?" Cian asked in alarm. "But the girl was already here...."

Cian's voice trailed off as he peered intently at Kianna. "Closer, lass."

Kianna stepped forward. Cian drummed his fingers on the armrest of his chair while he studied her.

"Ye may go, Kianna," Rolfe said at last. "Thank ye."

Kianna offered another reverence. It was a polished motion, and she had her hands folded so very perfectly in front of her. But there was a look in her eyes of uncertainty because she was still young enough to wonder if she was performing as her mother would want her to.

The moment the door closed behind her, his father growled. "Neil Chattan owes me a debt. Why would he send such a...child?"

"Because he takes the debt seriously," Rolfe answered his father. "According to Jasper Chattan, Neil sent the girl while her mother was away. I imagine his wife is nae too pleased with him."

Cian didn't grin. He wasn't ready to let the matter go. He slapped the arm of the chair, mumbling as his temper flared.

But there was nothing to do about the fact that Kianna was simply unsuitable.

"Well, I am still not giving me blessing to ye keeping that English tart."

"Annis is a good woman, Father." Rolfe bit the argument back that he wanted to voice over his father's use of the word tart.

"Ye are no untried lad, Rolfe. Do nae be blinded by how well she warms yer cock."

Rolfe returned to facing his father. He gripped his belt until he felt the edges of the thick leather digging into his fingers.

"Oh...ye do nae care for me talking like that?" his father asked when Rolfe held his tongue.

"I do not," Rolfe confirmed.

"Come now." Cian opened his arms wide. "The door is shut. Speak yer mind."

"There is naught to say."

Cian leaned forward. "Do nae treat me like an old feeble man, Rolfe. I am yer father and yer laird. Arranging a match for ye is me duty."

"And yet, ye did not do so until now," Rolfe spoke softly. "I wonder if that is on account of Sandra."

"Do nae speak her name," Cian snarled. "Ye know I have forbidden ye to say that name! No one is even allowed to name their daughter that name."

Rolfe didn't rise to the bait of his father's anger. Instead, he stared at his sire as Cian pointed a trembling finger at him.

"I had no choice," Cian mumbled after a time. "My father would not have any daughter-in-law except for yer mother. The choice was not mine."

"I have never coddled ye, Rolfe."

Rolfe drew in a deep breath. "No, ye have not."

He reached up and tugged on his cap before turning around and quitting the room. It took every last ounce of self-discipline he had not to return and blister his father's ears.

But respect was earned.

Such a simple idea. One Rolfe had been raised on. His father was firm in his opinions, but Rolfe was strong because of that unyielding nature. Leading the clan would have broken him and rent the Munro in half if Cian had been soft in his approach to parenting.

Rolfe stopped and grinned. Once more, he was noticing his lack of ability to deal with females. Aunt Euna had bent him to her whim with feminine tears. And Annis? Well, she drew him to her with her desire to stand up straight and weather the storm no matter the cost.

She'd tried to shield him as well.

He was stuck on that facet of her character. Or perhaps, it was more correct to say it attracted his attention when not a single other female had been able to do so. Pretty faces didn't do it. Soft song and musical talent hadn't managed it either. Cora was unbridled and flamboyant, yet he'd only been mildly drawn to her.

Annis wanted to stand alone.

It drew him to her, awakening a need to champion her.

She'll argue with ye over it, laddie.

Annis would. Rolfe grinned as he began walking again. Anticipation was brewing inside him, but he headed for his chambers instead of back to where Annis was.

He'd always shouldered the duty of his father's expectations. Now would be no exception. In fact, now was the most genuine test of his honor. He wouldn't have Annis until he had her without objections from his father.

How do ye plan to accomplish that, laddie?

Rolfe wasn't precisely sure. But that didn't mean he was stopping until he accomplished his goal.

She was his woman.

﷽

"I'M GOING TO enjoy helping ye lose yer innocence, lass."

Annis heard his words in the darkest hours of the night. She opened her eyes and discovered her bed was far more lonely and cold than she had ever felt.

So strange.

Her bed had always been her sanctuary. The single place where no one looked at her. There was no need to guard her expression inside the folds of darkness. There, in the night, she was finally free to be herself.

Now, she felt alone.

Honestly, she was stunned. Annis rolled the idea around inside her thoughts as she tried to grasp it.

She wanted company.

Well, you want Rolfe's company.

Her memory offered up what she'd been thinking about before Matterson had taken her away. The measuring tape lay somewhere forgotten, and the piece of paper she'd intended to use for Rolfe's measurements was likely a ball of mush in her skirt pocket.

But tomorrow was another day.

Another opportunity to go to Rolfe, as she'd been intent on. Joy filled her, as well as anticipation.

Oh yes, fate was finally being kind to her at last!

﷽

Duncan land…

LUCAS DIDN'T HAVE to ride out to face Goron.

No, he might lock the gate now that he had the votes behind him.

He knew it and felt the Duncan Retainers watching him as he mounted his horse. Behind him, forty men were making ready to ride out.

It would be a fair fight.

Terin Campbell stood on the top of the steps which led into the largest tower.

Goron was a short-sighted ass for leaving her a maiden. That shortcoming had led to Lucas gaining the upper hand in claiming enough votes to become laird.

It was an oversight that would affect the entire clan, though, and he wanted those who had voted against him to know he'd take the position head-on, not cowering behind a gate because his opponent had made strategic mistakes.

All right, he was looking forward to the fight, too. Goron and his mother, Benedicta, had ruled ruthlessly, bending everyone to their whims. The chance to rise up and face his tormentor was something Lucas wasn't about to miss out on.

It might go badly. He wasn't fool enough to overlook that fact. But he was riding out to meet Goron Duncan, and that was that.

He reached up and touched his fingers to his cap before he turned and dug his knees into his horse. The day was brisk but fair enough, and his stallion took to the road, eager to stretch its legs.

He was about to meet his destiny.

⟫⟫⟫⟪⟪⟪

ANNIS WOKE TIRED.

All she wanted to do was roll over and cover her eyes with the blanket and go back to sleep.

But there was sunlight on the floor.

She looked at it and groaned. The floor was chilly, and the air brisk when she opened the shutters. But outside, there was bright sunlight. After days of sleet and gray clouds, it was a marvel.

One not to be wasted.

Annis started to turn away and seek her clothing, but something caught her eye. Below in one of the side yards of the older portion of the stronghold, Kianna was sitting on a swing. The girl moved her legs and glided back and forth in a lazy pace. No one was near, only a few hens pecking at the ground.

The girl was forgotten.

Annis felt her mouth go dry. She knew the feeling of being someplace where she was not accepted. Like so many brides, Kianna had been separated from everyone she knew, and now, she faced the life of being an outsider.

It wasn't completely cruel intentions on the part of the Munro. Kianna fell into a strange category as far as the hierarchy of the stronghold was concerned. If Rolfe's mother were alive, it would be her place to take Kianna in hand since the girl was born of the mistress of another house. Finnea was the Munro Head-of-House, as such, Kianna would someday be her mistress if the wedding proceeded. So Finnea wouldn't take the girl in hand for fear it would lead to festering resentment.

Which leaves you.

Annis pursed her lips. But her hesitation only lasted a moment before she turned around and began dressing.

Are you sure?

Actually, she was. Annis felt something new moving through her. A sense of confidence she'd never encountered before. Perhaps it had begun with Finnea giving her the keys to the solar wardrobe.

No…be honest.

Her cheeks heated as she realized it all centered around Rolfe. He'd always treated her…well, and he'd always made her felt cherished. There was a word she'd never really felt the meaning of. She'd learned it, heard it used, and yet, Rolfe was the first one to make her understand what it felt like.

Perhaps she was opening herself up to a more significant hurt, but Annis didn't allow that fear to stop her. She went down the stairs and headed for the yard to find Kianna.

⫸⫷

THERE WOULD BE a line outside his study.

Rolfe woke to the sunlight and felt his belly tighten.

He had duties.

Responsibilities.

All he wanted to do was seek Annis out. His need for her was an addiction, and he had no desire to do anything but indulge his craving.

But he also wanted to be worthy of her.

So he headed toward his study. But he heard her voice floating through the passageway.

"No one has noticed me since I have been here," Kianna said.

Ahead of him, Kianna was following Annis.

"Today, you and I shall work in the solar," Annis informed Kianna. "Did your mother teach you…"

They disappeared around the bend.

"Seems yer English captive is settling in," Sholto remarked beside him. "Appears she enjoyed the attention ye paid her abovestairs."

Rolfe slapped his man on the shoulder. Sholto grinned, unrepentant.

"It's rather interesting to discover English women are nae the cold fish I've heard they are."

"Sholto," Rolfe warned. "Do nae test me when it comes to Annis."

He realized he'd rarely spoken truer words. They felt like they had risen up from his bone marrow. It was a simple idea. Irrefutable.

His.

And she was taking Kianna in hand and settling in.

Just as soon as his day was done, he was going to enjoy helping her settling more.

CHAPTER EIGHT

B Y THE END of the day, Annis had a far greater appreciation for mothers and nurses. Well, and any parent or tutor. Kianna was obedient enough, but the effort of being in charge of her was taxing. The hours flew by, and Annis discovered herself stunned to hear the bells ringing for supper, for it seemed they had just begun but an hour ago.

"I'll go wash." Kianna flashed Annis a bright smile and disappeared.

How often had Annis been the same with Aife? In a hurry to be finished. Never realizing that she would grow up right on time?

Annis sat for a moment longer, indulging the memories of days when she had been the young woman being schooled in stitches while lessons on language and mathematics were discussed. A noble bride was expected to arrive with the skills necessary to run a large estate. French, Latin, and English were the minimum number of languages she could be proficient in. Kianna's mother had done well with the girl, but she was still young.

Annis laughed softly under her breath. Kianna was young enough not to understand the necessity of being devoted to her studies.

"I thought I'd never get ye to meself."

Annis turned around to discover Rolfe in the doorway of the solar. He had that mischievous grin on his face as he looked around the room.

"The last time I was in here…" he said, "was when the Head-of-House marched me up here after I ate a full dozen tarts and lied with jam all over me face and hands."

Rolfe entered the solar. "Let's see." He reached behind the wardrobe. "Ah!" He withdrew a rod that had a thick layer of dust on it.

"Aife had one just like that," Annis said as Rolfe lifted the rod and brought it down on the open palm of his left hand.

"Aife was yer nurse?"

The question brought heat to her cheeks because Annis realized they'd never really discussed anything personal.

"Aife was all I knew," Annis answered softly. "She raised me. My mother died when I was four."

There was silence in the solar for a long moment. Rolfe didn't appear to have any more experience with personal conversations than she did.

"Oh well, it's good you are here," Annis said.

"Ye're happy to see me, lass?"

He sat the rod down, and his smile grew brighter. He was moving toward her, mesmerizing her. Her breath froze in her lungs, as she seemed stuck just watching him approach.

"Hearing ye say such makes every argument I had to sit through today worth it."

Rolfe was only a pace away now. He reached out and stroked her cheek with the back of his fingers. The contact was jolting. She jumped and shivered. Heat swirled through her belly, and the surface of her lips tingled with anticipation.

She was nervous, though. A bundle of impulses as she tried to decide what to do, how to respond. There was a tempest inside her, making her want to chatter while at the same time, she wanted to be kissed.

"Yes, I need your measurements," Annis said. "For a shirt."

He'd slid his hand along her cheek and onto her nape. Rolfe had been leaning down, tilting his head so he could fit his mouth against hers in a kiss.

He stopped just shy of that contact.

Annis shivered, her body screaming in frustration as he lifted his head up and locked gazes with her.

"A shirt?" he asked softly.

"Aye. Finnea said you wouldn't let the last tailor measure you."

He massaged the back of her neck for a moment. His expression became hungry. His lips thinning as he leaned back down so that their mouths were only an inch apart.

"I'm guilty of no' wanting to take me shirt off for the man."

Rolfe sent a look into her eyes, which made that heat swirl once more through her belly. There was something flickering to life at the top of her sex, and it made her recall in vivid detail the burst of pleasure he'd given her before. How satisfying it had been.

She craved more of it.

"Come," Rolfe said.

He was suddenly in motion. Annis had been so caught in the moment, she found herself being pulled out of the solar and down the stairs while still attempting to think.

She really didn't want to think.

No, she wanted to feel.

And be kissed.

Yes, that, too. But Rolfe had clasped her wrist and taken her to the bottom of the tower. He was moving at a brisk pace, pulling her to the base of another tower and then up the steps. By the time they reached the top, she was out of breath. He let her go inside his chamber and turned around to firmly close the door.

"I can nae be taking off me shirt in me mother's solar." Rolfe chuckled.

There was wicked suggestion in the sound, and a moment later, he'd tugged his shirt up and over his head.

Annis never did catch her breath.

His chest was sculpted to perfection. Hard and covered in golden hair. He closed the distance between them as she drew in a little breath and let it out.

"Take all the measurements ye like, lass," he said.

Thinking was proving so extremely difficult for Annis.

Impossible, really.

She wanted to feel. Experience. Not think.

But one of his eyebrows was raised as he waited on her response.

"The measuring tape is...um...back in the solar." Her voice was unrecognizable. It was husky and needy.

"Well, in that case." Rolfe leaned down. "We'll just have to deal with that tomorrow."

She didn't need to ask why they couldn't complete the task right then, for he pressed his mouth against hers.

Nothing mattered but kissing him back.

And touching him.

The need was all-consuming. Annis lifted her hands and placed them on his chest. Her fingertips were suddenly extremely sensitive. The connection between their skin a new jolt of sensation, which went through her like a bolt of lightning.

"That's the way, lass, touch me."

It was an order and yet, a plea. His voice was dark with need, unleashing a desire to press up against him.

But her clothing irritated her.

She was too hot, and her dress unbearably tight. Annis pulled the tie out of her cleavage this time, popping open the knot and loosening the front of her bodice.

Rolfe watched her. His eyes glittered. He had her backed against the wall, but the way he watched her empowered her. She rolled her shoulders, and her bodice and sleeves went slithering down her arms to the floor. She was left in her smock and stockings.

"My turn."

Her breath caught again as he reached for the buckle on his belt. A quick motion of his hand and the wool was loose. It dropped down to puddle around his ankles, leaving his nude body in full view.

You shouldn't look at his...

The thought was too late, for her gaze had already lowered to his cock. The truth was, she'd never actually looked at one. It stood up, hard and rigid.

"Touch me, Annis."

She set her teeth against her lower lip, but the invitation was just too tempting. There was such freedom in the ability to reach out her hand and close it around his member. It was hot and smooth. He shuddered as she closed her hand around it and drew her grip up to the top.

Her gaze flew back to his.

Rolfe was watching her, his blue eyes glittering.

"Aye, lass, I enjoy being touched there just as much as ye do."

He leaned one hand against the wall and lowered his head until his face was in her hair. She heard him inhale her scent, and another shudder shook her.

So many little details. How had she never realized there were so many facets to intimacy?

"Stroke me, Annis."

She reached down and drew her hand along his length once more, well now, she was encountering a whole new meaning of the idea of lust.

You aren't married...so it's a sin.

Rolfe made a soft, male sound of enjoyment, and nothing else mattered. Annis toyed with his length. Drawing on it while she listened to the sounds he made. The staff grew harder, and a drop of liquid formed in the slit on the top of it. His breathing became raspy as he slid his hand down and cupped her breast. The thin fabric of her smock did nothing to shield her from how good it felt to have her breast cupped. Somehow, she had never noticed just how sensitive her body might be.

"We fit together well, Annis."

She raised her face so she could look into his eyes. Passion was smoldering there, promising her more of the pleasure he'd given her before.

And she craved it.

"Take me to bed," she voiced her craving.

His lips rose as she spoke. A moment later, he'd pulled her smock off. Then he carried her to the mattress and took a moment to pull her shoes off before she turned over and crawled up the bed.

She wanted to be there.

Passion warmed her, and she smiled with pure delight.

Rolfe finished pulling his boots off and turned to look at her.

"I've thought about seeing ye in me bed. Now that ye are here, do nae ever think I will let ye go, Annis."

He crawled up after her. So big and powerful, her belly twisted as she watched him. He covered her, resting his weight on his elbows as his body connected with hers from top to bottom.

"And never worry that I will fail to share the pleasure with ye, lass," he whispered next to her ear as he kissed the side of her neck. "Ye are my woman."

And she wanted to be.

Annis didn't think anymore. Their limbs were entangled, and it didn't feel awkward. No, there was perfection to the way they fit. She needed to touch him. To slide her hands along the sides of his chest and up into his hair.

His kissed her with a hunger that matched her own. She moved her mouth in unison with his. Tasting him as he teased her lower lip with the tip of his tongue and then pressed her lips open so he might kiss her deeply.

Her thighs spread naturally to cradle him. She clasped him to her as the head of his cock slipped between the folds of her sex. She was wet, and it made so he could press forward with ease, the movement of penetration lacked pain or even discomfort.

Instead, there was delight.

He filled her, and it soothed the need gnawing at her.

But she wanted more.

More motion.

His hands were in her hair as he worked his hips, sending his length into her body as she lifted her hips to accommodate him. Pleasure was building with every stroke, brightening, becoming more pressing. Nothing mattered but lifting her hips for his next thrust. Her heart was hammering away inside her chest, and she didn't care if it burst so long as she kept pace with him.

Annis felt the climax approaching. For a moment, she was desperate to reach it, half fearful it would elude her. But Rolfe didn't disappoint her. He drove deep and hard into her, continuing until she gasped, the moment upon her. It was gripping and consuming, the pleasure wringing her and exploding in a bright, hot flash that raced from her belly outward to the end of her fingers and toes. Her nipples contracted into tight little nubs before she felt Rolfe begin to flood her with his seed. A deep wave of satisfaction left her gasping and spent on the sheets.

》》》《《《

HE'D MEANT TO go slower.

Rolfe opened his eyes as he caught his breath and growled at the canopy which covered his bed.

He'd meant to awaken her passion with kisses and soft touches.

Now?

He growled at himself, frustrated with his lack of self-discipline.

Annis stirred beside him in response. Rolfe turned and gathered her close. She made a soft sound as she settled into his embrace and something snapped inside him.

It was a good thing he was lying down because emotions flooded him. He hadn't experienced such a level of feelings since his mother had died, and he'd realized he had to grow up. As a fourteen-year-old boy, it had seemed like a good thing. Now, Rolfe realized he'd sealed his emotions behind a wall in order to be everything the clan and his father wished him to be.

Now...now there was Annis.

She was precious in a way he hadn't understood another person might be except for his father. Her scent was filling his senses, settling the restlessness he hadn't even realized was bothering him.

Like he'd found an answer to some dilemma.

She muttered in her sleep, shifting away from him. He frowned and eased her back toward him. A frown marred her face as he placed her head on his chest once more. But he smoothed his hand over the top of her head and watched her lips ease into a contented line.

She'd get used to him.

Because he wouldn't stop until she did.

>>><<<

SOMEONE WAS IN her room.

Annis drew in a deep breath and stretched. The sheet was smooth against her bare skin.

Her eyes opened in shock as she realized she was wearing only her stockings. She blinked at the canopy overhead.

Aye. Only her stockings.

More importantly, her passage was just ever so slightly sore.

Well, you went and did it.

Her cheeks heated, but her lips rose in a smile as a little giggle escaped her.

186

Two more giggles answered from across the chamber. Annis flipped over like a freshly caught fish. She grabbed the bedding, clutching it up to her chin as someone snapped their fingers.

"Mind yer manners."

Finnea scolded two maids. "Do ye think I can nae find others to take such a good position? Girls who know to keep their opinions to themselves? At least until the mistress gets to know ye a wee bit."

The two girls caught Annis looking at them. Both of them sunk into reverences, one of them pointing to her. Finnea turned swiftly around.

"Forgive me, mistress, for waking ye." Finnea was quick to snap her fingers again at the maids. They both hurried to open the window shutters.

Bright sunlight flooded inside the chamber along with fresh air. Annis quickly sat up.

"I am ashamed to be wasting the light," Annis muttered, horrified by how late in the morning it was.

"There is no reason to be concerned. Ye do nae answer to me," Finnea assured her. "This is Holly and Mia. If they do nae please ye, I will send someone else."

The girls began to hurry around the chamber. Finnea considered them with a practiced eye.

"I'm sorry ye were tasked with me today," Annis spoke to the Head-of-House. "I know you have a great many demands on your time."

Finnea had a small smile of satisfaction on her lips. "Well, ye can be helping me with this house. Once ye settle in. Up with ye. There is still food on the tables in the hall."

Finnea looked back at her maids before she nodded and left the chamber.

Everyone knows you are Rolfe's mistress now.

Was it wrong that Annis didn't feel a bit of shame over the matter?

Oh, her cheeks heated as she came out of the bed but not because she believed she'd sinned. No. It was just a bit of shyness over being bare. Holly and Mia were quick to help her wash.

They'd brought up some warm water and a half barrel. Standing in it, Annis was treated to several cups of water poured over her before a little soap was rubbed along her limbs and then more water to wash it all down. The brisk air raised goosebumps on her skin, but a length of linen was handed to her as Holly guided her to stand in front of the hearth where a new fire was crackling away.

Luxury.

It truly was.

A fresh smock was dropped over her head before Holly leaned over to secure the padded roll which would go around Annis's hips. Commonly referred to as a bum roll, it kept the weight of the skirts from being too taxing, and it also held her skirts away from her feet a few inches to aid in movement.

Mia had a new underskirt in her hands.

"Where is my dress?" Annis asked.

"It's down in the laundry," Holly answered. "Finnea found another which should fit ye well enough."

Another luxury.

Annis might have argued, but the dress they brought to her was a lovely cranberry color. It was lighter weight wool, and she'd find it much more comfortable than the dress she'd selected to keep her warm on her journey away from the Duncan stronghold.

You are well and truly away now.

And a fallen woman.

Fallen? Well, she'd done what she should so often and never felt as happy as she did at the moment.

So perhaps she would just start doing what she dared instead.

The idea made her very happy. In fact, it felt like there was so much happiness inside her, it was just going to spill over and illuminate the room like the sunlight.

Her belly rumbled.

Holly hurried to finish arranging her hair before the two maids smiled at her, looking for approval.

"Thank you," Annis said. "Thank you both very much."

They flashed her grins, and Annis realized she was famished. She headed for the door but stopped when she realized the maids were beginning to clean the chamber. Finnea had clearly changed her mind on Annis's standing.

She wouldn't feel guilty. Annis chided herself as she descended the steps. She didn't think she had ever been so happy in her entire life, so there would be no regrets.

None.

Instead, she would savor every precious second of happiness.

Her belly rumbled long and low.

And she'd eat, too!

She hurried toward the hall to break her fast.

Most of the tables were empty by the time she arrived. But there was ample fare. Annis gathered up a bowl of porridge and a broken round of bread before settling down at one of the long tables in the middle of the room.

⋙⋘

LAIRD CIAN MUNRO contemplated Annis from the high ground.

She sat straight and didn't return any of the looks being cast her way.

Well, as a bastard, she'd likely learned to keep to herself through the years. He drummed his fingers on the arm of his chair, more alarmed by the way his people seemed to be accepting her than by the way she acted.

Matterson was looking anywhere but at him. Cian grumbled. His own man was tolerant of the girl. Such a fact was something that would make getting rid of her harder to do. Two women passed close enough to where the English girl sat that Annis looked up. Cian's eyes widened when his clanswomen lowered themselves.

English.

The word was an idea that left a sour taste on his tongue. Seeing her sitting at his tables when her brethren had laid so many of his own blood in their graves was something Cian couldn't stomach.

By Christ, he wouldn't see her as Mistress of the Munro.

⋙⋘

SHE HADN'T TAKEN the measurements for the shirt.

As her hunger was sated, Annis recalled how she'd ended up in Rolfe's chamber the night before.

Something moved off to her right, and she looked over to see two Munro women. They were looking at her and leaning toward one another as they chatted.

About you...

Well, that shouldn't have been surprising. The Head-of-House had been in the chamber when she awoke, proving the entire household knew Rolfe had bedded her.

You enjoyed it.

She had. Annis discovered herself still attempting to wrap her head around that idea. The surprise hadn't worn off, leaving her smiling because she was just so very happy to discover life held such moments of joy.

Lonn had been a selfish bastard. Honestly, even if he'd had no affection for her, would it have been too great an effort to at least allow her to be comfortable when they were in bed? A few soft kisses, and she would have gladly tried to return his attention.

The two women froze when Annis looked at them. Life wasn't finished with surprises, it would seem, for they both lowered themselves before continuing on their way.

It was unexpected.

Annis looked back at her meal, trying to absorb the gesture of respect.

That wasn't the word.

Kindness.

She felt herself brightening again. Sitting still was impossible, so she stood and recalled the task Finnea had given her.

The Head-of-House had set the example on how Annis was to be regarded. Now it was Annis's turn to show how she would proceed now that she'd caught Rolfe's attention.

Caught? He captured you.

Indeed he had.

She'd be productive, just like every other member of the household. For earned respect was the best sort. Annis turned and went toward the tower where the solar was. She'd collect the measuring tape and the small travel desk so she might write down Rolfe's measurements. Finnea would see Annis wasn't going to earn her place on her back.

No, but you plan to make sure Rolfe likes bedding you.

That was very true. In fact, Annis was likely going to put quite a bit of effort into making certain she was as alluring to her lover as he was to her.

Becoming a seductress now?

Apparently, she was, and yet, there was no shame gnawing at her over admitting it. No. None.

Annis heard a giggle.

It was light-hearted. The corners of her lips rose because the sound was quite simply a reflection of the way she felt.

But an icy hand closed around her heart when she turned to see the sound had come from Kianna. The girl was smiling from ear to ear as her face reflected her happiness.

And she had her hands wrapped around Rolfe's arm as she looked up into his face.

And he was grinning down at her. That rakish half-smile she knew so well herself.

Annis leaned back against the stone wall of the passageway. Her heart was barely beating as her knees felt weak.

"Hurry, Rolfe, before we are seen." Kianna was tugging on his arm.

"Aye, lass, I'm at yer disposal," Rolfe answered.

Annis felt the need to retch. Tears were burning in her eyes as she curled her fingers against the hard stone of the passageway wall.

She felt gutted. Tears were flooding her eyes, and she couldn't seem to fend them off. She needed to think the situation through, but her emotions weren't interested in allowing her the time. Instead, she was left battling doubts and recriminations.

He's had you, so now he'll move on.

You know men are heartless.

Kianna is his bride. You are the mistress who will sate him until she is old enough to wed.

Annis reached up and patted herself on both sides of the head in an attempt to get her mind to stop whirling. She needed to stop and get a grip on herself. Things had been so very perfect just moments before. She mustn't panic.

"Rolfe is a fine son."

Annis sucked in a startled breath and opened her eyes to discover Cian Munro standing in the passageway next to her. The Munro Laird was looking in the direction Rolfe and Kianna had gone.

"Aye," Cian Munro muttered again as he looked toward Annis. "Rolfe had to shoulder his duties young, but he has done well. Very well. Rolfe always puts the clan first."

Annis didn't miss the way the Munro Laird looked at her. He swept her from head to toe. "However, ye know a thing or two about standing straight and doing what is expected of ye. Do ye not, lass?"

Annis was caught in the grip of horror. She could only lean against the passageway wall and stare back at him.

He chuckled and coughed.

"Aye...aye...ye know how to keep yer mouth shut. A good trait. No man likes a babbling female," Laird Munro said. "After all, the only two women a man is duty-bound to suffer their chattering from is his mother and his wife. A mistress...well, ye keep to yer place, lass, and I'll not bother ye. Me son works hard, I suppose I should not begrudge him a mistress since his bride is too young for the moment and winter is here."

Cian Munro went on his way, Matterson and Daeg following their laird down the passageway after hearing every word their laird spoke. The stone wall at her back was cold, but it was nothing compared to the chill Annis felt gripping her heart.

And try as she might, there was nothing she might think of to console herself. Rolfe had brought her home as his captive, but it was better than wedding Torian Leslie.

Better than returning to Goron Duncan.

And you went to his bed.

She had.

So, she'd struck her bargain. Why did it hurt so badly?

>>><<<

Duncan land...

SEVERAL DAYS ON the road and Lucas pulled his horse to a stop. Ahead, a column of Retainers was riding hard.

And they were Campbells.

Damn Goron for a fool.

Or maybe not. There was something very satisfying about know-ing Goron was going to get everything he deserved for neglecting his duty as laird. Leaving his vows unconsummated while flaunting his mistresses was something the Campbells were clearly not in the mood to suffer silently.

Lucas waited for the Campbells to reach him. The ground was too wet for there to be a cloud of dust when they pulled up.

"I am Lucas Duncan."

The man riding at the head of the column had two feathers sticking up on the side of his bonnet. "Kendric Campbell. I'm here to take my sister Terin home."

"I've secured a majority vote among the Duncan," Lucas informed him.

Kendric's features eased a tiny bit. "And ye are on the road...why?"

"Because I'm going to finish the matter personally."

Kendric looked at his captain. A moment later, he returned his attention to Lucas. "Me laird would likely tell me to witness such an event with me own eyes. So long as ye are making it clear ye value an alliance with the Campbell."

"I do," Lucas assured him.

"Then I will ride with ye, Lucas Duncan."

Lucas kneed his horse forward. He hoped Goron felt them coming. The damned bastard didn't deserve a quick end.

But Lucas wasn't planning on wasting his time drawing the matter out either. He wasn't a man who enjoyed the suffering of others. He didn't plot it, as Benedicta and Goron had always seemed to be doing. If there was a way to avoid killing, Lucas would have liked to hear it.

But he knew there wasn't one.

Goron wouldn't give up the lairdship, and Lucas wasn't planning on allowing him to continue in the role. Now that the clan had voted, Goron would never allow Lucas to live because he was the one man who the clan would back.

So it would be a fight to the death.

⇥⟫⤬⟪⇤

Munro land...

THE MEASURING TAPE felt wrong between her fingers.

Stop being so emotional.

No matter how hard she tried to listen to her own words of advice, Annis failed. She ended up sitting down on a bench while tears escaped her eyes once more.

She had never cried so easily.

Not until you fell in love with Rolfe Munro.

Her eyes widened as the truth came from inside her. It wasn't something she decided upon. No, just like it was foretold in poems and music and lore, love just happened. Sweeping aside all logic as it gripped her and claimed her as a victim of madness.

But it hurt.

Another fact foretold by lecturing clergy and wise, old women.

To love was to enter into madness where your emotions swirled out of control. Annis found her thoughts jumping from those moments when Rolfe had held her against him in the dark hours of the night to the sight of him smiling down at Kianna.

She was his bride.

Annis discovered that fact tormenting her. It sliced into her heart, drawing blood, and then returned to slice her again. There appeared to be no end in sight either.

Your circumstances are better than ever.

They were, and she should have been able to make peace within herself. But just as love was fabled to do, it made her want more.

You are being unrealistic.

She was. Acknowledging her faults didn't help, though. It simply made her ache more.

"Mistress."

Holly suddenly appeared in the doorway of the solar. She stopped and lowered herself. Annis struggled to mask her unruly emotions as the maid entered the chamber.

"The laundress found this…in yer underskirt." Holly placed a bowl on the table next to Annis. "Is it yer dowry?"

"Do nae pester the mistress with personal questions, Holly," Mia scolded her.

The bowl was filled with the gold and silver coins Annis had carefully quilted into her underskirt. There were several silver spoons and a full set of gold buttons she'd clipped off her best doublet. The doublet had been made of velvet and not likely to suffer the Scottish rain well. But gold was gold. She'd spent hours hunched over in the corner of her room with the window shutter open to utilize the moonlight so none of the Duncan maids would see a candle flickering beneath her closed chamber door. She'd lost count of how many coins there were. Now, the bowl was quite full.

"Thank you," Annis said.

The two maids lowered themselves. "Finnea sent along a key and says we're to show ye the new store room, for ye need clothing. It's in the manor house."

Reality was showing her that life went on. The needs and requirements of the day would progress, no matter the personal dilemma she might be experiencing.

That is why you should not fall in love.

Annis stood and followed Holly from the solar. Remorse would do her little good. The best she might hope for was to maintain her composure. To suffer in silence.

Pride had its uses, after all, it would seem.

CHAPTER NINE

"JASPER!"

Kianna slipped off her mare before the animal had completely stopped. She was a flash of ankles and billowing skirts as she ran toward her brother.

Rolfe dismounted as Jasper picked his sister up in a huge hug. Kianna was sniffling against her brother's chest a moment later.

This is what me father needed to see.

Rolfe couldn't help but think the thought. Kianna had done well. She'd represented her clan and blood kin well, but she was still so young. Being reunited with her brother had reduced her to tears.

Ye knew she was too young, laddie.

Aye. Even his father had seen it.

Not until ye forced him to.

True, but parents were to be respected, so Rolfe wouldn't dwell on just how it had come to pass, only that his father would have to accept that Kianna needed to go home. Rolfe cast a glance at the sky. Dark clouds were starting to gather. The wind was more than brisk. It had an icy bite now. The leaves were dry, and the wind made a rattling sound as it went through the bare tree limbs.

Winter would give his father time to accept Annis.

It will also give ye time to win her heart.

Rolfe was eager to finish with the Chattan. Jasper sat his sister on her feet and ruffled the top of her head. He looked over her shoulder at Rolfe.

Rolfe reached up and tugged on his cap. Marriage alliances were good, but there were other sorts of relationships to be forged between clans, too. Jasper wouldn't forget the favor he owed Rolfe. More importantly, though, the Chattan heir would know Rolfe was a decent man. That was the sort of thing that would keep a third party from building distrust.

"Aw well," Jasper said in his jovial tone. "It seems I will nae have an excuse to fight with ye again. Too bad, really. I enjoy a good fight, an ye did...decently enough."

"If ye take yer sister off to any more weddings before she's grown, I will happily thrash ye for it," Rolfe said.

Jasper's eyebrows rose. "Is that a fact now?"

Rolfe nodded. Jasper extended his arm. Rolfe clasped his wrist with more strength than necessary. Jasper returned it. They held still for a moment, both of them making sure their men saw it.

"Forgive me for being brief, but I should probably go home and rescue me father," Jasper declared.

Kianna suddenly frowned. Her expression became stressed as she worried two handfuls of her skirt between nervous fingers. Jasper's face tightened. Rolfe caught the look of rage in his eyes and understood the man's position. As a good son, his father had to be respected, his word obeyed.

"Yer sister is always welcome here," Rolfe lowered his voice so it didn't carry to the Chattan Retainers. "I mean that. There will be shelter for her here, but I cannot wait to wed. Ye have seen my father's condition."

"Aye. I have," Jasper replied. "Yer father will have happier last days if ye settle on a wife soon."

Kianna had ventured closer. Her eyes widened. Protected by her youth, she hadn't foreseen any complications with returning to her home if Rolfe released her. Now her young mind was grasping reality and its harsh edges. Her home wasn't really a safe haven. As the daughter of the laird, it was her duty to marry with an eye on the alliance it would forge. Her father would be looking for another match for her. The days she had left with her family were in short supply.

Rolfe wished he might have spared her that knowledge.

"I have a feeling me father will have seen the error of his ways," Jasper grumbled with a return to his brash humor.

"Unlike you," Rolfe said.

"Me?" Jasper made a soft sound under his breath. "Did I not give ye one of the best fights ye have ever had? And in front of yer woman? I hear she was in yer bed last evening. Shouldn't ye be grateful to me for allowing ye to appear gallant?"

Kianna gasped and looked at her brother. Jasper seemed to have forgotten she was there. His face darkened as half his men groaned. Kianna's eyes had begun to fill with tears, but she blinked them away.

She was growing up quickly now.

"Father should be grateful I am willing to return," Kianna stated firmly.

Jasper locked gazes with his sister. "He is our father and laird." There was the unmistakable ring of duty in Jasper's tone.

Kianna's expression tightened. "I obeyed him, did I no'?"

"Ye are a good daughter, Kianna Chattan," Rolfe said clearly for all to hear. "If me father was not so ill, I'd have kept ye, for ye are his choice of bride, but me father does not have the time to wait for our wedding. I hope the Chattan will understand me dilemma."

His words were crafted skillfully. Years of shouldering the weight of the Munro were echoing in his statement, for it would afford all parties to save face. There was no need to point out that the Chattan Laird had erred in sending Kianna. No, Rolfe would simply take the burden of not completing the contract.

"We do understand." Jasper made it clear how he expected his kin to think on the matter. "Me father didnae think he might refuse yer father's dying request."

"Aye," Rolfe finished the conversation. "It is all understandable. And there is no need to discuss the matter again. Our fathers should be respected."

There were rumblings of agreement from both Chattan and Munro Retainers. Rolfe caught a flicker of respect in Jasper's eyes before the man winked at his sister.

"There is snow in the air. Let's get home, brat."

Jasper helped his sister up and onto the back of a horse, then touched two fingers to the side of his bonnet before he wheeled his horse around and took command of his men. They rode out of the village in a neat column, Kianna secure in their mist.

She had the makings of a fine woman.

That was the last thought he spared for Kianna. Rolfe was far more interested in thinking about the woman waiting for him at home.

Is she waiting, laddie?

Rolfe grinned, refusing to allow doubt to pester him.

Annis was waiting.

His memory offered up the tiny sounds of enjoyment she'd let out the night before. The way she had moved with him. It had been purer than any experience of his life. Honestly, he was no virgin, and guilt did arrive to nip at him over the way he'd causally indulged in passion.

He'd never realized how intimate it should be.

No one might have prepared him for the way he felt about last night. It was as if he'd started seeing colors for the first time. The world was vibrant now, where it had only been monotone. He stood facing the fact that he'd cheated himself out of the feeling by bedding women he didn't have an emotional attachment to.

Ye are nae as bad as many.

No and yet, the fact that he'd kept his liaisons out of his father's stronghold didn't quite absolve him of guilt.

Repentance is good, laddie.

It was, and he was planning on devoting himself to making amends. His father wouldn't budge easily, but the wind blew again.

Rolfe felt it cut through his clothing. A nice long winter was precisely what he needed. His father would see fine Annis's attributes, and the weather would ensure she was happy to share his nice warm bed.

He turned back for his horse, but two of the village elders were hurrying toward him. Rolfe knew the look well. There was some matter which required mediation in the village. He swallowed his impatience. There were still several hours of daylight left.

And darkness was suddenly the best friend he had, for it would afford him the opportunity to retire to his chamber and woo his captive. It would seem there was a silver lining to everything because he was suddenly looking forward to foul weather.

⇒⇒⇒⇐⇐⇐

"Finnea said to take whatever ye wish." Holly was excited by the Head-of-House's offer.

Annis couldn't hardly blame the maid either. On the upper floor of the manor house was a store room. It was as large as the chamber Annis slept in.

And it was full.

There were bolts of wool in every hue—lengths of hemp linen. A large worktable was in the center, so the fabric might be laid out and carefully straightened before being cut. Annis had only ever seen so much fabric in the town market where multiple merchants had shops that were well stocked.

"There are buttons, too." Mia encouraged Annis to come and look at a cabinet with dozens of drawers. "Not as fine as the buttons ye have, though."

Most of the buttons were copper. But there were some made of silver, too.

"And there is thread...and needles...and pins," Holly continued to exclaim.

Annis suddenly felt shame nipping at her. How could she be so unhappy?

Rolfe treated her far better than anyone ever had.

You enjoyed being in his bed.

He had a bride. Honestly, it would have been remiss of his father to neglect to arrange a suitable match for his only son.

Are you finished being emotional?

Yes, she certainly was.

The two maids were looking at Annis, clearly out of ideas to cheer her up.

"It is a fine storeroom. I have never seen better," Annis assured them.

"The laird's son had instructed his secretary to make sure we were ready for the tailor to spend the winter with us," Mia explained. "No expense was spared to ensure the man had ample fabric to work on. Now, well, it seems we shall enjoy the bounty."

"I see that is so," Annis remarked. "I believe that tailor just might regret his choice."

"You are here now, mistress, Mia continued. "We shall have a fine winter together."

Holly and Mia grinned. Annis couldn't ignore that the Head-of-House had clearly decided that Annis's standing was higher now than when she had first arrived. For this workroom was for the mistress of the Munro. The older solar was very nice, but the workroom had glass-paned windows and padded seats. There a place for a musician to sit while the noble ladies of the household sewed.

The Head-of-House had been charged with keeping the keys to the room. Allowing Annis into it was a clear declaration of what standing Finnea believed Annis now had.

You know full well to enjoy what you can, when you can.

She did. Annis forbid herself any further gloomy thoughts.

"I must make a shirt for the young laird first," Annis declared with a smile. "Finnea tasked me with the duty."

The two maids immediately went to the stack of linens. They'd selected one and began to position it on the table before Annis recalled that she didn't have the measurements she needed. The two maids were back to looking between one another in an attempt to decide how to handle Annis's temperament.

"Forgive me, mistress, but ye need a smock as well since ye arrived with naught." Holly took the intuitive and voiced her opinion.

"With the three of us, we'll have it done today or tomorrow, and ye could get the measurements for the shirt tonight," Mia added.

"That is a fine idea," Annis agreed.

The two girls smiled. The image of Kianna smiling up at Rolfe attempted to rise up, but Annis forbid herself to be so petty.

Or perhaps greedy was the most appropriate word.

Jealousy would rob her of the happiness to be had. And Laird Munro had made a very good point.

Rolfe was a fine son. He would shoulder his duty just as Annis had done when she wed Lonn. It didn't mean they could not be happy.

Finnea hadn't given her lack-wits as companions, either. The two girls took careful measurements and helped Annis to mark the fabric before they dared to cut it. Not a bit was wasted. Once the pieces were ready, they all rolled and tucked the edges with careful, practiced stitches before they began to assemble the undergarment. Holly fetched their lunch, so the light would not be wasted. Annis rolled her shoulders to relieve the ache in her neck as the day wore on. By dusk, each maid had assembled a sleeve with a neat cuff and underarm gusset. Annis had put the sections of the body together and attached the collar. When the supper bells began to ring, they were all content with their progress.

"The hall will be cheery, Mistress." Mia encouraged Annis to leave the workroom.

There were candles in holders against the wall, but the stacks of fabric didn't need to be exposed to smoke. Rain had started to fall in the late afternoon, so all the windows were shut.

"That sounds delightful," Annis agreed.

The manor house was a good way from the older towers of the fortification. Annis went back to where the buttons were stored. She took a small pouch and placed ten of the silver ones inside it.

"Since the young laird conducts business in the tower, I will make his shirt in the solar," Annis explained. "Tomorrow, all three of us can't work on this smock at the same time."

Holly and Mia nodded. They put everything away carefully and happily escorted her to the lower floor and great hall. Finnea had her staff serving the tables. Cian sat on the high ground. Annis took a seat at one of the long benches. There were more than a few curious looks cast her way. But Holly and Mia were quick to send their kin warning glances. With the rain falling outside, everyone was coming in to enjoy a warm meal and a dry spot to relax in after a long day of work. Several musicians struck up at the far end of the hall, adding a delightful element of joy to the evening.

But Annis wanted to freshen up. She wrapped the second part of her meal in a broken round of bread and left Holly and Mia to the music and their well-earned personal time. The passageways were cold, and the rain was beating down almost sideways outside. There was something in the air. A sense of specters and restless souls from eras past. Goosebumps rose up along her limbs as she listened to her own footsteps on the stone floor because it was so quiet.

Suddenly there was a growl.

Annis jumped. She was near one of the doorways, which opened out into the side yard. The door wasn't closed all the way. The low light showed her a dog.

She relaxed. The dog let out a whimper, lowering its head as its nose twitched, and it began to whine.

"Hungry?" Annis asked. The dog was coming toward her, begging for food. Beneath its belly, its tits were heavy with milk. "So, you have a litter to provide for?"

Annis leaned over and gave the piece of chicken she had in her bread to the dog. It grabbed it off the floor and swallowed it after only two chomps. The begging began again.

"I have only the bread now," Annis tried to reason with it.

The dog's nose picked up the juices from the meat on the bread. Annis leaned forward, offering the bread to the animal. There was a soft clink as the little pouch she'd put the buttons in fell out of the pocket she'd made with her skirt.

The dog clamped its jaws around the pouch.

"You cannot eat that," Annis spoke softly.

The dog suddenly turned and bolted out into the yard with the pouch still held in its teeth.

"Wait," Annis cried.

But the animal was long gone. Annis grabbed her skirts and hiked them high so she might give chase. Ten silver buttons were worth more than Holly or Mia would make in a quarter. The wind whipped the rain into her face, soaking through her skirts as she scanned the yard for the dog. There was only a sliver of light cast by the setting sun, but it was enough to show her the tail end of the dog as it went into one of the far buildings.

Annis charged after the dog.

⇛⇚

"YOUNG LAIRD."

Rolfe turned to discover Daeg watching him from the shadows.

"Is me father looking for me?" Rolfe asked.

Daeg was his father's man to the bone. But tonight, he had an odd look on his face. As though he was torn.

He looked both ways, ensuring they were alone before he stepped closer to Rolfe to keep his words from carrying.

"I ken ye are likely no' too happy with me on account of me touching yer English woman," Daeg began. "I did nae hurt her."

"Ye are loyal to me father," Rolfe remarked carefully. "He is the Laird of the Munro. And ye did not harm her, or there would be an issue between us."

Daeg tilted his head to one side. "Ye run this clan, and I am no' blind to the facts. Now that I've thought the matter through, I should no have taken the little English miss away. She is decent enough and respects yer father."

A chill touched Rolfe's neck. It rippled down his spine as his father's man still appeared to be chewing on something that he was having trouble getting past his lips.

The darkness beyond the stable door suddenly alarmed Rolfe, for he'd neglected to set any of his own men on watching Annis.

Christ. His father would certainly have heard that he'd bedded her. *Ye bloody fool.*

"Daeg?" Rolfe squared off with his father's man. "Where is Annis?"

"I do nae know."

"But?" Rolfe pressed the man for whatever was bothering him. "Ye are here because…why?"

"Because the little miss is no' at supper."

The chill was back, and it tied his belly in a knot. Rolfe was positive he'd never felt so near to puking over fear.

"What else?" Rolfe pointed at him. "Spit it out, man. I am dangerously close to losing me temper with ye."

"Today in the passageway, the lass saw ye with young Kianna. And yer father was there. He said some things to the little miss that while they were no' lies precisely, they were far from kind. Maybe some women might suffer being yer mistress while yer bride matures, but I imagine a woman of royal blood would no' be willing to suffer the slight."

Rolfe hadn't thought he could feel worse.

He did.

He'd left without speaking with Annis. He'd been intent on getting Kianna on her way. Focused on removing one of the last things between him and claiming Annis. Once his young bride was gone and winter fully upon them, his father would have to bend.

He'd forgotten Annis was strong-willed. If she thought her trust betrayed, she'd leave on her own.

His mouth was dry, and his belly knotted. But something else flared up inside him.

"Get the lads out here, and find my captive!"

⋙✕⋘

ANNIS CHASED THE dog through the smaller stable, which was behind the manor house. The animal moved fast, making it an effort to keep up. She hiked her skirts higher to gain more speed and catch the dog.

It ran out of a side door and across another section of yard. Annis followed it, splashing through the mud as the icy sleet hit her neck.

At least she was hot enough from running to enjoy the temperature.

Behind the stable were three more buildings. Inside it was dark because hay and thatch were stored there, and no one dared to leave a candle burning. The dog became a shadow, darting along the wall and then up to the loft. Annis heard it panting as she took to the steep stair ladder leaning against the edge of the loft.

At last, the dog had stopped. In the corner of the loft, the dog dropped the pouch. There was the sound of soft whimpers as its puppies begged their mother to allow them to nurse. She panted for a moment before turning around and settling down. Her young immediately nuzzled against her belly in search of a teat.

Annis let out a sigh.

But a moment later, it was a startled gasp as someone encircled her with a hard arm.

"Where do ye think ye are going, Annis?"

The scream which had started to escape her lips died as she recognized Rolfe. He turned her and pressed her against the wall of the loft, caging her with his arms.

"I will never let ye go, Annis!" his tone was harsh, and in the darkness, he was a creature of shadow. "Can ye not see I treat ye better than anyone else?"

He didn't give her the chance to answer. He tilted his head to the side and pressed his lips against hers. The kiss was hard. This time, he discarded his restraint, releasing his passion. She gasped, and he took advantage of her open mouth to deepen the kiss. His tongue swept inside to tangle with hers.

She groaned.

Now that she'd tasted passion's ultimate pinnacle, her body was quick to warm to his advances. She didn't want to resist; even if, in her thoughts, she wanted to know why he'd been upset with her, nothing mattered at the very moment except for kissing him back.

So that was what she did.

Annis wrapped her arms around his neck. Her senses were suddenly full of him. The scent of his skin was intoxicating. She needed to be closer to him, so she pressed herself against him as he closed his arms around her and stroked her sides.

Her new dress had a square neckline. He kissed his way down her neck to where her breasts were pushed up by her stays. She leaned back, pleasure rippling through her as she heard the sound of her breathing filling the space.

Why did it seem as though it had been ages since she was in his embrace?

Each touch from his lips sent another ripple of delight through her. It all began to pool in her belly as she stroked his neck, desperate for more contact between them.

"Ye are mine, Annis...how can ye doubt it?"

Part of her wondered why but the truth was, she just didn't want to talk.

No, she wanted to have him.

She reached for the edge of his kilt, tugging the fabric up so she might get her hand beneath the wool. His member was hard, and closing her hand around it shattered some barrier inside her. There were suddenly no rules. She wanted him, and she was going to drive him to the edge of his control so that he was just as needy as she was.

"Christ, Annis!" Rolfe exclaimed.

His breath was raspy, and he lifted his head, looking up at the ceiling as she drew her hand along his length. She felt him shudder, heard the rough sounds of male enjoyment escaping from his lips, and smiled. Confidence flooded her, awakening a memory of something she'd heard Lonn say.

"I'm going to get me cock sucked...by someone who is nay frigid..."

She opened her eyes, contemplating the idea. Rolfe's neck was corded, and the sight only encouraged her to be even bolder. Something inside her was feeding on the idea of reducing him to the same mindless state he'd left her in the night before.

She wanted him to crave only her.

Annis sunk to her knees. Rolfe drew in a stiff breath, but she had already gotten into position. She opened her mouth and took the head of his cock inside.

"Annis..."

Her name came out as a groan. The sound fanned the flames of her determination. She closed her lips around the head of his staff and sucked. His hips thrust forward. Another sound came from his lips, which she might have once mistaken for a sign of pain.

Now she understood he was caught in the grip of need. A pleasure so intense, it straddled the border between agony and ecstasy.

Annis opened her mouth and took more of his length. She cupped the remaining portion of his member with her hands as she sucked and drew upon him. What kept her at it were the sounds he made. His hand cupped her head, tightening in her hair.

But he suddenly pulled her away.

She let a cry of frustration, sensing she'd been denied complete victory. Annis wasn't willing to be taunted, so she clasped his flesh and stroked him. Up and down, pumping her hand in quick motions.

"Annis..."

He let out a strangled cry as his seed erupted. He turned just enough so it spurted off to the side as Annis stroked his member through the moment. He let out a growl before he was bending his knees and lowering himself. He tipped her head up as he locked gazes with her in the semidarkness.

"Who taught ye to do that, Annis?"

There was a dangerous note in his voice. Something rippled through her, and she realized he was angry on her behalf.

"Lonn said it once...I never did it...but I thought you might like it....so...I wanted to try it with you."

His lips twitched into a half-grin.

"Did he ever do it to ye, lass?"

Annis felt her eyes widen. "No."

He chuckled softly at her shock. The hand he had on her nape was suddenly massaging the muscles of her neck.

"Oh aye...I can happily reciprocate."

There was a wicked note in his tone. Annis felt her cheeks catch fire at the very idea of him putting his mouth on her.

"Well...maybe some other time."

She was suddenly on the floor. Flat on her back in a smooth motion. Rolfe handled her so easily, it shocked her, and then he flipped her skirts back. The night air teased her bare thighs above the top of her stockings. He smoothed his hands along the inside of her legs, sending a jolt of anticipation through her core.

"Rolfe...you must not."

"Why no'?" Rolfe had settled between her spread thighs. He pressed a hand down on her lower belly, making her clit pulse.

How could an idea be so acutely arousing?

Even if understanding eluded her, the heat flickering in her clit was something she knew the meaning of. Desire was building inside her at a huge rate, like a flood coming down a dry river bed. She knew what she craved and that Rolfe could give it to her.

"Because I'm sure it's not correct behavior," she offered breathlessly.

He smoothed his hand over her belly, his grin widening.

"Ye are me captive, Annis. I have no intentions of behaving properly with ye. Not a bit."

She didn't get time to argue with him further. He pressed her legs wider apart. The folds of her sex separated, leaving her exposed and at his mercy. She'd never felt so sensitive. The first touch of his breath made her surge away from him. It was an unconscious reaction, instinct, but he held her down and leaned forward to press his mouth against her slit.

She let out a cry.

It bounced off the roof as Rolfe chuckled ominously. There was warning and promise in that chuckle.

His mouth was incredibly hot. Against her flesh, it was nearly searing. Yet just at the edge of her endurance. He began to suck, gently at first and then with more power. Pulling at the little pearl at the top of her sex. Need built at a crazy pace. Her passage began to ache as he used the tip of his tongue to drive her even further into insanity.

She was lifting her hips, seeking that burst of pleasure that would leave her glowing with satisfaction.

He suddenly filled her with two fingers. Thrusting them deeply into her body as he sucked upon her clit. The combination was her undoing. Pleasure snapped through her, breaking her apart as she cried out with the intensity of it.

"So, that is how ye like it, lass..." Rolfe rose and covered her.

She was still pulsing with the release, but his weight rekindled her passion. There was a hunger brewing in her belly, which had not been fully sated.

No, she wanted him deep inside her.

It was such a blunt, carnal admission. She should have worried about it but, in that moment, there was only Rolfe and the fact that he was close enough to reach for.

She wound her arms around him, pulling him down as she clasped him between her thighs. She didn't care where they were, only that they were together and hidden away from the rest of the world.

"Aye, lass. I want more as well."

Nothing would do but to have him.

He growled, beginning to move as he drew in a deep breath against her hair. Need was a pulsing tempo inside her. There was no thinking, only reacting.

When the end came, it was hard and blunt. Pleasure snapped through her, as bright and hot as a bolt of lightning. She ended up straining upward as Rolfe spilled his seed inside her. For a long moment, they were frozen in the final throes of passion.

Rolfe rolled off her, pulling her with him as he clamped her to his side. Her head ended up on his chest as they both began to regain their breath.

"I cannot do without ye, Annis," Rolfe said as he stroked her hair. "Best ye set yer mind to staying with me."

Annis blinked. She lifted her head so she might look at his face. Moonlight was coming in through an open window shutter and washing over him. His expression was hard. His lips set in a thin line.

"Do nae look at me like that, Annis," Rolfe muttered as he sat up. She was lifted up along with him and ended up sitting beside him. "Ye like being mine. Half me men just heard ye enjoying being mine."

"What?" She gasped as she looked at where she'd climbed up to the loft. One side of it didn't have a full wall. Which meant it was open to the stable floor below. If anyone was below them, they would have heard…everything.

Rolfe stood. His kilt fell back down to cover him as he reached down and grasped her by her upper arms. She was on her feet a moment later, her skirts settling into place, leaving them both appearing as though nothing had happened.

"Why didn't you tell me…someone might hear?" Annis demanded.

"I have never held a captive before, Annis," he informed her gruffly. "But I swear I will set me men on ye since ye appear to still think to run away from me."

"What are you talking about?" she asked, perplexed by his disgruntlement.

Rolfe pointed at her. "Ye were running, Annis. I saw ye with me own eyes. Are ye daft to go out in a storm? And dressed like ye are? When ye ran from the Duncan, ye used sense."

"I did not run away," Annis defended herself.

"Ye had yer skirts clear to yer knees, woman!" Rolfe growled at her. "Half the kitchen staff saw ye going across the yard."

"I was chasing the dog." Annis pointed toward the corner where the dog was still curled up with her litter.

Rolfe opened his mouth, but he shut it, clearly surprised by her comment. He turned and looked toward the corner.

"Ye were chasing the dog?" he asked, clearly not understanding why she'd do such a thing.

Annis walked over and picked up the pouch. The dog no longer had any interest in it because it knew there was no food in it.

"She thought there was food in this and took off. So I chased her, for I was not about to lose a dozen silver buttons on the first day Finnea allowed me into the manor house storeroom."

Rolfe was struggling to understand. "Why would a dog take a

pouch of buttons?"

"Because I had food in my hand, and the fabric smells like meat." Annis finished. She held the pouch up as evidence.

Rolfe looked between the pouch and her face. His lips twitched into a grin. She was so relieved to see his expression soften, but right on the heels of that feeling, she recalled what he'd said about setting his men on her.

"You will not set your men on me, Rolfe Munro."

His expression hardened. "I should have done it already, Annis. Before me father upset ye. I will never leave yer safety in doubt."

"Do not." The words came out in a near wail. Rolfe's eyebrows lowered as he stepped toward her.

Annis jumped back but not fast enough. He clasped his hands around her upper arms to hold her close to him.

"It seems ye still have a mind to leave me, Annis."

She shook her head. "No, that is not it."

She was struggling against his hold. He released her with a snort of frustration but planted himself between her and the ladder.

"Annis? Help me understand, for I swear ye have the ability to drive me mad."

There was true longing in his tone. It touched off the same need tearing at her insides.

"This is the first time I've ever been free." She struggled to form her thoughts into words. "I can make choices here. With you." She shrugged. "I know you must understand. As the only son of the laird, you have shouldered duty as long as I have."

At least she wanted him to feel the same.

Ha! Men do not think as women do.

How could they? It was ridiculous to even think such a thing. Men had power while women were controlled.

Annis gave a little sigh. "I do not want to argue."

She turned and made her way down the steps. Rolfe was behind her, but what startled her was Sholto. The burly veteran captain was standing near the bottom of the steps. He had his back to her, but Rolfe's prediction of half his men hearing them was suddenly impossible to refute.

Rolfe came up behind her. He clasped her wrist and pulled her past Sholto. By the time they reached the yard, her cheeks were flaming because they passed six more Retainers. And not a single one looked away, or even halfway pretended to not be fully aware of what they had been about in the loft.

"I have her," Rolfe spoke clearly to his men.

"Aye, no doubt of that," Sholto remarked as he followed them.

Annis wanted to curl into a ball, but first, she'd need to get to a dark place where she might hide. She increased her speed, passing Rolfe as his men chuckled at her expense.

Her ordeal wasn't over, though, for there were maids clustered around the doorway, which led back into the kitchens. They smiled at her, their expression full of knowledge.

By the time she made it to the passageway, she was nearly running again.

Rolfe caught her wrist, tugging her away from the steps to her tower chamber.

"Enough, Rolfe." She pulled on her wrist. "I am tired."

"Ye sleep in my bed, Annis."

She gave another yank on her arm, but he only pulled her toward him despite her effort. He lowered his shoulder, and she tumbled over it as he straightened and carried her up the steps to his room.

"Rolfe Munro!" she sputtered as he turned her loose.

He placed himself in front of the door and crossed his arms over his chest.

Sometimes, she forgot how large he was.

The chamber felt filled with him standing there.

Still, she propped her hands onto her hips and refused to be intimidated. Her stance earned her a grunt from him.

"If ye want to yell, Annis, I will be happy to give ye something to scream about." There was a dark promise in his voice.

"We already…"

"Do ye not think ye can make love more than once a day, lass?" he asked.

"Well…I suppose I never really thought the matter through. Honestly, I've had always been intent on getting the duty over and finished," the words came out in a rush. Once spoken, she listened to what she said and gasped.

A gleam entered Rolfe's eyes. "In that case, I am going to enjoy tempting ye to share me bed often."

"How…often?" Perhaps she shouldn't have asked such a question, but she truly was curious.

"Ye have an intense effect upon me, Annis. Why do ye think I allowed me men to hear ye?" His expression was serious. "I want them to know that ye belong to me. I have never needed to do such a thing before."

There was a rap on the door.

Rolfe frowned but turned and opened it.

"Laird."

Holly and Mia both lowered themselves before they slipped right past Rolfe and into the chamber. One had a tray while the other held a pitcher and plates. They sat them on the table in the receiving portion of the chamber.

"Good night," Rolfe told the maids pointedly.

"We must see to the mistress," Holly argued.

"She cannot unlace her dress herself," Mia said.

"I will tend to her," Rolfe told them firmly. "Go."

The two headed for the door, but they failed to hold their giggles in before the door was closed. Rolfe followed them, shutting the door firmly.

"I do understand what ye mean, Annis." Rolfe's voice was quiet. He turned and contemplated her for a long moment.

"About what?"

"Freedom," he said as he came around behind her and began to unlace her dress. "The clan expects access to me at all times. Privacy is not something I taste very often."

He pulled the second lace free and helped lift her bodice up and over her head. Rolfe closed his arms around her waist and clasped her to him. He drew in a deep breath against her hair.

"I do nae want to share ye, lass," he muttered softly.

She turned in his embrace, reaching up to open his doublet. She wanted their clothing gone so they might take solace in one another's company, just for a while. The sun would rise soon enough, until then, she wanted to be his.

She pushed his open doublet over his shoulders and smiled. He started to say something, but she pressed her finger against his lips. Their gazes locked. The candlelight cast a soft glow around them and seemed to offer them a refuge from the rest of reality.

The night ahead was suddenly a secret little joy that she was going to be able to share with him.

Making love?

She suddenly understood what it meant. He swept her off her feet and cradled her against his chest as he carried her to the bed.

His bed.

And tonight, it would be *their* bed.

>>>><<<<

"He brought her back."

Cian Munro tapped on the armrest of his chair. Matterson didn't answer him, but the Retainer rarely did.

"Bring Finnea here."

Matterson tugged on the corner of his cap before he left to go in search of the Head-of-House. Cian was left alone with the crackling of the fire.

Cian...

He blinked, but the air in front of him was wispy.

"Cian..."

He heard Sandra's voice as the image of the woman he'd loved one spring so very long ago began to materialize.

She wasn't real.

Couldn't be.

Yet her face was there. The same sweet smile that hadn't faded with the years which separated them.

"Are ye ready to join me, Cian?"

"Ye're dead," Cian muttered.

Pain filled him again. It was something that didn't seem to fade with time either.

"I'm partially to blame for it. Yer death," he confessed in a bitter tone.

Self-reproach filled him. He blinked and squinted at the face of his beloved. His heart felt tired in his chest, as though it didn't want to continue beating.

"I said what I said...so ye'd be free and love another," Cian said.

"Ye are my love," Sandra informed him. "I am waiting for you, Cian."

She was reaching for him. Cian tapped the armrest, torn between reaching for her and staying to guide his son.

There was a rap on the door and the vision dissipated.

Would she wait longer for him? It had already been so many years.

"Laird." Finnea lowered herself in front of him.

Cian focused on his Head-of-House and the matter at hand. Sandra was something from his past, and there was no going back in life.

No matter how much he might wish to do so at times.

꘎꘎꘎

GORON DUNCAN WAS pushing hard for home. His horse was wet and still, he maintained the speed. The terrain was rocky, but he'd crossed onto Duncan land and wouldn't let up. Most of his men had fallen behind, unwilling to keep such a reckless speed. His horse was spent, though, the animal beginning to slow.

Goron growled. He pulled up on the reins and jumped out of the saddle. A single Retainer had kept up.

"Give me yer horse!" Goron demanded.

"Laird?"

Goron didn't have time to debate the issue with the man. He punched the Retainer, sending the man over the side of the horse, and he was mounting the animal a moment later.

He had to make it back to Duncan land before his bastard cousin called for a vote. He cursed himself for not bedding his wife, for if Terin had a child, she'd have held the clan in check to ensure the inheritance rights of her babe.

He'd remedy that oversight very soon.

He leaned over the neck of the stallion and used the slack of the reins to slap the animal on its thick neck. The horse plunged forward.

His horse suddenly let out a scream as one of its legs folded. Goron was tossed from the saddle, but the animal came rolling down on top of him. Beneath him, there were rocks. The animal's weight pressed him onto those rocks, breaking his ribs and crushing his organs.

It was over in the blink of an eye.

One moment he felt himself tumbling toward the ground, and in the next, he was gasping for breath, only to discover that his lungs couldn't seem to hold air. Pain was the only thing filling him. But without air, he couldn't scream. He withered, fighting to get the air he needed to feed his burning lungs. Instead, he felt his blood soaking into his clothing. It was hot against his skin while desperation tormented him, lashing him with helplessness.

By the time his men made it to his side, his vision had darkened. The pain receded. No, he was rising up and away from the torment. Death closed its grip around him, blackness encompassing him until there was nothing else.

Nothing else at all.

>>>><<<<

LUCAS DUNCAN COULD only thank fate for giving him a heavy load to bear.

Born out of wedlock was bad enough. He'd also been the son of the youngest brother, so insignificant at best.

And Benedicta Duncan had made sure he knew he owed her for every mouthful of food he consumed.

Lucas looked down on Goron's body and wondered just how circumstances had changed so very dramatically in the last month. What Benedicta and her sons had always deserved had at last come around to land on them. Lucas admitted, he'd doubted it would ever come to pass. For good didn't triumph over evil, not when those doing the evil acts held the power.

Today, though. Fate seemed to have delivered the reckoning so richly deserved.

"I suppose that is one way for the matter to end," Kendric Campbell remarked. "A fool's death. I pity the poor horse. The animal had no choice."

No choice.

Lucas understood that plight well enough. Now, though? He looked at the men who had ridden with Goron. The news of what had happened back at the Duncan stronghold while the laird had been away was known by them all now. Perhaps they might have chosen to maintain their loyalty to their laird, but now he was dead.

"Laird." One of the older Duncan Retainers tugged on the corner of his bonnet as he looked straight at Lucas.

"Laird."

"Laird."

The rest of the men followed suit. A few appeared frustrated, and Lucas made sure to remember their faces. They were the men who had enjoyed privileged positions, and those spots had been secured through pressing down Goron's opponents.

Lucas had been one of them.

He was alive by his own tenacity and the will to fulfill his mother's last wish. That he live and never allow Benedicta to triumph completely.

CHAPTER TEN

Munro land...

ANNIS SMILED.

She didn't think she'd ever been so comfortable in bed before. She drew in a deep breath and sighed. The sheet felt perfect against her bare skin, and Rolfe was lying next to her. The scent of his skin filling her senses with every breath. Sharing the bed with him was another surprising joy, one she had never thought would please her so very much.

Now? Well, now she couldn't seem to be close enough to him.

"I like the little sounds ye make, Annis."

She opened her eyes to discover Rolfe watching her. His expression was relaxed, offering her a peek at the private side of his personality.

"Are you saying I snore?"

He chuckled. "Sholto snores. And the only thing worse than that is when he breaks wind."

Annis frowned at him.

"Does me pillow talk need a bit of refining?"

Annis pushed herself up. The morning air was brisk, but Rolfe's lips thinned as his gaze lowered to her bare breasts.

"I agree, lass, actions speak far louder than words."

Rolfe rolled her over onto her back. He was hard and hot, and a bolt of excitement went through her.

But someone knocked on the door.

"Be gone!" Rolfe bellowed.

He flashed Annis a wicked grin before beginning to lower his head down towards her, his attention on her lips.

Whoever was on the other side of the door knocked again.

Louder.

Rolfe drew in a frustrated breath.

"As you said, you have a limited amount of privacy," Annis muttered. Disappointment was prickling along her limbs.

"Aye," Rolfe groused, but he rose and shrugged into his shirt. He tossed her smock toward her.

"Come," he said, once Annis had pulled the garment down to cover herself.

Finnea appeared when the door was opened. The Head-of-House lowered herself before she strode forward into the chamber. Holly and Mia were hovering on the landing outside the door, but they didn't enter. Instead, they closed the door firmly behind Finnea.

"Finnea?" Rolfe asked.

"The laird has set me the task of delivering a morning brew to Annis each day."

Annis drew in a stiff breath.

She should have thought of it.

Why hadn't she thought of it?

Because she wanted Rolfe's baby.

Rolfe looked at her and then back to Finnea. The Head-of-House held a cup in her hands that she had a cloth wrapped around because it was hot.

"My father told ye to serve that to my...Annis?" Rolfe demanded.

"He did," Finnea answered firmly.

"And ye are going to do it?"

"It's the truth I spent a good long time thinking the matter through last night after yer father summoned me to his chambers and gave me his instructions. For I never thought to be caught between the pair of ye. He is the laird, and yet, ye are the young laird. Fortunately, it occured to me to bring it here, when ye are here, too, and therefore, I would not be doing anything behind yer back, while still following yer father's orders."

So the matter would become Rolfe's to decide. Annis felt her heart freeze.

"Take it away," Rolfe ordered tightly.

"Do not." Annis rolled out of the bed and came around the foot-board. "I should have thought to take it myself."

Annis reached for the cup. For some reason, her eyes filled with unshed tears.

Rolfe is the son of the laird. He will have to marry for an alliance.

She knew it well. So there was no reason to be emotional.

Rolfe plucked the cup away from Finnea.

"Leave," he ordered the Head-of-House. "Ye have delivered it. I have taken it from ye. Yer obedience to me father is finished."

Finnea lowered herself quickly and turned around. She was out of the chamber in a moment, leaving Annis facing Rolfe.

He was furious.

"Why do ye not want me children, Annis?" he asked quietly. "I stole ye, and yet, do I not treat ye kindly?"

"Aye," Annis answered him. "You treat me so well, do you think I would cause trouble between you and your father?" She tightened her resolve and walked toward him. "I will take it. I will accept that there are some things you cannot give me and that someday you will have to wed."

Her voice caught, betraying how much she didn't want to see him marry another woman. But she drew in a stiff breath and tried to take the cup from his hand.

"This is poison, Annis." Rolfe held the cup out of her reach. "If the mixture is not just right, ye could die."

"I understand precisely what it is, Rolfe, and what it does." Annis tightened her hands into fists. "I know how to make it."

Rolfe's eyebrows lowered. "Did ye take this before, then?"

Annis locked gazes with him. "I did."

Her voice held all the pent-up rage she'd never been able to vent toward Lonn and his family.

Rolfe's expression darkened. "And yet, ye would treat me in the same way ye did the Duncan?"

He threw the cup across the chamber. It hit the wall and shattered.

"I would never make you choose between me and your father!" Annis declared. Tears were trickling down her cheeks, and she seemed to have no way to stop them. "Do you not think I want the child of the man I love? To, at last, have a family and a home and everything? But not without your father's blessing."

"Love?"

Annis stopped to draw in a breath, and Rolfe asked the question in a whisper-soft voice. She looked at him, more exposed than she had ever felt in her life. One harsh word and she'd surely bleed to death from the wound, but there was no taking it back now.

"Do ye love me, lass?"

Rolfe had closed the distance between them. Stalking closer, reaching out to catch her chin between his forefinger and thumb. She was suddenly trembling, so fearful of rejection and yet, filling with the hope that he might reciprocate.

"I love you, Rolfe Munro. In a way I never believed possible before meeting you," she said softly.

He was silent for a long moment, studying her intently. Fresh tears escaped her eyes as she was stuck in that moment of silence without companionship in her confession. But it was too much. She blinked and looked away from him. She tried to step to the side, seeking shelter from the disappointment beginning to tear into her exposed heart.

Rolfe clasped her to him with one of his hard arms, and cupped the back of her neck to raise her face back toward his.

"I know love is not something men believe in," Annis mumbled.

He nodded, and it felt as though he'd reached in and crushed her heart with the single motion.

"I never believed in it," he confirmed.

Annis shuddered. She'd never realized her emotions might hurt so very badly.

Rolfe tightened his arm around her because she was attempting to step back from him, pushing against his chest as the need to escape became unbearable.

"I never believed in love until I saw it shimmering in Cora Mackenzie's eyes," Rolfe explained. "I was so happy that I did nae wed her, for I would have prevented her from finding the man she truly loved, and I would never have had the chance to see ye looking at me...as ye are."

It was enough.

Well, it will have to be.

Annis blinked back more tears, trying to remind herself that reaching too high was a good way to fall. No man wanted a woman who brought trouble to his house.

"I will handle me father," Rolfe spoke with hard determination.

"You mustn't argue with your father over me."

Rolfe's expressions darkened again. "When it comes to matters which involve yer health, Annis, I will no' allow me father to order something that will harm the woman I love."

She stiffened. "Love?"

One side of his mouth twitched up. "Aye. Do ye think I'd argue with me father over a woman I did not love?"

She balled her fingers into a fist and hit him. So close, the blow carried little force. "Why did you not tell me before?"

"Because I was too dumbfounded by discovering ye loved me to speak."

"Oh." It was the only word she managed to say. Everything else seemed to be insignificant compared to his confession.

"I love ye, Annis, and it is a fine thing that ye love me in return for otherwise, ye would live yer life as me captive, for I will never let ye go."

He sealed her reply inside her mouth, kissing her softly and then harder. As always, the moment they touched, passion flickered to life, growing until it consumed them both. The window shutters remained closed as Rolfe carried her back to bed.

And it was noon before either of them raised their heads up again.

⊁⊱⊰⊀

Duncan land…

LAIRD GORON DUNCAN was laid next to his father. It left the clan quiet, as many wondered whether or not they were cursed.

But there were many who breathed a sigh of relief to see the last of Benedicta's spawn beneath the ground.

Perhaps there might be a future without suspicious deaths.

Then again, with power went struggle.

Lucas found the walk back to the Duncan stronghold to be one of the longest in his life. Along the way, his shoulders felt the weight of the lairdship settling on them. The expectations didn't bother him; he was more than ready to face them. What he loathed was the certainty of knowing the plotting wouldn't end with Goron's death.

There were many who had profited from handling dirty work. They were all in positions he couldn't just take from them without evidence. And the sort of people who performed dark deeds in the small hours of the night were the kind who made sure there were no witnesses.

Lucas drew in a deep breath as the gates came into view.

His mother would have wept for joy, for Benedicta had always made certain she knew she was nothing.

He grinned because it was true he was enjoying knowing that somewhere, hopefully in hell, Benedicta and her sons were watching him walk through the gates with the clan supporting him as their laird. He pulled his bonnet off and stopped. The senior captains who were walking near him paused, as well. Lucas took a moment to withdraw three feathers from the inside of his doublet. There were several smirks on the faces of those captains when he attached them to the side of his bonnet and made sure they were standing up straight. He tugged the bonnet down on his head before he started forward again.

Something shifted inside him. A sense of purpose.

Aye, the road ahead was filled with uncertainty, but he discovered he was eager for it because when he emerged on the other side, his life would be worth living at last.

From bastard to laird. It wasn't unheard of in the Highlands.

So perhaps his mother had been right about his destiny to sit in his father's seat. Lucas vowed to make sure no one missed his arrival.

><<

Munro land...

"MUST YE RISE?"

Annis looked at Rolfe.

"What is that look supposed to mean?" he inquired.

"I am thinking I like ye looking like this the best," Annis answered. It was a wicked thing to say. She felt heat tease her cheeks as she smiled at him in a way she was certain she'd never looked at a man before.

Saucy.

"I could nae agree more," he said as he reached out and caught her close so he might kiss her.

But Annis wiggled away after a moment. "The day is wasting."

Rolfe grunted.

"And Sholto is likely sitting outside the chamber door making ready to laugh at our expense," Annis continued.

"He's a good man, Sholto," Rolfe declared as he found his shirt. "I want every soul on Munro land to know ye are mine."

Rolfe dressed far faster than she did. By the time he had his kilt pleated and belted around his lean middle, his expression was tight.

"I will speak with my father," he informed her gruffly.

"Do not." Annis sent him a grin as she pulled a brush through her hair.

"Annis—"

She moved across the floor and stretched up on her toes to press a kiss against his mouth. "I believe I should spend some time with your father. So he can get to know me." She winked at him. "Don't worry, Rolfe, I have more patience than most, and I am very, very good at making the best of sour situations."

Rolfe stared at her for a long moment. But he slowly grinned at her, and there was a flicker of anticipation in his eyes. "Well, in that case. He keeps his private whiskey stash in the right-hand corner of his chamber, behind the books."

Rolfe turned, but he stopped and looked back at her. "Me father still manages to throw those books fairly well."

Annis kissed her fingers and blew the kiss to him before she wiggled her fingers in a farewell wave. "We'll do just fine."

Rolfe lifted his hand to his cap and tugged on the corner of it. "I believe ye just might at that my English lass. Besides, if ye deal with him, I can go make arrangements for our wedding."

Annis felt her playful mood shatter. "Rolfe, we can't marry."

He'd started to reach for the door handle. Rolfe turned on her, his expression hard with determination. "And why not?"

"Well, I am…English."

He flashed a grin at her. "Aye, well, we Highlanders have been known to take a few English lasses as our captives."

"Rolfe."

He turned and pulled the door open.

"Rolfe Munro," Annis raised her voice.

He stopped on the landing and looked back at her. "Enough, woman! I know ye crave me, but ye shall have to wait until tonight for more!"

Her face burst into flames as Sholto began to laugh. Holly and Mia dashed through the door, shutting it firmly as Annis shook her head.

Captive?

Well, it was the truth that she was enjoying it full well!

⇶⇇

Duncan land…

TERIN CAMPBELL SAT up in her bed.

The chamber was still and quiet. Her bedding was clean, and there was the lingering scent of rosemary clinging to it. The staff was doing their best to gain her favor now that Benedicta was no longer their main focus and making it clear that her daughter-in-law wouldn't ever be the mistress of the stronghold.

She didn't belong.

It was a feeling she was very used to. She'd expected it to fade in the first year of her marriage, but it never had. Benedicta and her sons had seen to that. Could she have fought harder? Yes. But she'd just never been quite able to make herself grovel to Goron the way he'd insisted she do. There were plenty of people who would tell her she'd squandered her opportunity to be the lady of the house. If she had a son, she'd have a position. Somehow, Terin just couldn't lament her choice.

Was it so wrong to think a child should be born into a happy home? Just because she was born the daughter of a laird, did it mean her future was to be one riddled with scheming and power plays?

Well, you have spent four years pondering the matter.

She had. Terin stood and walked over to the window. She opened the shutters and looked out into the yard. Night was losing its grip. The sky was brightening as the stars began to disappear. Still, the first birds had yet to sing.

She felt like those birds. Nestled into her bed while waiting for the morning sun to awaken her.

She was so tired of waiting.

In fact, she was sick of waiting. It felt like poison in her veins. Either she fought it off, or it would kill her in the worst possible way.

Slowly. Allowing her to notice every drop of her life dripping away.

No...fortune favored the bold.

Terin turned around and walked to the wardrobe. Inside there was a spare length of wool. Some maid had placed it there in case Goron ever passed the night with her and needed a clean kilt. It was an extravagance to have a length of wool going unused. But Goron had expected such luxury.

So perhaps she would make use of it.

What are you doing?

Terin wasn't precisely sure, but once she began, there was no stopping herself. She pleated up the wool on the floor and then went back to the wardrobe in search of a shirt. It was too large on her, but she moved the buttons on the cuffs so they would close tightly around her wrists.

She lay down on the wool and used her belt to secure it around her waist. When she turned to look in the mirror, she saw a lanky lad, if she discounted her waist-long hair. Her legs hadn't been on display in a decade since she became too old to run wild with her brothers. If the Church discovered her dressed like a man, there would be dire consequences, but that didn't dissuade her.

She'd done all the things she should.

Now, she was going to do the things she dared.

Determination flared through her. Terin reached for her sewing scissors and hacked off a foot of her hair. She tied a section back from her eyes and tugged a bonnet down over her forehead. The last thing she did was to press her fingertips into the soot at the edge of the hearth. She smeared the black ashes on her face to disguise how soft her skin was. A quick look in her mirror showed her a grubby youth. Or at least it might hold up if she kept her head down and her mouth shut. She gathered up the money she'd hidden around the chamber in case she needed to escape. It wasn't much, but she wouldn't starve so long as she wasn't too picky.

The first bird sang as she walked out of the stronghold.

Terin smiled. The most genuine smile she'd experienced in four years.

⪻⪻⪻✦⪼⪼⪼

Munro land…

"GET OUT!"

Cian Munro shook his fist at Annis.

Annis smiled at him. Matterson didn't move, proving the Retainer realized his laird was being dramatic.

"I am keeping you company," Annis replied sweetly. "For Rolfe's sake, you and I must become better friends."

"Ye are English!" Cian railed at her.

"Yes," Annis said with a sigh. "It's true that I was never consulted on the matter of where I was to be born. It's a terrible injustice. Perhaps you might take up my cause with fate and right the wrong done to me. I would be most grateful."

Cian scowled at her.

"No?" Annis smiled at him. "Well, I suppose it's a lost cause, as I am here."

"Are ye daft, woman?"

"I admit I love your son," Annis said. "Many claim love is a form of madness."

Cian pointed at her. "Ye are nae allowed to love me son."

"Why not?" Rolfe suddenly appeared in the doorway of the chamber. "I love her, so why can she not love me, Father?"

"Because…" Cian grunted. "Because ye are me only son, and ye need to wed and produce an heir."

Rolfe tilted his head to one side. "Well, as to the matter of begetting, ye are the one who sent Finnea with a brew to keep Annis from conceiving. I would be very happy to see Annis rounding with me child."

"She is English!"

"She is me captive," Rolfe insisted quietly. "What better business is there than a Highlander stealing the finest-blooded mare the English have and making her his?"

Annis felt her cheeks heat. Cian made a strangling sound beneath his breath, but Matterson suddenly spoke up, "Seems a fine bit of work to me."

Cian turned his head to look at his subordinate. "How can ye take the side of the English?"

"I take the side of the young laird," Matterson replied.

"Father, with James likely to inherit the throne, what better grandson can I give ye than one with royal blood in its veins?"

Cian looked at her. He seemed to be considering the idea.

Well, that's a step in the right direction.

"I am no' agreeing to it," Cian declared, but his tone had lost some of its hardness.

Rolfe reached up and tugged on his cap. He winked at Annis, though, before turning around to leave.

"Take her away," Cian demanded of his son.

Rolfe looked back at his father. "Well, Father, it's like this. I will nae allow her to take that brew ye ordered for her, and we've both told ye that we love one another. So, if she leaves with me, ye'll have to get used to the idea of yer grandson coming from an English woman."

Cian growled. "Have ye no shame to say such a thing in front of yer father?"

Rolfe looked at Annis before he shook his head. Her cheeks were smarting from how hot they were, and it only grew worse when she heard Matterson trying to stifle his amusement.

"She stays," Cian ordered.

Rolfe was gone a moment later, and Cian looked at her, his expression disgruntled.

"Shall I fetch the whiskey?" Annis asked quietly.

"Aye."

It was far from bending, but Annis realized she didn't want the crusty old Munro laird to be anything other than he was. She went across the study to where the bottles were hidden and retrieved one from the back of the stash. Unlike the ones in the front, this bottle didn't have a layer of dust on it. The clean condition proved it was Cain's favorite and only residing in the back in order to hide.

She carried it back and poured a measure of it for him. Cian lifted it to his nose and drew in a breath.

"Well, since ye are here, I will teach ye a thing or two about whiskey. The English have no bloody idea how to enjoy whiskey correctly."

>>><<<

ANNIS HESITATED IN the passageway that evening.

It was dark now. Her belly was full and nearly bursting from the fine supper Finnea had served her personally. The rest of the staff took their cue from the Head-of-House and hovered over her until she begged to leave.

Rolfe had never arrived in the hall.

Finnea had insisted it was not uncommon, for the matters of the Munro kept him busy.

Now though, she stood in the passageway, nibbling on her lower lip as she tried to decide which chamber to go to for the night.

As if there is a choice to make, he told his father he loves you.

Annis smiled before she headed toward the steps which would lead her up to Rolfe's chamber. Three flights of stairs, and she crossed into the chamber feeling more at home than she ever had before.

"Ye made the correct choice, lass."

She gasped and turned around to find Rolfe closing the door behind him. There was a grin on his face as he tossed his doublet onto a chair.

"You were behind me?"

"Aye," Rolfe answered as he opened his belt, and his kilt fell down. "Ye are me captive after all. There are expectations of how I should treat ye, Annis."

He started toward her.

"Expectations?" Annis decided to join in his game. "What sort of expectations?"

"Right now." Rolfe closed his arms around her and lifted her up before putting her back against a wall. Her head was above his, and his body went right between her thighs.

"Right now, I am supposed to ravish ye, lass, but the truth is, I am yer devoted servant."

She laid her hands on either side of his face, needing to memorize every detail of the moment. But the desire to kiss him was stronger. She was drawn to him so strongly, there was no fending off the impulse.

Aye, she'd never felt so very much at home.

>>><<<

"WHAT IS ON yer mind, lass?"

Annis turned her head, but Rolfe still had his eyes closed. He was on his back, the wee hours of the morning offering them the opportunity to savor being together in his bed.

He opened his eyes and looked at her. "I hear yer thoughts churning."

"You told your father about my blood, but since you stole me, I doubt the Duncan will be giving you anything to prove my parentage. So…"

"I can't prove you are a descendant of Margret Clifford's line?" Rolfe finished for her.

"Yes."

He reached out and smoothed the hair back from her face. "Good."

Annis was surprised. "But…"

Rolfe pressed his finger against her lips as he rolled onto his side to look at her.

"James will not lose the English throne to an old woman who is a descendant from the younger sister of Henry VIII when James is from the elder sister's line. Documents signed seventy years ago will not hold up against his desire to have both crowns. It's better ye are not someone he thinks he needs to go through, Annis."

"But if that is so, I bring you nothing."

He pulled her close. "Ye bring me love. The only thing I did not have. There is a fine manor house for ye to move into next spring, lass. I have managed the Munro well. What I need is a woman who will stand up to me father while treating him kindly."

"But there will be no alliance."

Rolfe nuzzled her temple. "In that case, best we produce a fine litter of descendants to marry off."

She wanted to argue.

But there was no point because he was everything she had never even dared to dream she might have.

➤➤➤◄◄◄

IT SNOWED ON their wedding day.

The wind howled, and the snow made a perfect carpet of white. It was so pristine, Annis almost forgot that her nose was turning numb. Rolfe wed her in the great hall of the new manor house. His father watched from a large chair as he sat wrapped in thick furs.

But there was a grin on his face.

The Munro were clustered around them. At least the tight conditions kept everyone warm. When it was over, though, Holly and Mia swept her away and up the new stairs.

Finnea was standing in a huge chamber, which was located over the great hall. Beeswax candles were lit, filling the air with the scent of honey. The Head-of-House was smiling as she directed half a dozen maids around the chamber. The bedding was pulled back, and rosemary sprinkled on the sheets. Holly and Mia brushed out Annis's hair until it shimmered in the candlelight.

This time, her belly wasn't knotted with dread as Annis was taken to her wedding bed. She climbed into the sheets in her smock and felt gratitude welling up inside her.

Thankful.

It was more than a word. It was a complete idea.

The Munro weren't going to be denied the celebration of their young laird's nuptials just because it was common knowledge that she and Rolfe had already shared a bed.

Such a trifling matter didn't matter to the Munro. Rolfe was delivered to her by a howling group of Retainers. The women fled the chamber just before Rolfe was stripped and dropped beside her in bed.

But they parted to allow Cian Munro to look at them both. Annis let out a little squeak of surprise as she tried to tug the sheet up. Her new father-in-law was dressed completely for the first time in her memory. His kilt was fresh and pleated expertly. A doublet was buttoned over his chest, every button polished. A fine velvet bonnet with a gold broach was on his head. He looked at them for a long moment, a smile on his face.

"Good night, then," he said before he turned, and Matterson helped him toward the chamber door. "And the rest of ye, get out! We are not the bloody English who stay around to watch."

The memory of her first wedding night rose from the dark corner of her mind where she had banished it. Annis didn't shy away from it, though. She wanted to notice the contrast between the two moments of her life.

She never wanted to forget how wonderful her life was.

"Do ye like the chamber, lass?" Rolfe asked.

Annis turned her attention to him completely, the memory dissipating as she looked into Rolfe's blue eyes.

"It's a new chamber, for the new chapter of our lives," he said.

"Does this mean I am no longer your captive?"

His rakish grin appeared. "Ye will always be mine, Annis. But feel free to test me on the matter every now and again, for I enjoy reminding ye."

He pressed her down onto her back, leaning low to kiss her. She clasped her hands behind his neck, letting out a little sound of enjoyment as she kissed him back.

"I enjoy your lectures, husband," she said softly.

>>><<<

Summer…

"WHAT A STRONG laddie…"

Cian Munro declared as his new grandson clasped his tiny hand around the tip of his pinky finger. "Ye are a perfect child."

The baby began to fuss. Turning its head, seeking his mother.

"Ah well...back to yer dam," Cian muttered as Holly lifted the baby up and cuddled him close. "Matterson, go with the girl. Make sure me grandson is delivered into the keeping of his mother."

The Retainer hesitated, but Cian waved him after the maid. Matterson tugged on the corner of his cap, a twinkle entering his eyes.

"I will bring him again," Holly promised before she was out of the doorway. Matterson was close on her heels, and Cian suddenly realized his devoted man was sweet for young Holly.

Ye should have noticed before. Matterson is a good man, who spends too much time with ye...old man.

Matterson should have a son, too. The Munro needed sons and daughters for the next generation.

The baby was a breath of fresh air in the old chamber. One Cian hadn't realized he missed so very much until he felt it dissipate after he couldn't hear Holly and Matterson's steps any longer. The old tower was something from the past. The new manor house was proof that Rolfe would guide the Munro into a promising future.

The Munro had an heir.

Rolfe was no longer the last of the line.

Cian grunted. It was good. Very good.

He felt his heart struggling to beat again. As though it simply lacked the strength to lift his chest any more. He saw specters, too. Right then, a mist was forming into a person in front of him. A tingle touched his nape as he recognized the girl he'd never told he loved. She was still so bonny. Her cheeks full and rosy.

But he'd wanted to see his grandchild born. Cian grinned. The summer had been full of a renewed breath of life for him as he watched the heather bloom and his daughter-in-law's belly rise up, plump and round. His son had helped him finish off the last of his whiskey as they waited for the birth.

Good.

So very good.

"Are ye ready, then?"

Sandra was back now. Clearer than ever before.

He reached for her and felt her grip his hand. A soft sound crossed his lips because he actually felt her fingers closing around his. Such a wonderful sensation. How long had it been? Far, far too long. He blinked, and she was still there, more real than a moment ago.

"Come Cian, I have waited so very long for ye."

"But...me son needed me...."

"Cian," his love admonished him. "Yer son is a man."

"He is," Cian muttered. "I'm proud of him."

"Ye must come now. There is no more to be done."

She was right. Cian struggled only through another couple of breaths before he surrendered.

But now, the woman he'd been denied was there, her hand in his, and there was no reason not to go to her.

So he did, taking a step forward, feeling the weakness drop away. And he wasn't alone.

⟫⟫⟩⟨⟨⟨

Chattan land...

TERIN ENJOYED THE summer sun on her face.

She refused to ponder the harsh possibilities that the Chattan would turn her out. Her Aunt Davonna might not welcome her at all.

Especially dressed as a boy.

Well, there is no turning back.

That wasn't precisely true. Terin was a Campbell. She was still a maiden, too. Even if her dowry was in the Duncan coffers, her clan was too powerful to ignore.

But she was finished with having her body used to further the interests of the Campbell clan. Oh, she knew it was her good fortune that Goron had never consummated their union. In fact, she stood on a hill overlooking the Chattan stronghold because she understood so very well how fortunate she was to have escaped her marriage.

Now? Well, now she wasn't sure what to do.

But Davonna had never been meek or mild. In fact, her aunt was an unbridled female who had been held up as an example of how not to behave.

It sounded like a perfect place to begin with getting on with her life.

Or at least a place to gain a different perspective on how to live, now that Terin had tried the path her family and clan had set her on.

Terin had been obedient.

Now she wanted to be bold.

So she stepped forward.

About the Author

Mary Wine has written over twenty novels that take her readers from the pages of history to the far reaches of space. Recent winner of a 2008 EPPIE Award for erotic western romance, her book LET ME LOVE YOU was quoted "Not to be missed..." by Lora Leigh, New York Times best-selling author.

When she's not abusing a laptop, she spends time with her sewing machines...all of them! Making historical garments is her second passion. From corsets and knickers to court dresses of Elizabeth I, the most expensive clothes she owns are hundreds of years out of date. She's also an active student of martial arts, having earned the rank of second degree black belt.

Printed in Great Britain
by Amazon